What's a Girl Gotta Do?

What's a Girl Gotta Do?

Sparkle Hayter

SOHO

Published by
Soho Press Inc.
553 Broadway
New York, NY 10003

Library of Congress Cataloging-in-Publication Data

Hayter, Sparkle. 1958–
What's a girl gotta do? / Sparkle Hayter.
     p.   cm.
ISBN 1-56947-000-6 :
1. Women journalists—New York (N.Y.)—Fiction.   I. Title.
PS3558.A879W43   1994
813'.54—dc20   93-17896
CIP

Manufactured in the United States
10 9 8 7 6 5 4 3 2 1

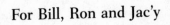

For Bill, Ron and Jac'y

Many a good hanging prevents a bad marriage
—William Shakespeare
Twelfth Night

What's a Girl Gotta Do?

Chapter One

ON THE LAST DAY of the year, I got this weird phone call. It's not every day a dame like me gets a call from a mysterious stranger.

Well, actually, it is almost every day. I'm a reporter and I get a lot of phone calls from mysterious strangers, most of whom are clearly a few bees short of a hive. It's a fact of my life.

But it's not every day I get a call at home from a mysterious stranger who knows my childhood nickname, Red Knobby, something very few people know, I assure you. He knew my childhood nickname, he knew my mother's medical history, he even knew when and to whom I'd lost my cherry in high school.

So I knew this guy wasn't just another conspiracy buff calling up with a wild theory, claiming to have "evidence" of a link between freemasonry and Lee Harvey Oswald or some other scandal that was going to rock our republic to its very roots. This guy knew some strange stuff about me, and when he said he was a private investigator and wanted to meet to give me the rest of a report he'd done on me, it naturally piqued my interest.

I tried to get as much information from him as I could over the phone, of course, but he was a tough nut to crack. He wouldn't tell me why he was investigating me, or who hired him to investigate me. To every question, he answered, simply, "Meet me at the Marfeles Palace Hotel tonight. I'll find you."

My company was having its New Year's Eve party that night at the Marfeles in midtown Manhattan.

I hung up the phone and asked myself: Who would investigate me, Robin Hudson, a lowly, third-string correspondent at the All News Network with a floundering career and a failed marriage? Sure, my estranged husband and I were divorcing, and I won't kid you, I was angry with him and I was hurt. But I'd agreed to the divorce and I wasn't seeking alimony. It wasn't like Burke had any need to dig up dirt on me and it wasn't like there was much dirt to be dug up. What could this mystery man find?

But I have secrets, like everyone else, embarrassing secrets I'd just rather people didn't know about me, and I was especially vulnerable to embarrassment at the moment. See, the last six months of the year weren't very good for me.

In July, a faux pas at a White House news conference effectively ended my brief career as a Washington correspondent. Shortly after that, another faux pas, involving a cannibalism story, sent me into TV news Siberia, the Special Reports unit. Murphy's Law, right? Once my career was pretty much destroyed, my husband, Burke Avery, left me for another woman, and not just any woman but a much younger woman.

In light of all this, what could anyone dig up that would possibly make me feel or look worse? Well, there were a few other humiliating incidents I'd like to leave behind me, thank you very much, and a few shameful acts I don't want the whole world to know about.

So I'd meet the guy at the Marfeles that night. The location was good; there'd be a lot of people at the ANN party to make me feel safer, just in case the guy was some kind of sicko who wanted to get me alone in an underground parking garage, Deep Throat–style, to rape and flay me.

The ANN New Year's Eve party was an annual apocalyptic event, a costume ball where employees dress up as their favorite news story and generally get wrecked. This year was our tenth anniversary and the theme was a salute to ten years of twenty-four-hour television news, a very big deal.

Yet, before I got that phone call, I planned to skip it. Why? Maybe because my estranged husband was going to be there. Maybe because he was coming with Miss Amy Penny.

Miss Amy Penny. During her relatively brief life thus far, Miss Amy Penny had done a lot. As co-host of ANN's *Gotham Salon*, a morning magazine show, she provided a steady diet of celebrity news, fashion guidance, and other soft features for homemakers who'd taken the Mommy Track.

Before becoming a "television personality" (which may or may not be an oxymoron), she was a Miss Mason-Dixon Line and a TV and trade show spokesmodel for that upscale, low-dust baby powder, Gentility. You may remember their ad campaign two years ago, the one where a woman with caramel-colored hair and big tits lolled around on a beige carpet with a baby-for-hire and two of those little wrinkled-up dogs, Shar-Peis. Amy was the one with the big tits.

All this, plus the fact that she aspired to "serious journalism," I learned from a recent, half-page, kissy-face article in

People, which failed to include the accomplishment most pertinent to my own life: She'd managed to break up my marriage.

Miss Amy Penny. Just the sound of her name was enough to burn a hole in the lining of my stomach. I'd seen her around the network and caught a few episodes of her program but, as Burke worked for a rival station, I'd never had to see her on the arm of my husband before. Friends of Amy's made sure I knew they'd be there. Presumably, they thought I'd opt to avoid further humiliation and take a pass on the party, which had made sense to me. But then the guy called and I changed my mind.

As the ANN party was a costume party, I toyed for a while with the idea of going as Ronald Reagan's colon, a story that had special meaning for me. But in the end (no pun intended), I opted for something simpler and less offensive, as one of my New Year's resolutions was to try to offend fewer people in the next decade and thereby escape from the century with my life. I decided to go as Ginny Foat, a prominent feminist tried for murder and acquitted in 1983. On a practical note, it was easy to put together. All I had to do was wear a "Support Your Local Feminist" button and carry a tire iron around.

It felt oddly appropriate to me. Maybe because my estranged husband was going to be at the party. Maybe because he was bringing Miss Amy Penny.

Understandably, it took some serious motivational exercises to get up my courage to go. I poured myself a glass of lemon Stoly on the rocks, put some music on, and sat down with my ancient, battle-scarred cat, Louise Bryant, in our favorite arm-chair. Together, Louise Bryant and I pondered the comforting lyrics of our favorite postmarriage song, Nancy Sinatra's "These Boots Are Made for Walking."

I don't know why but this ritual, that song, and the act of hitting the palm of my hand gently with my tire iron seemed to bring order to my thoughts. A kind of serenity came over me and I found the nerve to go.

Murphy's Law again. When I got outside my apartment building, I ran into my downstairs neighbor, Mrs. Ramirez, an eighty-year-old bully with a blue rinse, who was out walking her high-strung Chihuahua, Señor. God, I hate those dogs. They look like rats with a glandular problem, they're dumber than a sack of hammers, and they're bad-tempered—a horror movie just waiting to happen. What is the attraction?

In Mrs. Ramirez's case I could kind of see it, though, because she and the dog shared the same snappish temperament. Not all old people are sweet and wise. Even assholes grow old. Mrs. Ramirez, for instance, has this nasty habit of cornering me in the elevator, calling me a whore, and rapping my head with her cane. She complains constantly about me to the landlord, the super, and the few good Catholics left in our East Village neighborhood. If she wasn't so damned old, I'd press charges.

With Señor's leash in one hand and her carved cane in the other, she shuffled towards me menacingly. "I couldn't sleep last night because of *you!*"

I'm always really sweet when I talk to her. It's kind of an experiment. I'm trying out that kill-them-with-kindness theory.

"Hello, Mrs. Ramirez!" I said, smiling angelically. "How's your little friend Señor? And how are you?"

Still got that very large, very rough stick up your ass?

"You had a big party last night! I was up all *night!*"

"I didn't have a party. I watched a movie and went to bed."

"I heard *dancing!*"

Mrs. Ramirez's problem, as I've tried to explain to her 354 times, is that her hearing aid is turned up too high, amplifying the noise in my apartment, which is above hers. The sound of a cap popping off a soda bottle sounds like the crack of a whip to her. When my cat, Louise Bryant, walks across the floor, Mrs. Ramirez thinks there's a naked mambo party going on upstairs and multiple commandments are being repeatedly and cavalierly broken.

"I was watching *Top Hat*," I said. "The volume was way down."

"It sounded like you had the Rockettes up there! It was so loud it scared me. I had to take a nitroglycerin pill. Next time, I'm calling the police."

"Please call the police next time, Mrs. Ramirez. Have them come up and arrest the Rockettes," I said.

"I'll call them now!" she said.

Suddenly, she picked up her cane and waved it at me. I held up my tire iron to ward off the blow. This was great. Get into a sword fight with an old woman in the middle of the street. Try to convince the police when they came that I had to bean a frail eighty-year-old lady with my tire iron in self-defense. I turned and started walking away from her fast.

"You young people have no respect. You're all going to get AIDS and die," she said, as if that were a just punishment for lack of respect. Then she shuffled brusquely past me with

8

Señor, who belatedly picked up Louise Bryant's scent and began yapping.

The glittering Marfeles Palace, a restored beaux arts building turned into a hotel and run by the imperious Eloise Marfeles, would normally be way out of ANN's price range, which was more along the lines of a Knights of Columbus bingo hall.

But Eloise Marfeles had defied centuries of superstition by allowing her building to have a thirteenth floor. No sooner had she opened the previous autumn than bad luck visited her with a vengeance. Fires broke out, unions staged job actions, elevators got stuck between floors, and other mishaps occurred almost daily. The tabloids were having a field day with it and business was bad.

As a result, ANN got a real deal on the place—the ballroom and a block of rooms on the thirteenth floor for use by company personnel the night of the party. For her part, Eloise Marfeles got a lot of cheap publicity out of ANN and a chance to debunk the superstition.

When I got there, I hesitated in the doorway and, with mixed feelings of curiosity and dread, scanned the crowd. Around me Dan Quayles, Jeffrey Dahmers, and Long Dong Silvers mingled with Hillary Clintons, Boris Yeltsins, giant condoms, and giant Tylenol capsules.

Frannie Millard, a robust matron done up as Margaret Thatcher, grabbed my arm and said, "Robin Hudson."

"Yes."

"I'm in charge of name tags tonight. Not everyone wants to wear one, but I hope you won't give me a hard time about it."

"What a drag, having to work at the party," I said, as she pinned me for easy identification.

"I like helping out," she said efficiently and left me for three members of the Standards & Practices division, also known as the network censors, a.k.a. the court eunuchs.

An ancient panic grabbed me as I stared into the social chaos ahead: Who would I hang out with? Tonight I needed a comfortable cordon of friendship to protect me both from mysterious strangers and from humiliation by my husband. I looked around for someone I recognized, someone sympathetic, and saw Louis Levin heading towards me. Louis was a news producer and a paraplegic and he had done his wheelchair up as an electric chair, complete with a leather and metal helmet.

"Hey, little girl," he said. "Wanna sit in my lap and play with Mister Microphone?"

"Who are you supposed to be?"

"Ted Bundy." He pushed a button and smoke came out of the helmet.

"You are an evil genius, Louis."

"Thanks. Who are you?"

"Ginny Foat. Say, Louis, have you seen my husband sliming around tonight?"

"Not that I know of," he said. "What's he coming as?"

"I dunno. I couldn't find out."

"I did see your second favorite person," he said. "Jerry Spurdle."

"What did he come as?"

"Himself."

"He came as a bucket of larvae?"

Spurdle was my boss in the Special Reports unit. I "be-

WHAT'S A GIRL GOTTA DO?

longed" to Jerry Spurdle, as he liked to remind me. He was part
of my humiliation, my punishment, my artistic suffering.

"No. He came as Richard Nixon," Louis said. "He came as a
dick. Get it?"

"Har har," I said slowly. "Just like Jerry to pick a story that
was over before the network ever went on the air." An exclusive
radio interview with Nixon in 1972 had made his reputation—
Jerry's, not Nixon's—and he liked to remind people of it.

"I'm sitting with some of the writers," Louis said. "Why don't
you join us?"

"Bless you. I will—later. First, I think I'll do some recon.
Map out all the people I want to avoid." And try to make
contact with my mystery man.

"Come sit with us. We're up in the balcony," he said, and
motored away.

I circulated, waiting for the man who knew my secrets to
approach me, while at the same time keeping an eye out for
Burke and Amy.

This being a costume party, it was hard to tell who was who
without reading name tags. Everyone was in disguise with a
few highly visible exceptions, including Dr. Solange Stevenson, ANN's psychologist with a talk show, whose only nod to
whimsy was a photo button showing her rival, Dr. Sonya
Friedman, with a large red X through her face. Also not in
costume, our fearless leader, Georgia Jack Jackson, chairman
of the board of Jackson Broadcasting System, our parent
company.

Solange was simply too dignified to wear a costume ("the
soothing Solange Stevenson"—*TV Guide*). But dignity was
something Georgia Jack didn't worry about too much. Since he
considered himself his favorite news story he came as . . .

11

himself. Legitimately, I might add. In the 1980s Georgia Jack unleashed an entertainment empire on the world, built a twenty-four-hour news network against the odds, dated half the women in the Screen Actors Guild, and created a great deal of controversy by buying up classic silent films and adding sound and dialogue to them, which filmmakers decried as mutilation.

Jackson was huddled at one end of the ballroom with the cream of the correspondents, the mediacrats, the cool kids at the prom who excited my envy.

The network's premier anchor and talk-show host, "avuncular" Greg Browner, was dressed this night as an MX missile. Greg was a prince of the Jack Jackson church, and ruled an autonomous fiefdom within the kingdom. His highly rated call-in show had taken on Larry King and made a respectable showing. Greg then moved his show up an hour to beat King to the punch, and was taking away huge chunks of the traditional call-in audience.

Next to him was "dispassionate and professional" Joanne Armoire, dressed as the late great Lucy. Beneath her red wig, Joanne was blond and beautiful in a Lufthansa stewardess sort of way. Her career had been meteoric. She'd been one of the few Western women to go into Afghanistan with the mujahedin and she'd taken a bullet in her leg when she was covering the ethnic war in Sarajevo.

This is who I thought I would be: a brave, trench-coated figure, looking serious and beautiful, standing in a war zone in some picturesque country, bringing the world my own brilliant and illuminating insights on the news. I saw myself as a hard-hitting correspondent, taking on world leaders, asking them tough questions, Oriana Fallaci in Rita Hayworth's body, bad men cowering and good men swooning in my wake.

That's who I thought I would be. This is who I am: a slightly rumpled, third-string reporter with ink stains on all her blouses and a small run in her stocking, who sneaks around with a hidden camera looking for seamy stories and petty scandals. The *National Enquirer*—in Rita Hayworth's body.

Joanne and I had started out at ANN around the same time, in similar lowly positions, and we had both been writers for Greg Browner when he was the anchor and managing editor for the six o'clock. Her hitch on the six had gone somewhat better than mine, in small part, at least, because she knew how to handle Greg's constant advances and his big ego. She knew when to speak, when to hold her tongue, and how to be diplomatic.

I did not. I told Greg to go fuck himself and was promptly given a new assignment—a better assignment, actually—another report on my "bad attitude" comfortably ensconced in my thick personnel file.

I watched Joanne trade bon mots with Mark O'Malley, a devilishly handsome business reporter wearing a barrel marked "1987 stock market crash," and Tom Charing, who wore an upright open coffin and a bad suit with a hammer and sickle on the lapel to represent a generic dead Soviet leader. Off to the side was Madri Michaels, a brunet anchorwoman with a premolded plastic kind of beauty who came as Madonna, wearing Mylar. So obvious.

These were the reporters and anchors who always dominated the A block—the first ten minutes or so of a news show—and brought prestige and respect to ANN. The Pantheon. They took risks, they knew how to use their sources, and they knew how to tell an exciting story. Because of this, they had considerable influence with lawmakers all over the world. Everything they did, everything they said, every movement of their heads, every earnest furrow on their brows said "Emmy."

God, I wanted to be one of them.

The pathetic thing is, I had been well on my way. I'd had the crime and justice beat, covering big Manhattan murder trials and other cases for the network. It was a second-string beat, but I didn't mind. It fascinated me and I knew it could lead to bigger and better things.

Then I got my big break. I was sent to D.C. on a temporary assignment to fill in as weekend White House correspondent. All right. It was only weekends and it was only fill-in, but it was that all-important foot in the door to the Washington power establishment—and the big stories. I could have parlayed that into a regular spot in the A block, guest appearances as a panelist on Brinkley, a column in the *Washington Journalism Review*, a Maxwell House commercial.

But I had this little problem, you see. I couldn't seem to keep myself from fucking things up.

After half an hour of mingling, nobody had approached me and I was beginning to think the guy who called me was just an old high school boyfriend playing a practical joke. Old high school boyfriends. There's a depressing subject. I needed a drink.

Traditionally, the New Year's drink at ANN parties was Jonestown Punch, which was not only in bad taste but was bad tasting, a sickening, strong concoction of grape juice and vodka. That was free. Anything else you wanted you had to pay for at the cash bar.

Which is where I found Jerry, one arm over the bar, his Richard Nixon mask pulled down around his neck, trying to offend a young bartender/actress.

I stood behind him and heard him say, "I'll have a slow screw up against the wall. Know what that is?"

The bartender gave him a shriveling look.

"Sloe gin, OJ, and Galliano," she said.

That's Jerry for you. He drinks slow screws, a drink whose only purpose is to shock cocktail waitresses and lady bartenders. So out of touch, that Jerry. Doesn't know that the new generation of drinks—Sex on the Beach, Safe Sex, Oral Sex, Orgasms—makes the old slow screw quaint and old-fashioned.

He didn't see me standing behind him, so he proceeded unwisely.

"I'm well hung," he said to the skeptical brunet. "Oh, I apologize. I suffer from a mild case of Tourette's syndrome. Do you know that disease? It makes me tell the truth all the time."

He thought he was so funny. The woman just stared at him.

"Just a mild case. I'm a producer. I could get you a job in TV. Nine inches. Oh, there I go again."

Yes, all Jerry's best lines sounded like they'd been picked up from liars in locker rooms. I wanted to tap him on the shoulder and say something smartass—I was spoiling for a fight—but Burke was going to be here later and I was saving myself for him.

Anyway, the lady could take care of herself.

"Get away from me, or I'll call security," she hissed.

Jerry turned and saw me there.

He hated that I'd just witnessed his humiliation at the hands of a female.

"Look, it's another member of the PMS Sewing Circle," he said, as he pulled his Richard Nixon mask up over his face and pushed past me.

I could tell he was really drunk, otherwise he'd never have had the nerve to talk to a pretty young woman like the bartender. Jerry has this little problem relating to women, you see. It's a very common problem. When he's sober and he comes face to face with a woman in a social setting, he tends to become focused on her breasts and can't look her in the eye. If she moves from side to side, his head moves from side to side too, like a dog watching a tennis ball.

I ordered a shot of lemon Stoly and downed it with a grimace and then grabbed a plate of hors d'oeuvres and went up to the balcony area overlooking the dance floor. Louis waved me over to a table by the railing.

There were about a dozen writers crammed around the rectangular table, one in Woody Allen wig and glasses clutching a doll, another as a giant condom made of papier-mâché, complete with ribbing and reservoir tip, the whole thing articulated into segments so the wearer could bend and sit. The rest were a mixed bag of Scud missiles, presidential pets, the usual buffoonish congressmen.

They looked up and said hi, and then resumed an argument I'd apparently interrupted on the moral imperatives of *Bewitched*.

"Look at it as an allegory about marriage," Helen Lalo said. "This young woman comes into her marriage with exceptional abilities, which her husband tries to stifle. He tries to make her conform, to sacrifice her natural gifts, her specialness. Endora, on the other hand, encourages her daughter to *express* her special talents."

I couldn't get into this conversation, so I sat down and watched people waltzing on the dance floor below, waiting for my anonymous source to make himself known. Just then, my husband danced into view with Miss Amy Penny.

What a cute couple—Burke as Oliver North and Amy as Fawn Hall. I thought maybe Donald Trump and Marla Maples or Jimmy Swaggart and a generic truck-stop prostitute might be more appropriate costume couplings. But even as I was sneering, I felt a painful twinge. Burke looked really good, like a younger, shorter, blonder Peter Jennings, and that snappy marine uniform didn't hurt a bit.

Burke was a lucky guy. With his sunny looks, he could only age well. As a woman, I fought crow's-feet, but no crow's-feet for him. Unh-unh. What he had, the television columnists called "an endearing correspondent's squint." My worry lines robbed me of a little bit of youth and diminished my on-air worthiness, but his gave Burke a look of authority. Personally, I think the best revenge is aging well, and in that respect, Burke had me beat, hands down.

I was quite sure young women would always find him attractive, young women like Miss Amy Penny, who sparkled tonight as Fawn Hall. Unaware that I was watching, she looked up at him as they danced and he looked back and their eyes glistened, full of each other. They looked like they were in love, but I couldn't tell—was it with each other, or with their own reflections in each other's eyes?

I blinked back tears and watched through the blur as Greg Browner brought George Dunbar over and introduced him to

Burke. Dunbar was president of ANN. Burke shook his hand energetically and said something. I don't lip-read too well, but I knew Burke's spiel for media bigshots. Look them in the eye, smile warmly, say, "I really respect your work," and then quote them back to themselves ("I *liked* what you said to the National Association of Whatever about blah blah blah"). But he never gushed and the technique worked for him, talented sociopath that he is. He was a rising star at Channel 3 and being groomed for network, or so the buzz went.

These golden people were standing almost directly below me but Burke still hadn't seen me. For a moment I had a childish urge to do something cartoonish—drop a flower pot, anvil, safe, or grand piano on him. Not having any of those items at hand, I threw a cocktail peanut at him instead, which bounced off his head and landed at his feet. He looked up.

"Sorry!" I hollered down. He gave me that condescending look of hurt I know so well. It's the look a progressive parent gives a demon child when child psychology has failed. I am very disappointed with you, that look says. You've let me down. But you're hurting yourself more than me.

Burke didn't say anything, he just moved out of peanut range. I could see Amy still, talking to Greg in this hyper way. She was a nervous little thing, but nervous in a way other people (other than me) find attractive. It's a mildly gushing, eager-to-please nervousness.

The men exchanged business cards and all shook hands, the ritual networking farewell. When the band started up again with Glenn Miller, Burke and Amy went back to the dance floor, the better to display their unbridled love for each other to the whole world.

I needed another drink.

Chapter Two

I DRAGGED MYSELF AWAY from the writers and went back down to the bar where I ran into Eric Slansky, the supervising producer (or super prod as he was affectionately known) for the Browner show. Tonight he was dressed as New Coke.

He saw my tire iron and said, "Do you ever go anywhere unarmed, Robin?"

"I try not to, Eric."

"I hear you're almost single," he said, and grinned. I love a man who grins.

"Almost."

"Why don't you lose the tire iron and dance with me?" he asked.

Before getting on with Greg—a cushy gig—the year before, Eric was the super prod for *Ambush*, a half-hour issues show in which newsmakers and pundits were grilled by liberal and conservative journalists. He was very funny, very smart, and he seemed very laid-back.

Oh yeah. And he was very cute.

No, cute was for puppies. What this guy was, was anachronistically gorgeous. Like a character in a Merchant and Ivory film, that pre-war Ivy League letterman-in-track look: tall, lean, with shortish dark hair, a strong jaw, and piercing, shadowy blue eyes. If that wasn't just what the doctor ordered, he was thirty-one, four years younger than me.

Perfect. If Burke could have a younger woman, the laws of fairness dictated I could have a younger man, at least for the duration of the party.

Eric was playing along nicely, being very witty and suggestive. I got into it and, modesty aside, parried back with aplomb. I didn't take it seriously, though. Come on, the guy was gorgeous and younger than me and he had hit on me before. I always got the feeling he was just casting a role for his memoirs, the Older Married Woman, who comes somewhere between the Danish College Student and the Lesbian Duo.

"I'd love to see you outside of work," he said when the Stones medley ended.

Before I could answer, the music started up again and a strange man cut in on us. Eric stepped aside graciously.

"I don't believe we've met," I said apprehensively to the guy, who was about my height, with ginger-colored hair and a florid complexion.

"No, we haven't met. I'm a big fan of yours, though," he said. "And I know a lot about you, Red Knobby."

He smiled and thrust an envelope into my hand before turning and walking away.

Momentarily caught off guard, I stood for a moment and watched his back as he disappeared into the crowd.

People were still dancing around me and I was being buffeted on all sides by clumsy, dancing drunks. I looked down at the Marfeles Palace envelope before opening it. On Palace notepaper he had written: Room 13D, 11:00 P.M. SHARP. Attached to that was a photocopied sheet entitled "Investigative Report" and below that, in block letters, was my name, ROBIN JEAN HUDSON.

Huge sections of it had been blacked out, leaving only my vital statistics—height (5'8"), hair (red), eye color (blue), date of birth, Social Security number—and two little tidbits wedged between the black blocks, which reported that I had smoked pot (big deal) and that my mother had once been arrested in London for trying to walk into Buckingham Palace as though she owned the place.

Everything else was blacked out, which made me more curious, especially since the footer on the bottom of the page said 1 of 3, and there was only one page in the envelope.

I shoved it into my purse and went to the ladies' room to splash cold water on my face, catch my breath, and to think about all this.

The guy was no old high school boyfriend. He may have been a private investigator, but how could I be sure? What if he was one of my sicko fans who had paid a P.I. to get the goods on me?

Then again, judging by their bizarre mash notes, my sickest fans were hard-core masochists. Not very flattering, that's for sure, but relatively benign. The only way I could get hurt by them was if I gave in to their demands. Then I might pull a muscle whipping them or something.

Still, it would be pretty stupid to go up to a strange man's hotel room late at night, right? On the other hand, the guy might know all my dirty little secrets, and how else would I find out what he knew?

I considered my options. I could tell someone where I was going and to call the cops if I wasn't back in twenty minutes, but everyone at this party was a journalist. They'd want to know what was going on.

The only two people I could trust with this—my mentor, Bob McGravy, and my producer, Claire Thibodeaux—weren't there. Bob hadn't attended an ANN party since he gave up drinking in 1986 and Claire was a no-show.

I'd have to go it alone and be prepared for the worst, I decided. I went out to the ballroom to retrieve my tire iron, a real confidence-builder, which I'd left leaning against the bar.

But when I got there it was gone.

"Did you see my tire iron?" I asked the bartender.

"Your what?" she asked. "Your tire iron? No, I haven't seen it."

She shook two aluminum cocktail shakers between her hands and said, "They took the garbage away a while ago. Maybe they took it with the trash."

Shit. I really felt safer with that tire iron.

I still had two backup systems in my purse, a bottle of cheap spray cologne spiked with cayenne pepper to approximate Mace and a battery-operated Epilady, which I realized after one use was a better offensive weapon than feminine aid.

But to be on the safe side, I swiped a knife from the buffet table.

"Oh, can I use that?" Sawyer Lash asked, taking the knife from my grasp and dipping it in butter, which he applied to his roll before handing the butter-smeared utensil back to me.

Sawyer was dressed as the televangelist Paul Mangecet. Sawyer, whose nickname was Ted (as in Ted Baxter), was the only guy in the network whose professional reputation was

WHAT'S A GIRL GOTTA DO?

close to mine. He was a third-string anchorman with a gift for the malaprop.

He had such bad luck. Take his costume, for instance. Paul Mangecet, the head of Millennial Broadcasting and the take-over king of Christian business, was indeed a big news story and his messianic-chipmunk look lent itself well to costume satire.

Unfortunately, he was also a vocal critic of ANN's global reach and our news policy and everyone figured he'd make a stock play at some point. It was a sign of Jackson's sensitivity about the subject that the word had gone out that no one was to come to this party dressed, even in an unflattering way, as Paul Mangecet.

Someone forgot to tell Sawyer.

On my way back from the bar, one of the two hundred people I was avoiding came over to rub salt in the wound.

Solange Stevenson put her hand on my shoulder and said, "You must be feeling terrible, dear. Your husband showing up at your company party with his younger mistress! I want you to know it's natural for you to feel bad, Robin, to feel inadequate and inferior. My God, if anyone has the right to feel inade-quate and inferior tonight, it's *you*, Robin."

She had come up on me from behind. Solange moved like an Apache; you never heard her coming until the hatchet was in your head.

"How sweet of you to point that out," I said. "Thank you for telling me how I'm allowed to feel."

It was Solange's TV-psychologist way of being bitchy, of telling me I *was* inadequate and inferior. Solange couldn't stand anyone to be happier than she was. You know the philosophy: I cried because I had no shoes, and then I met a woman with three thousand pairs and I *really* cried.

It was funny about Solange. Outside of ANN she was one of the network's best-loved television personalities, with a large television following, but within ANN she was only feared. According to the newsroom, ice water ran through her veins and came out colder. She'd never actually practiced psychology. She'd gone straight from the doctoral program at Columbia into broadcasting. Those who can, do; those who can't, teach; and those who can't teach work in television.

Her eyes could shrink-wrap and label you in under a minute—manic depressive, sex addict, co-dependent— and she had the wider world broken down into two basic categories, perpetrators and victims. If you ask me, everyone is a little bit of both but, hey, I don't have a Ph.D in the subject.

"You have to give yourself *permission* to feel bad," Solange said, patting her honey-colored hair, which was upswept tonight and trés soigné.

"Gee, thanks, Doc. By the way," I asked, "where's *your* ex-husband?"

I pointedly looked around and saw Solange's ex, Greg Browner, talking to Joanne Armoire.

Joanne saw me and smiled her Grace Kelly smile. Only Grace Kelly was Grace Kelly, of course, but Joanne was first runner-up. Tonight—her beautiful, white blond hair hidden under a red wig, her petite body cloaked in a polka-dot dress with Peter Pan collar, Late Lucille Ball Collection circa 1950s, when Lucy and Desi were still America's marital ideal—she looked unsophisticated, yet still intelligent.

24

Lucy and Desi. And look what happened to them. There's a sitcom allegory for modern marital expectations for you.

"Greg and I parted amicably," Solange said, and my mind snapped back from the black-and-white years.

Before I could challenge this distortion of fact, Susan Brave came up, looking for Eric Slansky.

Susan, a too-tall, big-boned tweedy woman, was Solange's new producer. Before that she had worked for Eric on the Browner show. Her dull brown hair was shaped into a blunt-cut page boy that screamed Holyoke '81, where she had played field hockey and majored in weepy women poets. Normally she wore a uniform of cardigan sweaters, pearls, and plaid skirts but tonight she was dressed as Tipper Gore. She was obviously pasted; her tortoiseshell glasses had derailed from the bridge of her nose and were slightly askew, as was her Tipper wig and her goofy grin.

"Robin!" Susan said, throwing a loose arm around me. A little Jonestown Punch sloshed over the side of her glass. "How are ya? I saw you with Eric earlier. Do you know where I can find him?" She had a crush on Eric.

"How are you, dear?" Solange said to her. "You've had a bit too much to drink, I think."

"Gee," Susan said, chastened. "I'mmm sorry. I never know how mmmuch is enough." She threw her arms open in a broad gesture of prostration to her boss. The paper cup of punch went flying and splashed all over Solange's very expensive lilac silk suit.

Susan had just redeemed herself in my eyes, but Solange was not amused.

"Susan, sometimes I think you're beyond hope!" she said. "Now I have to go upstairs and change."

25

Susan was distraught. After Solange excused herself, Susan said, "I didn't mean to spill my drink on her. I feel terrrrrible."

She looked terrible. A shade of avocado was creeping into her complexion. She pulled herself erect and with something resembling dignity said, "I think I'm going to have to excuse myself now for the ladies' room. It's time to throw up."

She wheeled around and staggered purposefully towards the john.

It was 9:45. I still had over an hour to kill before my appointment and I felt tense. I needed to work off some stress somehow, so I went looking for Burke and Amy, figuring it was time to make *them* feel uncomfortable and knowing it would do me a world of good.

At that moment, the two of them were dancing to a Beatles medley. After taking a deep breath, I summoned up every ounce of chutzpah in me and shimmied on over to the dance floor, where I inserted myself between them. I was holding the knife I'd taken from the buffet.

"Hi, Robin," Burke said, grimacing as though he'd just stepped in something squishy that smelled.

He stopped dancing and stepped around me to be beside his girlfriend.

"And Miss Amy Penny," I said, extending my free hand. She took it without enthusiasm and we shook. When she withdrew her hand, I noticed she was wearing a ring with a huge diamond in it.

"It's very nice to see you . . . again," she replied feebly in her honeyed drawl. With her smooth, peachy makeup, she looked remarkably like a Barbie Doll. Malibu Barbie. Adultery Barbie. Corespondent Barbie.

"You're so young-looking," I said to her, taking a leaf on the

26

civil insult from Solange Stevenson's book. "What are you, Amy? Twenty-one?"

"Twenty-three," she said defensively.

"Barely out of college," I said, because I knew for a fact that she hadn't gone to college and was self-conscious about it.

"If you'll . . . please excuse me. I'm feeling a little bit woozy," Amy said, with pained politeness.

She looked a little pale. I loved that I had this effect on her. Whenever I saw her in the hallways at ANN, she turned tail and ran from me. Well, maybe she didn't run, but her step was noticeably quickened.

"I'm just going to leave you two alone to hash this out," she said.

Burke looked at her with caring. Poor Amy, put in this awkward situation by the Wicked First Wife. He gave me that progressive parent look again.

"You have a lot of nerve coming to this party," I said after she left us.

Whenever I speak with Burke, I intend to be amiable, to take the moral high ground and behave with decorum. But all he had to say was the word *Amy* and I became vengeful. To actually see them together looking so happy was too much.

Burke claimed they'd met when she was doing a field report at the Toy Expo and he was covering it for Channel 3. But in fact, they'd met at this very same ANN party last year, when he had accompanied me. I remembered a look they gave each other, a kind of recognition between strangers. At the time, it registered subconsciously. Only later, with the addition of certain facts, did that hidden memory of mine emerge and become significant. This was kind of an anniversary for them, I realized.

Burke was about to say something, but just then Boris Yeltsin walked by with Mia Farrow and Ross Perot.

When they passed out of earshot, he said, "These are Amy's friends and colleagues too. You don't own ANN."

He paused while a spotted owl walked past, holding a martini in each hand.

"Of course, I wouldn't have come if I'd known you were going to be here. I would have thought, given all the embarrassment you've suffered this last year, you'd want to keep a lower profile," he said.

"Hey, discretion is a two-way street. Do you call that rock on her left hand low profile? It's like a floodlight."

Burke took a deep breath. I think he was counting to ten. Around seven he recaptured his temper and said, "It's just as well you came over, I guess. I need to talk to you anyway. I want to get this over with."

"Big hurry, huh? Am I right? *Is* that an engagement ring she's wearing?"

Amy returned and interrupted us.

"Burke, I'm feeling sick. I think I have that, you know . . ." Their eyes met. They were speaking in their own code. "That flu. I'm going to get a cab uptown."

"But I haven't met Jack Jackson yet and it isn't even ten. Can't you wait until I can take you?"

"Well, I *can't* wait, Burke," she said.

There was a perceptible pause.

It was impossible to get Burke away from a party until he'd met every single important person present who could help his career. As Jackson rarely showed up at company parties, this could be his only shot. I watched with interest to see who would win this battle, as I'd been there, and I'd never won.

"You're right. You stay and meet Jack Jackson," she said after a moment, a girl who put her man's concerns ahead of her own. "Madri is leaving early. Maybe I can share her cab."

This could only make me look bad by comparison.

"You're sure you don't mind?" he asked her, sounding sincere, full of empathy for his wench. This was not the same guy I'd been married to.

"I'm sure. No reason for both of us to miss this."

They made like they were going to kiss and I said, "Please. A little discretion."

After she left us again, for good this time, Burke turned to me and said, "Robin, I just want to put this behind us and get on with our lives. I have a lot of respect for you. I'd like for us to be friends. If not, well, I don't care what you say to me—or what you do—," he added, with less conviction. "But leave Amy out of it. She's an innocent bystander."

"Innocent, my ass! She dated a married man while he was still married, while he was still sleeping with his wife and telling his wife he loved her. She did it knowingly. I'm sorry, but that's against the rules."

"She can't help it. She loves me."

"Gag me with an oar."

He took another exaggerated deep breath. "Look, Robin, shit happens. People decide they want different things. People fall out of love. . . ."

"Then you should have told me. You shouldn't have claimed to love me. You lied, you cheated, and she encouraged you, and for that," I paused, "you have to die."

I raised the butter knife slightly for emphasis and was gratified to see that, for a split second, Burke took me seriously enough to put an arm in front of his face defensively.

"I'm joking," I said with contempt. "You're such a weenie. I mean, what a cliché, leaving me for a younger woman. Did you really think I was going to stab you? Do you really think you're worth a crime of passion? Get real."

"You've been known to go nuts every now and then," he said.

"Oh please, we're divorcing. I'm allowed to lose my god-damned temper. It's one of the perks."

He was getting pissed off. "It's your sanity I'm worried about, Robin, not your temper. Your *sanity.*"

What a difference a few years of marriage makes. "I'll never sign the papers," he told me once, shortly after we were married, when I mentioned that insanity ran in my family (it came straight down the maternal line) and confided my deeply held fear of ending up in an asylum somewhere, muttering to myself about the state of the world with spittle building up at the corners of my mouth. Or wandering the streets telling strangers I'm a member of the royal family, as my mother often does.

I'd pushed him too far. Now he was using that fear as a weapon against me, just as I use his fears against him. On the day we split up, he'd told me I was a hysteric, a doomed woman, certifiable.

And what had I done to incite this heartless assault? Merely tried to feed him a pie—in which I'd baked his lucky shirt, a beloved silk Perry Ellis, cut into strips and enclosed in a light, flaky pastry. That was the same day, as I recall, that I learned of his affair with Miss Congeniality, Miss "My future plans are to find a cure for cystic fibrosis or else become a television anchorwoman."

He continued to probe this sore spot. "Do you still keep that morbid scrapbook of dead people you don't even know?"

"Murdered people."

"Oh, murdered strangers. So much more rational than just dead people. Do you still grow poison ivy in the window boxes?"

"It's too cold for window boxes. I have it in hanging planters inside the windows now and in vases on top of all the major appliances and valuables. In case of burglars. If they rob me and the police don't catch them . . ."

"You want them to suffer a painful rash at least, I know," he said. "You've explained this to me a dozen times and it still strikes me as nutty. You don't think this behavior is a little strange?"

"This from a man who rubs sheep-placenta cream into his skin every night. A man who refers to his genitalia as 'Uncle Wiggily.' A man who won't read a magazine until he wipes down the cover with disinfectant."

"You know how many people's hands a magazine goes through before it gets to your door? Do you know where their hands have been?"

"I'm surprised you were willing to kiss me without wiping me down first."

"It's no use trying to talk to you civilly," Burke said. "You'll excuse me."

"Sure, Heinrich," I said loudly. He looked around nervously. I know lots of his secrets: that his given name is Heinrich Albert Stedlbauer IV, changed to Burke Avery for television; that at home he belches without excusing himself and secretly reads Judith Krantz. I know his guilty pleasures and his annoying habits. I know his blood type, his allergies, even which foods give him gas (raspberries and coconut were the worst offenders). I wish I didn't know so much about him, and I wish to hell he didn't know so many things about me either. That's why I said his name—to remind him to keep his mouth shut about me.

"You promised not to tell anyone that my name—"

"You promised to love, honor, and cherish," I said, but he looked so hurt by my threat that I gave in. "I won't say anything. Jeez."

"Thank you," he said. "Let's get together and talk one of these days. I really do want to be friends if we can." He kissed my cheek and as soon as he did I wiped the kiss away with my hand.

I looked for Eric—unsuccessfully—while worrying about my imminent meeting with the ginger-haired guy. At 10:55, I headed to the elevators. As I got on, Solange, changed into a fresh blue suit, came out.

"Oh, are you staying here tonight, Robin?" she asked.

"Uh—no. I'm going up to meet a friend."

"Oh, I see," she said suggestively.

I smiled weakly and let the elevator doors shut her out. Great. A rumor of some kind would be circulating around the ballroom in about a minute and a half. I wondered who my name would be linked with. I wondered who I could get to tell me.

I walked down the corridor and when I reached the door marked 13D I opened my purse just slightly so I'd have easy access to my Epilady and my cayenne cologne if I needed them, and I kept a good grip on my knife.

I knocked and waited for a moment. There was no answer. I knocked again harder but there was still no answer.

I figured maybe he was just late. I'm a late person myself as a rule, so I leaned against the wall and waited for another fifteen minutes.

While I was standing there, Joanne Armoire came out of a room down the hall. She gave me a quizzical smile. "Who are you waiting for, Robin?" she asked. Journalists are shameless.

"A friend," I said, looking away because I was lying.

"Oh. Well, happy New Year—almost."

"Yeah, you too." I watched her walk away and disappear into the wall where the elevators were.

I knocked one more time, louder and longer, just in case the guy had fallen asleep or something. But there was still no answer.

What kind of weird joke is this? I wondered.

Yep, that's what it was, I realized. A joke.

I'm known as kind of a . . . prankster at ANN, which was crawling with them. And somebody was getting even with me and in a way that would naturally appeal to my troublesome curiosity.

Let's face it, a few phone calls around my hometown could have yielded the information he'd fed me on the phone.

Hell, if he'd caught my own mother on a bad day, she would have quite innocently told him anything he wanted to know about me, and forgotten about it as soon as she hung up the phone.

It was a pretty good setup, I had to admit. Page 1 of 3. Very clever. I wondered who had masterminded it and when and how they'd reveal themselves. I started gleefully plotting my revenge as I returned to the party.

I was hoping it wasn't too late for me to catch up with Eric Slansky.

Chapter Three

I HAD MORE THAN A slight hangover as I rode the subway down to Jackson Broadcasting the next day, New Year's Day, a working day in the news business. An electrical storm cracked and thundered at regular intervals inside my skull.

It was one of those days when everything on the subway seemed slightly unreal, when I thought of the city as New York: the Movie. Everything and everyone seemed self-conscious and surreal. Across the aisle, this kid was staring at me and in spite of my imploding brain I smiled at her. Suddenly, she burst into tears.

I turned to the guy next to me and said, "Kids just love me." The man looked surprised that I had spoken to him, like he too might start bawling at any moment.

I'd dressed, fed Louise Bryant, and boarded the subway on autopilot, and only now was the night before returning to me, in flashes. Burke . . . Amy . . . Eric Slansky. Oh God.

Had he really told me he was HIV negative and liked "slightly" older women? Had I really mentioned that at thirty-five I was at my sexual peak? Had we really discussed all the different places we'd had sex?

And that practical joke. The ginger-haired man who'd never showed. After waiting around outside room 13D I'd gone back down to the party and had another lemon Stoly, so the rest of the night was still kind of blurry around the edges.

I vaguely remembered Jack Jackson on stage toasting the new year and leading us in a countdown to it. Some asshole who thought he was being funny randomly shouted nonsensical numbers to confuse us, which, thanks to our inebriation, he was able to do briefly, until Jackson restored order.

When midnight struck, with corks popping and confetti swirling in the air above, I kissed Eric Slansky.

Yeah. I remembered that kiss pretty clearly. In fact, the memory of it was so fresh in my mind it gave me a pelvic contraction. Eric and I danced and kissed until about 1:30 A.M. Shortly after that, with everything around me wobbling, the air wavy like hot air over a fire, I vanished from the screen.

The subway stopped directly beneath Jackson Broadcasting headquarters, a massive black-and-pink granite building in the east fifties, and I got off with a horde of waxy white people who worked nearby, including a few JBS types whose names I didn't know.

JBS is really three networks: DIC, the Drive-In Channel; JNC, Jackson Network Corporation; and ANN. DIC is a movie channel aimed at the beer-and-gun-rack crowd, while JNC is a bit of everything, including tractor pulls, a highly rated if critically ignored wrestling show, and plenty of *Mr. Ed* reruns. ANN, however, is the prestige of JBS, the all news network nobody thought would fly but did, bringing honors and black ink to our esteemed founder and chairman, Georgia Jack Jackson.

We'd come a long way, baby. In the early days of ANN, there were only two kinds of people there, old-timers with checkered careers rescued from the fringes—and drunk tanks—of journalism, and newcomers, right out of college and willing to work for peanuts. The freshly scrubbed and the nearly washed-up. Back then, it took a peculiar mix of genius and low self-esteem to work for ANN. The low self-esteem allowed them to work us long hours for low pay without dissent. The genius kept us on the air and built the quality of the network.

I read somewhere about this Afghan tribe that could build a Kalashnikov from a Chinese bicycle. That's sort of what we did in those early years. Back then our equipment was cheap and broke all the time. We broadcast an entire interview with Henry Kissinger in various hues of green, klieg lights fell in the middle of newscasts, and one day someone came and repossessed the set while we were on the air.

We were hapless but we had this sense of mission: to scoop the other networks and to present the news as unbiased and unfiltered as possible to the people, the unpolished news, warts and all. Every once in a while we'd scoop the Nets on something important. We'd rush out of the bushes, muss the networks' hair, and rush back in again, laughing.

Ten years later, we are all glossy and well manicured and every prime minister, president, and dictator in the world watches us. It's scary. Especially if you're not all glossy and manicured, like me.

I was a little late for work, but not so late that I couldn't stop to scan Democracy Wall, a ten-foot bulletin board that covered the left wall in the hallway leading to the newsroom.

Under the heading FAN CLUB was a letter from one of Madri Michaels's crazy fans, asking her to please send a pair of her freshly worn panties, autographed. There were contests to provide captions for wire-service photos, goofy stories, and a little bit of legitimate news, although the primary purpose of Democracy Wall was to provide labor with a forum to spoof management, world leaders, and anchors. I'd been the butt of a few Democracy Wall jokes myself.

That day I was looking for a note referring to the joke played on me. But there was nothing.

It was ten minutes to the top of the 10 A.M. show and just outside the newsroom anchorman Patrick Lattanzi was speed-smoking a cigarette before he went on. He smiled at me, but didn't waste any smoking time in salutations.

"Hi, Pat," I said anyway, as I went into the newsroom. A desk assistant ducked between us with freshly ripped copy while an editor veered around us with a freshly cut videotape.

If you've never been in a television newsroom, it's a little like being inside a giant pinball game. Tapes whirred, typewriters clacked, computer screens hummed, phones buzzed, lights flashed, and images flickered. Along one wall were bright monitors showing what the other networks were running as well as our own picture and the feeds we were pulling off the satellites. Underneath the monitors was the assignment desk, manned by one African-American woman and a half dozen harried-looking and overweight white men in their shirtsleeves.

The assignment desk branched off into the satellite desk on one side and the international desk on the other, forming a wall of desks around the room's perimeter. In the middle of all this were the writers, who sat at circular "pods" with a copy editor on an elevated area in the center. Producers were at the producer pods, associate producers at associate producer pods, and lower forms of newsroom life without a pod to call their own were eeking past each other like bats careening around a cave.

Across the newsroom, Bob McGravy was standing by the supervisors' desk, talking to the day super. He saw me and waved, then he held up a small Slinky and grinned. Recently, he had completed a smoking-cessation program kicking a thirty-five-year-old cigarette habit he picked up as a copy boy for Edward R. Murrow in the 1950s. Every day he had some other substitute in his hand—a dollop of modeling clay, a harmonica, even a rosary. I'd given him the Slinky, wrapped in paper made up of supermarket tabloid headlines.

We had a good relationship, McGravy and I. He was my mentor, but despite the company rumors to the contrary, our relationship was strictly platonic. Even if I had had lust for him, I never would have acted on it; the guy was my boss's boss, and I'm just not that kind of girl.

At that moment, someone sidled up to me and blurted, in a whisper, "Turk alert!" and I fixed my eye on the far exit and headed straight for it.

All over the newsroom, people scattered, looking for edit rooms to hide in or frantically hitting typewriters or picking up phones in order to look busy. But I reacted a little too slowly; just inches from the doorway, I felt the large hand of Turk Hammermill on my shoulder.

"Robin!" he said.

I turned around slowly, working up a polite smile as I did. "Turk. I didn't see you," I lied.

Turk was wearing what he wore every day, a Mets sweatshirt

over jeans. As a sports producer he didn't have to worry about what he wore, and he didn't.

"You know what I did this weekend?" he said, not waiting for an answer. "I watched a tape of the Mets-Expos game from last September. Did you see that game?"

Then I made my second mistake. I hesitated before answering.

"Man! It was brilliant!" Turk began. "Okay, Mets are up, it's the bottom of the ninth, score is seven-three 'Spos. Two down, three men on, and . . ."

By now I was trying to devise a new strategy for escape, looking around the newsroom for someone to rescue me. But everyone had seen Turk by now and they were avoiding my eyes. Cowards.

". . . first pitch is a strike, second pitch is a strike, and the third—oh, first I should tell you about the 'Spos pitcher. This pitcher, his name is . . ."

In a business that specializes in them, Turk was the biggest bore. Not only was it impossible to get a word in edgewise, but he digressed from the main story before completing it and then digressed from his digressions, constantly interrupting himself to go off on tangents, each less interesting than the one before.

". . . his father used to pitch in the Carolina League. Of course, that was long before major league baseball went up to Canada . . ."

Widely told newsroom joke: What's the least heard sentence at ANN?

Answer: I'm looking for Turk.

What kept me, and legions before me, from saying "Turk, shut up!" was that he was really a nice guy, a little on the sensitive side and not too bright, and nobody could bear to hurt his feelings. Oh yeah, and he was Georgia Jack Jackson's nephew.

Relief for me came from an unlikely quarter. As Turk was reciting the History of Major League Baseball, Jerry Spurdle came up beside me and began chewing me out.

"Jesus, Robin, we're waiting for you. The production meeting was *supposed* to start half an hour ago. Jesus. Excuse us, won't you, Turk?"

Spurdle led me out of the newsroom and down the hall to the Special Reports offices, which were housed in what was once an extraneous set of men's and ladies' bathrooms. The stalls and plumbing had been removed and replaced with three large offices and a central conference area and it had all been repainted, but we still had ceramic tile on the floor and you could still see the outline of the word "Gents" where it had been on the swinging door to the hallway.

Occasionally someone from another floor would walk in, expecting a urinal, and be surprised to see people working in there. Frankly, a lot of people at ANN still considered it the biggest urinal in the building. Special Reports was where stories like "Sex for Sale," "Hollywood Hunks," and "Your Child and Satan" were done, "investigative" shows that were rating grabbers, heavy on clichés and light on investigation. It was also where I was paying my debt to journalism for professional gaffes committed in the last year.

When we got to the office, Claire, the producer, was waiting with a box of chocolate frosted doughnuts and a fresh pot of coffee. She did it for us, bless her soul, and not for her because she never let refined sugar or caffeine cross her pure lips.

"Your phone messages," Claire said, handing me a couple of

pink papers. Two calls from Elroy, one of my "special fans," who sees me as his dominatrix and gets off by calling or writing me to describe the many ways he wants me to punish him. This time he wanted me to spank his bare bottom with a razor strap and then glue his eyelids shut with Krazy Glue.

And they say romance is dead.

I crumpled them up and pitched them into the wastebasket by the coffee machine, where they hit with a satisfying ping.

"I didn't see you at the party last night," I said to Claire as I got coffee.

"I flew back late last night and by the time I got to my apartment, it was after midnight and I didn't see the point." She brushed her thick black hair with her fingers to get it off her face. "Was it fun?"

"It was weird. Burke was there with Amy Penny," I said as we sat down at the conference table and waited for Jerry to quit stirring his coffee, which he drank in a cup that said CHIEF MELON INSPECTOR, WTNA TV AND RADIO.

"Sorry I missed it," Claire said. "Was it terrible? Did you maim him?"

"Nah. I think they're engaged, although Burke wouldn't give me a straight answer."

I pulled at a chocolate doughnut, breaking off a sticky, doughy piece. "Well, what the hell. I had to see them together sooner or later. Now it's behind me. Anyway, I made her feel more uncomfortable than she made me feel, so I won the party."

Jerry sat down between us at the conference table, still stirring his coffee loudly. "Where were you last night?" he asked Claire.

"I had a family thing," Claire said. "My people celebrate

New Year's with an animal sacrifice. My mom expects me to be there, you know." This was for Jerry's benefit.

"I don't believe you anymore," he said, scowling.

"What did you sacrifice?" I asked. "A small child?"

"God no, a small rodent. Robin, you *know* human blood used in a sacrifice stains."

Around the newsroom, the Spurdle-Thibodeaux production team was known as Beauty and the Beast. Jerry had what is commonly known as "a great face for radio," which is where he came from. He had a soft and sinister look, pale and blond, gone to fat, "a mediocre sack of Aryan genes," as Eric had put it the night before. I'd said that Jerry looked like that unmarried uncle who hung out in the shed during family gatherings, the one your mother always warned you in a whisper not to be alone with.

What made Jerry even uglier was his habit of trying to disguise it by adopting the personal styles of famous handsome men. For a while, he went through a Don Johnson phase, where he moussed his hair, slicked it back, and sported a five-o'clock shadow all day long. He looked like Goofy.

Claire, on the other hand, had the kind of exotic beauty that made grown men in responsible positions stutter when they talked to her. She was half African-American, a quarter French and a quarter Cherokee, and when Jerry first hired her—to prove once and for all that he wasn't a bigot—he speculated that it was really something for someone like her to actually graduate from college and he asked her a lot of questions about voodoo. To her credit, Claire took it, and him, as a joke and went along with it, and every day she'd feed him some shit about animal sacrifices and black masses. By implying that her poor, illiterate swamp-trawling parents needed every cent she could give them, she actually squeezed a raise out of him.

Claire knew a lot about Cajun folk magic and she even believed some of it, the way I believe astrologers, but the truth was, Claire's father was a dentist in Metairie, Louisiana, and her mother was a dental hygienist. And they were Baptists.

"Enough chitchat, you two," Jerry said, leaning back into his chair. *Please, God,* I prayed, *make his chair fall over,* but it remained perfectly balanced.

"The holidays are over now and so it's time to get back to work on our sperm bank series. I've done some thinking and I've decided we will have to go undercover on this story."

I groaned. I hate undercover work. Sometimes it's necessary, but I hate it. It's dishonest, it's often gratuitous, and I didn't think it was needed for this story as we had a half dozen disgruntled same-race couples with mixed-race children—to make the point.

"Robin and I will pose as man and wife and go in with concealed cameras," Jerry said.

"God, you're not going to make a donation, are you?" I asked, horrified.

"Well, Robin, I think I might have to, for credibility."

"Credibility?" I asked. I made a face.

"Give it up, Robin. We are not doing that special report on death you want to do so badly."

"It's a good idea, a no-nonsense look at what happens to you when you die, your body, I mean, and what it costs. Boomers are facing the last half of their lives and it's starting to become an issue. I thought we could demythologize it."

"You want to do it because it's morbid."

"No, I want to do it because . . . ," I began.

"Because you fear death," Claire said.

"It's morbid," Jerry said. "And how are we going to get someone to sponsor death? No company wants its products associated with that subject—except funeral homes and places like that."

"And arms makers," Claire said, although she didn't really like the idea either. Her area of interest was exotic diseases. At the last editorial meeting, she fought for a series on a virus emerging in Africa that made your blood boil over until you kind of exploded.

"Don't go running to McGravy again, crying about how I'm a sexist sleazeball who makes Edward R. Murrow turn over in his grave," he said, reading my mind. "At least I never belched during a White House news conference carried live over national TV. While the mike was right above me."

Touché.

And he went on. "At least I never asked a woman who ate her dead companion after their plane crashed what he tasted like."

(Like tough, fatty chicken.)

"At least the mailroom still delivers my mail." It was the best retort I could come up with as I stomped off, the office door swinging behind me, and went to find McGravy to lodge my daily complaint about Jerry Spurdle.

God. If I close my eyes I can still see that mike hovering over me; I can feel the eyes of the other reporters on me, the eyes of the vice president, and on the other side of the television screen the eyes of thousands of hard-core ANN viewers. It is the first question I've been called on to ask (and now, for the life of me, I can't remember what it was). I stand, I open my mouth—and I burp. Not one of those delicate, barely a hiccup, burps. A ripping Richter-registering roar of a belch. After that, all I remember is tumultuous laughter and a hot chill of mortification.

All right, so I belched during a White House news conference carried live to half the globe, thus aborting my brief career as a Washington correspondent. Consider this: Everybody belches. It's natural. The queen and the pope belch.

The trick is not to do it when there's a high-powered mike hovering right above you.

And yes, I asked a woman who survived a plane crash by eating her dead companion, Bud, what human flesh tasted like. She was very open about the incident and I am a curious person. Don't you wonder about things sometimes? Don't you ever say things you regret?

Somehow, though, I got a reputation as being sensational, grotesque in my thinking, and with my career spinning out of control, down towards the hard earth, Bob McGravy convinced the powers to be at ANN, the network mandarins and the court eunuchs, to give me another chance. I thought they'd give me my old beat, Crime & Justice. Instead, they plugged me into Special Reports.

I never thought I would end up like this, writing and reporting on such gems of journalism as "Grannies Who Like Sex" and "The He-She Report," with everything given an extra sensational twist in the copy-edit process by Jerry Spurdle.

But Jerry's all-time low, the worst series he ever did, was "The Cancer That Dare not Speak its Name," on colon cancer, before I worked for him. A previous special reporter, now in our London bureau, told me about it. It wasn't a bad idea really, looking at colon cancer as a sidebar to the Reagan polyps story, dispelling some of the myths, encouraging people to have themselves checked out.

The mistake was asking viewers to send samples of their excrement on a Popsicle stick implement available in kits distributed free at outlets of a popular drugstore chain. Actually, ANN asked them to send their Popsicle sticks full of shit to a lab on Long Island to be analyzed at ANN's expense.

It was a humanitarian gesture that backfired, so to speak. On part one of the series, Jerry neglected to include the full-screen graphic with the lab address, which was to be run at the end of each "Cancer That Dare not Speak" segment, and as a consequence thousands of people with bowel problems throughout the tri-state area just sent their shit samples to ANN. Most didn't even bother with the Popsicle stick. They just wrapped up a good-sized hunk and slipped it into a padded envelope.

Needless to say, the folks in the mailroom have had it in for Jerry Spurdle ever since.

After roaming the byzantine hallways of ANN for forty-five minutes, I finally learned that McGravy was tied up in meetings with the mandarins. But just as I was about to abandon giving Jerry his RDA of grief, I saw Turk in the hallway outside the newsroom.

"Turk, how are you?" I said. "You should have been over in Special Reports five minutes ago."

"Yeah?"

"Well, Jerry and I were talking about the '69 Mets."

"Is he still there?"

"Sure. Why don't you go over?" I suggested.

Turk took off like a man on a mission.

I felt much better now.

In the afternoon, we had an interview with a white woman

whose husband banked sperm with Empire Semen before he died of cancer, and who had given birth to an Asian-looking child, leading her troublesome in-laws to believe she'd had an affair with an Asian man while her husband's body was still cooling.

The sperm bank's lawyers played up this theory in order to get it off the hook, and there was no way she could prove otherwise. She loved the child dearly, she said, but she wanted her reputation restored and she wanted her late husband's sperm found so she could try to have his child as well.

After that, we interviewed a doctor who did genetic typing on another baby conceived from Empire Semen semen. While he was 99.6 percent sure it was the wrong semen, he couldn't prove the woman hadn't slept with other men.

With those two in the can, we went back to the office. We had another such interview to shoot later that week, along with at least one undercover shoot, before we'd start writing and assembling the series, so at the moment I was rather under-employed. The pace could get kind of slow in Special Reports between interviews. I missed the action of general news.

I logged into the computer and an E-mail message blinked in the corner of the screen. I retrieved it. It was from Eric.

"Stairs?" it said.

I laughed. The night before, I'd quizzed him on his sex life, where he'd done it, in what position, how many times, etc. Now he was reciprocating. I hesitated before answering, but then decided it was okay, it was safe to proceed.

I typed back, "Not yet." I sent the message and then typed, "Public transportation?"

From his computer terminal in a far corner of the building, he answered, "Yes. Please be more specific."

"Subways, buses, trains, planes, helicopters, elevators, escalators, moving sidewalks, the Staten Island Ferry?" I typed. "Yes yes yes yes no yes no no yes," he beeped back. "And the Verrazano-Narrows in a moving vehicle," he added.

Around five o'clock Claire came into my office and said she wanted to discuss her career strategy in a more relaxed setting. Greg Browner was thinking of adding *Nightline*-esque backgrounder pieces profiling the celebrities on the show, and that would mean a reporter slot. Claire was dying to report.

"Keggers?" I suggested. Keggers, our usual hangout, was cheaper and more convenient than Kafka's, where she wanted to meet, and much less pretentious, or at least pretentious in a different way.

"Expand your horizons," Claire said. "You might even like the place. Besides, I want to talk about Greg and reporting and I want to do it away from the radar ears of journalists."

"Kafka's then," I said, and went back to the computer.

For another hour, I scanned the wires for interesting murder stories, and then went off to find McGravy. The early evening, after the day shift was gone, was the best time to catch him in his office. I found him there carefully winding one of the twenty or so windup toys on his desk: lizards, wind-up sushi, kangaroos, robots, chattering teeth, and so forth, all of which seemed to be moving. More tactile replacements for cigarettes.

"The great thing about quitting smoking," McGravy said without looking up at me, "is that you can get away with all kinds of childish behavior under the banner of quitting smoking. I don't think I've had so many toys in my life, or enjoyed them so much."

Not exactly dignified behavior for the network vice president in charge of editorial content, God bless him. Although he blames this behavior on giving up the toxic weed, calling this his second childhood, the truth is it's more of a recurring childhood, and quitting smoking is just his latest excuse.

He looked up at me now, pushing his glasses up the bridge of his nose, and laughed this grumbling kind of laugh. "What can I do you for?" he asked.

"Jerry Spurdle . . ."

McGravy rolled his eyes. "Now what?"

"He sickens me. He wants to go undercover on this sperm bank story. He wants to donate sperm."

A pair of walking sneakers were winding down on his desk and he picked them up and rewound them before answering. To his side, a marching baseball walked off the edge and fell into the wastepaper basket, where it flailed its legs helplessly against the trash. McGravy bent over and retrieved it, then rewound it and sent it towards the other edge.

"Sperm," I reminded McGravy.

"Well," he said, rewinding the chattering teeth. "It might be necessary and there's no way it can cause the kind of problem colon cancer did. You have to learn to bend, Robin."

"Bend, or bend over? Bob, it's too hard for me to work for him," I said, weariness in my voice, trying to appeal to his respect for individual personality. "He makes me so mad I want to pound him into the ground sometimes. It takes seven major muscle groups just to hold my tongue. Can't you get me out of there?"

"No, Robin, I can't. My hands are tied," he said, gesticulating with a toy duck. "Jerry wants you in that unit, and what Jerry wants, he gets. I'm sorry, Robin."

"Jerry *wants* me there?" I echoed. "What a sadist."

"Some people who know your temper, Robin, might say he's a masochist," Bob said. "He knows you're smart and can get the job done. The fact is, you're not exactly a hot commodity right now, and he is. As long as he keeps his overhead low and his profit high, he'll be Dunbar's fair-haired boy and he'll get what he wants. You know Jerry has turned a huge profit in Special Reports ever since he took it over."

George Dunbar, the president of ANN, had been hand-picked by Georgia Jack Jackson for his ability to squeeze dollars from dimes, and he *loved* Jerry Spurdle.

Puzzled by Jerry's success, the J-school grads down in the newsroom came up with two theories about how he'd made it to his position: Either he had color videos of network executives performing sexual acts with members of endangered species, or he performed those sexual acts on network executives himself.

But I knew the truth. While the journalists of the network disdained him, the accountants loved him because he was cheap and the salesmen loved him because his series were easy to sell to sponsors. He made them that way; he aimed the shows at the sponsors as much or more than the viewers. He knew a famous maker of tampons and sanitary napkins would appreciate the concentrated female audience tuning into a series on Hollywood hunks, for instance. Spurdle bragged that his unit's reports were the only ones never sponsored by anything that flashed an on-screen 800 number. He had real sponsors, no small boast at the network built by Slim Whitman and Ginsu knives.

"Robin, let me tell you something I learned over the years I've been lucky enough to make a living in this business," McGravy said.

Uh-oh. I smelled a "When-I-worked-with-Murrow" story coming. This usually involved a homey anecdote or parable about some character he knew in the early days of television, culminating in an odd moral.

Sure enough, McGravy told me about a man he used to work with at CBS, back in the olden, golden days before color transmission, who had a lot of talent but a bad temper. He could never compromise and not only did it make him unpopular around the office but it ruined several of his shows. One day, just as his show was about to go to air, he had a massive coronary and died. It was like a bad smell was removed from the place, McGravy said. Nobody missed him.

He paused and I knew the big finish was coming.

"The thing is, if you're talented you can get away with being a sonofabitch, but nobody misses a sonofabitch when he dies."

Oh, like when I'm dead I'm going to care, I almost said. But then I remembered that I respect this man, so I held my tongue.

I knew what he was trying to tell me, and I knew he was right. I had to be nicer to other people, be cooler, panic less, cuss less, smile more. Deep down, I knew all this and yet it galled me—it absolutely galled me—to have to take orders from Jerry Spurdle, a man for whom I had no respect, for whom I had nothing but contempt, a man who believed a woman was only a vehicle for the transport of her breasts.

"I could make Spurdle fire me," I said. "ANN would have to pay out my contract."

"I have no doubt."

"He shouldn't fool with a woman who knows his credit card number. Because living well is not the best revenge, Bob. The best revenge, in my opinion, is huge crates of Depend undergarments delivered to his apartment door. Or live chickens maybe . . ."

"Don't do it, Robin. Nobody will hire you in this town right now. Nobody will hire you in Washington or L.A. either. You'll end up doing paid programming or pollen stories on the Weather Channel for the rest of your life." He stood up and leaned over the desk for emphasis.

"No, I won't."

"You'll be selling tooth whitener at four in the morning on Nickelodeon. If you're lucky. Because there are guys like Jerry everywhere, and sooner or later you have to learn how to deal with them. You'd better do it sooner, Robin."

"I'm not going to kiss Jerry's ass. . . ."

"I'm not asking you to kiss his ass. I expect you to stand up to him, to fight to lower the sleaze factor. But quitting is backing away from a fight just because it isn't turning out precisely the way you want at the moment. Don't chicken out. If you stay here, do your time in Special Reports, pretty soon everyone will forget about the . . . belch and the cannibalism thing, and I'll be able to safely move you back to general news—*maybe*. But be patient, and remember, as the old saying goes, you get more flies with honey than with vinegar."

"Well, if you *really* want flies, you ought to try bullshit," I said. "It's an old folk remedy."

"I have faith in you, Robin, for whatever it's worth," Bob said. He wound up a monkey with cymbals and sent it towards me.

"It's worth a lot, Bob."

The monkey clanged its cymbals.

Chapter Four

BEFORE I WENT TO KAFKA'S, I had to stop at home to change clothes and to feed my dictatorial cat. Louise Bryant greeted me at the door with a contemptuous howl.

"Relax, you're not starving," I said to her.

Knowing that tone of voice, she adopted another tactic, kissing ass, rubbing her back against my leg and looking up at me with something almost like affection. If I didn't feed her soon, she'd move to more punitive action, taking a clawed swat at the back of my leg. Louise Bryant was very Machiavellian.

Louise Bryant came to us, to me, late in her life. It was like this: Burke wanted a baby, I didn't. Some people are meant to be parents, and some of us, those with long histories of insanity in the family, for instance, are not. In the end it was moot, because it turned out I was infertile. Children just weren't a realistic expectation without tens of thousands of dollars of costly and chancy in vitro. Burke needed a more fecund field than me (which he apparently thought he'd found in Amy Penny).

So Burke and I compromised on a cat. Actually, we'd decided on a kitten but at the SPCA we changed our minds and took home this ancient, battle-scarred alley cat with a taste for restaurant dumpster food and roses, a strange fear of harmonica music and a less strange fear of thunderstorms. After an unknown number of years as a street cat she took to being a house cat surprisingly well, as though she was born to luxury. But right away, the battle of wills began between Louise Bryant and me over her diet. She refused to eat anything from a can unless I stir-fried it with greens and oyster sauce.

Oddly enough, I do this every night for her. I open a can of Hill's Science Diet and stir-fry it in a little olive oil with some bok choy. I do this for a cat I'm not even sure likes me.

As soon as I put the plate down for her, she immediately forgot about my existence and buried her face in her food.

I searched through my closet for something sort of chic and sort of bohemian to wear, something that would qualify for Kafka's. I hadn't been to Kafka's, but I'd heard of it. It was the club of the minute, the newest mecca for young, stunning New Yorkers, like Claire. She ran with a gang that always included a lot of really beautiful, pseudo-bohemian actors, models, writers, and cerebral rock musicians who seemed on the verge of huge breaks. They all had respectable success at an early age, appearing in good off-Broadway plays or in small art films by promising young directors and they were very much in love with themselves. One of their number was making a documentary about them and their lifestyle, so whenever you'd see them in clubs, you'd see this cameraman and sound tech in their orbit, recording their every pithy bon mot and existential glance into space.

I shouldn't be so contemptuous, because the truth is, I'm

jealous of them and their easy confidence. When I'm around hot young people I feel kind of cold and old. I often wish I could turn off that deep, dark neurotic part of myself at will and be breezy and shallow when I need to be, such as when I am facing the bouncers at some trendy club, worrying that they won't let me in.

Fortunately, red hair is very trendy now and I have a long, stubborn mass of it. Club bouncers, who are people I should not want to impress but do, love it and usually wave me right in.

But when I got to Kafka's, the two borderline IQs at the door made no move to admit me, although I was the only one waiting behind the red cordon.

Housed in what was once a meat wholesaler's warehouse, Kafka's was an example of seedy chic, a fashionable bar located in New York's meat district near the Hudson River waterfront. Ten years before, the neighborhood was the heart of the gay S & M district known as the Meat Rack. Since then, many of the leather bars had gone out of business, but the transitional transsexual prostitutes, half man half woman, the chicks with dicks as they called themselves, still worked the area.

While I stood waiting for the bouncers to let me in, a car pulled up just down the street. There was a baby seat in the back. The front door of the station wagon opened, two long stockinged legs stretched out, and a tall, beautiful transsexual stepped into the spotlight of a street lamp.

As the car squealed away, she slithered back into the shadows of an iron awning to wait for the next trick. I couldn't even make her out in the darkness, she blended so well into the shadow, no doubt a useful skill in her dangerous profession. But then there was a bright flash of a lighter, which quickly died out. A few minutes later the lighter flashed again, first a yellow flash and then a quick blue-white flash. The lady was a crackhead.

At this point, satisfied that they had demonstrated their power over my social destiny, the bouncers abruptly unfastened the cordon and waved me out of reality and into surreality.

Inside, the bar was lit by blue-white halogen lights that shone vertically in cylinders from the floor, like some kind of force field. The place was busy for a weekday, and the beautiful people were three deep around the pale, glowing blue bar. Despite *Vogue*'s admonition that black was boring, almost everyone wore black as a base, accessorizing with bolder colors.

"Can I get you something?" the bartender, a tall Oriental woman, asked. She had an English accent.

"Vodka martini, dry, made with lemon Stoly, no garnish, on the rocks, lightly stirred," I said. I love ordering that. Name's Bond, James Bond. However, the pretension was lost on the bartender, who dutifully and absentmindedly stirred it up and handed it to me in a Lucite glass with a cockroach cleverly embedded in its base.

Down at the end of the bar Claire's usual gang of friends were hanging out but Claire was nowhere to be seen. One of them, an actress named Tassy something-or-other, waved at me absently, like she knew me from somewhere but couldn't remember if she liked me or not. I waved back and turned away to spare her having to make the judgment.

Claire was late, which was unusual. It was a quarter after nine before she finally got to Kafka's. Although the crowd was thick, it parted easily for her as she made her way through the blue-white force field to the bar. Right away, I knew something was wrong.

Claire, who was always perfectly put together, had failed to accessorize.

"Sorry I'm late," she said breathlessly. "But I just had a call from one of your old sources. The police are looking for you. They want you to turn yourself in."

"Turn myself in? Why? What is . . ."

"I stopped back at ANN to pick up a tape I wanted to watch later and while I was there this woman called," Claire said. "Desirée."

That was Nora, a police department flack who used to work at ANN and was a very reluctant source. "Desirée" was her nom de fink. I privately referred to her as Sore Throat.

"They found this guy dead—killed—at the Marfeles Palace. You were seen with him or something. Desirée was vague on details, but it sounds like you're a suspect, Robin."

"Oh sweet mother of . . ."

Words were flashing at me like neon signs: ME. A SUSPECT. FOR MURDER. ME.

For once, I was speechless. Speechless *and* paralyzed. Even with my rotten luck, this was going too far.

Claire ordered herself a double Dewar's neat, which she emptied in one large swallow. She rarely drank.

"I've got a taxi waiting outside. Do you want to call a lawyer and have him meet us at the cop shop?" She slid her hand over mine and gave it a squeeze. "Or do you want to sit a while and get your bearings on this?"

"No," I said. "Let's go."

When we were in the taxi, I thought of this story I read about Vaclav Havel, then president of Czechoslovakia, shortly after the Communists fell and he and other dissidents came to power. A year earlier, Havel had been in jail, as had many of his colleagues. Now they were running the country, making decisions on everything from freeing the press to how to distribute a shipment of East German brassieres.

During cabinet meetings, when the absurdity of the situation became too great, Havel would stop the meeting and say, "Let's all laugh for a moment."

I love that. I love the idea of a world leader taking a moment away from history for a hearty guffaw. I think it's good, all-purpose advice. I tried to follow it as the taxi rumbled over the narrow streets towards Manhattan South.

Within the hour, I was sitting at a table in a room at Manhattan South, which looked after everything below Fifty-ninth Street in Manhattan, with Detective Joe Tewfik, whom I knew slightly, and Detective Richard Bigger, whom I did not know at all.

I did not call a lawyer, because I felt my best shot was just to go in and tell the damn truth, or as close to the damn truth as I could get. I hadn't killed anybody, so why did I need a lawyer to speak for me, to conceal my crimes? For $350 an hour at that. I'd had a hard enough time with my divorce lawyer, who kept trying to goad me into going after a big piece of Burke's earning and inheritance potential. In my settlement meeting, she and I kept saying conflicting things. Finally, we burst into heated argument with each other, while our ostensible "enemies,"

Burke and his lawyer, watched, amused, from across the conference table.

I hated the way she made me look, like some kind of pitiful victim, being economically punished for *his* adultery when he took his income and left our marriage. I am not a victim, I told her. I earn my own living and plenty of men want to sleep with me too. I do not need Burke Avery, got that?

So I didn't trust a lawyer to tell my side of the story. Besides, I brought the tape recorder I used on stories with me and when I sat down at the table at the cop shop I whipped it out and said, "You don't mind if I record this, do you?"

"Uh—no," Bigger said, surprised.

Tewfik wasn't surprised. "Miss Hudson is a reporter. Like Brenda Starr," he said. "She keeps a record of everything."

"How do you know Larry Griff?" Bigger asked me.

"Who is Larry Griff? Is he the dead guy?"

Bigger nodded. I thought they might do a good-cop/bad-cop routine, so I planned to be sweet to the bad cop and rude to the good cop, just to muck up their rhythm somehow. But Tewfik was just sitting back watching, letting Bigger represent the duality of man single-handedly.

Lawrence M. Griff, a licensed P.I., Bigger informed me in a tone of voice that implied I already knew all this, had been bludgeoned to death in Room 13D of the Marfeles Palace with a blunt metal instrument. The body had been discovered a few hours earlier by the night maid.

"What do you know about it?" he asked.

"Did this guy have sort of short, gingery red hair?" I asked, knowing even as I spoke that Bigger was sure to say yes.

So I told him everything I remembered. Then I dug into my catch-all purse and after some rummaging, actually retrieved the note Griff had given me. Bigger held the hotel stationery envelope by its edges and handed it to Tewfik.

But I broke my damn truth rule: I did not hand over the other page Griff had given me, the first page of the investigator's report, and I did not make any mention of it. Because it spoke of my mother's arrest in London and alluded to her mental illness, I felt it would not help me any as a suspect, nor would it help them except to build a case against me. They had the note and the envelope. That seemed enough.

"What did this guy know about you?" Bigger asked. "How did he lure you to his room?"

"When he spoke to me, on the phone . . . he knew my childhood nickname."

Bigger and Tewfik both looked at me expectantly.

"Red Knobby," I said. "And he knew, you know, embarrassing stuff. Who I lost my virginity to, okay?"

"Was he trying to blackmail you?"

"He didn't say. I honestly don't know why he was investigating me or what he expected from me."

"You are reputed to be bad-tempered and eccentric, some might say a little paranoid," Bigger said.

"That's probably true to some degree at least. But I'm not *dangerous*."

"Well, witnesses say you threatened an old woman near your apartment building with a tire iron and later raised a knife to your husband. . . ."

"Look," I said. "I know I would make a fine suspect, but I didn't kill this guy. I got a phone call from him, he gave me a note, I went up to the room at the appointed time. He never even answered the door."

Tewfik took over from Bigger. "Why did you leave your tire

iron on the premises?" he asked. "Were you frightened? Did you panic and drop the weapon?"

"Why would I leave the weapon in his room? Give me some credit."

"I didn't say it was in his room. I said it was on the premises. How did you know it was in the room?"

He was getting the better of me. I was starting to think hiring a lawyer wasn't such a bad idea after all.

"I assumed . . . Look, I didn't know the tire iron was in the guy's room. I just assumed when you said premises you meant the crime scene, where the guy was found. It was a lucky guess, really." I sounded guilty. Shit.

"It wasn't found in the bedroom. We're still looking for the murder weapon—but a tire iron would fill the bill."

"Oh." I was relieved, yet felt oddly miffed that Tewfik had tricked me into establishing my innocence this way.

"Besides, one of your colleagues who saw you outside Griff's room said you weren't carrying your tire iron. You appeared, however, to be carrying a small knife of some sort. . . ."

"A butter knife. To protect myself."

Bigger still looked skeptical, but Tewfik smiled at me. Nice-looking man, Tewfik, a one-time Brooklyn hunk who, at forty-five, was settling nicely into middle age. His dark hair was graying and he was getting soft around the edges, but that just made him more accessible and thus more attractive. I'd known him professionally for a couple of years, marginally, through Crime & Justice. Used to have a little crush on him. But, alas, he was married to a cookbook writer and had two kids.

As for Bigger—imagine a weasel, upright in a sports jacket. A nice sports jacket, okay, and he had blow-dried hair, a cop for the Cops TV-show age. But he had a weak, mean mouth he tried to disguise with a feeble moustache that looked like it was just resting and might crawl off his face in search of a sunny rock at any moment.

"So who would want to kill this guy and who would want to frame you? Was somebody out to get you, or did they just see you put your tire iron down and then seize the opportunity?" Tewfik asked.

"I have no idea. Why was this guy investigating me?"

Now that I was off the hook as a suspect, at least for the moment, I had a few questions of my own.

"And who else was he investigating? I mean, he asked me to meet him at the Marfeles, where ANN was having its New Year's party. Coincidence? And when he gave me that note it was before nine thirty and he wanted me to meet him at eleven. So maybe he had the goods on somebody else at ANN."

"Who?" Bigger asked.

"I don't know. I'm asking you guys. He could have the lowdown on anybody—or everybody. Everybody has secrets." I smiled at the aloof Detective Bigger. "What are your secrets?"

Bigger didn't answer.

They reviewed my account of the evening before letting me go. I tried to find out what they knew about Griff, so I could maybe find out who the hell was checking me out. But they were on to me and wouldn't go into specifics.

"We may have to ask you some other questions," Tewfik said.

"My door is always open to men with badges and/or warrants," I replied.

Claire was waiting for me outside in the hallway, staring at herself in a window, and she didn't see me when I came out. If you ask her she'll deny it, but looking at herself is kind of a hobby of hers. Compliment Claire on what she's wearing and she looks down with some surprise, as though she never really gave a single thought to what to wear while she was dressing, she just "threw this on." She likes people to think her beauty is effortless, like if she really worked at it, really applied herself, look out—she'd be dangerous.

But I know the truth. When she walks past any vaguely reflective surface—a mirror, a window, a polished piece of granite—she can't resist looking at herself. Not only does she look at herself but, liking what she sees, she smiles at her reflection, like she shares a secret joke with it or something. Claire, a one-woman mutual admiration society.

"God, you're ugly," I said.

She jumped a little in her skin. "I didn't see you come up. How did it go? Do they have a case against you? Should I bring you an eclair with a file in it?"

"I'm not a suspect. Just a witness."

When we walked out the door into the street, lights flashed in our faces, blinding me temporarily. I heard voices shouting at me as the shadowy figures before me filled out and regained detail.

"Did you kill Larry Griff?" someone called out. Another voice called, "Why did the police want you, Robin?" It was a *New York Post* reporter I knew vaguely. There were a bunch of them.

Christ, I was in the middle of a gang bang, the vulgar term the news media uses to describe a mob of journalists descending upon an unsuspecting victim. I'd been part of the mob before, but never the object of its affections. It was frightening.

Claire pushed me back into the building. We said nothing. I was willing to spill a lot of stuff for the cops, but I wasn't fool enough to speak with the news media. Inside, a uniformed cop, drooling over Claire, directed us to a little-known exit.

Murphy's Law. One step out the door we ran right into my devoted husband, who was staked out with his crew on the sidewalk.

"Burke," I said.

"Robin! What are you doing here?" he asked. "Where's your crew?"

"What are you doing here?" I asked.

"Are you here on the story?" he said, guarded.

"What story?"

"What story are you here on?" he asked. A dialogue between reporters, all questions and no answers.

"You're here about the Marfeles Hotel murder, aren't you?" I asked.

"Yeah," he said. "I can't believe you're on this story too. Kind of a funny coincidence, isn't it?"

"Or an accident of nature, like when masochists marry each other."

"Robin, can't we please be friends, or colleagues?" he said. "Do we have to fight?"

"I'm sorry. I always mean to make nice, Burke . . ."

"I know you do . . ."

". . . but then I remember what a slimy piece of shit you are and I can't help myself."

"For Christ's sake, Robin, it happens," he said.

"Yeah yeah yeah. Life's a bitch and then you die."

WHAT'S A GIRL GOTTA DO?

He took a deep breath. His eyes looked glazed and unholy in the blue-white of the streetlight.

"Yes," he said. "Life's a bitch and people fall out of love with some people and into love with other people. Quit making a federal case out of it."

His camera crew was watching us, amused. Claire acted as if she wasn't listening and pretended to be engrossed in her reflection in a car window.

We were in public and I should have held my tongue at that point, but I didn't.

"So, what?" I said. "So just because people have been falling out of love for centuries, just because people have been cheating on their mates and lying to their mates since the beginning of time, that makes it all right? Yes, it is a federal case, in the United State of Robin and Burke. Fucking right, it's a federal case. It's treason."

"I can see there's no reasoning with you," Burke said. He changed the subject. "I heard they had a suspect up there. D'you see him go in?"

"No," I answered truthfully. The suspect Burke had heard about was me, and I loved that he didn't know it.

"Well, there was that tall guy . . . ," Claire interrupted, then stopped, acting as though she'd almost let the cat out of the bag.

Burke smiled, thinking he had weaseled this out of her with his masterful reportorial technique.

"White guy?"

"Not as white as you," I said.

Let him harass big, swarthy guys all night. I was tired and wanted to go.

Before I left he extended the olive branch. "It was nice seeing you again, Robin," he said. He almost got me with that voice of his, that great damn, deep, slightly gravelly voice that made me want to cross my legs and bounce my foot.

But then I realized his motives. Sure, he wants us to be friends, I thought. It'd make *his* life so much simpler. There's nothing Burke hates more than a loose wire, especially one that carries high voltage, like me. Why the hell should I go out of my way to make his life easier when he'd made mine so crummy?

So I said nothing. I smirked and turned and left with Claire.

"Do you feel like you need to be alone, or would you like to go somewhere and talk?" Claire said, as we hailed a cab.

"To tell you the truth, Claire, I'm starved. Do you want to grab something to eat?"

"Sure. I know a great vegetarian restaurant near here."

"How about Old Homestead? Expand *your* horizons." Old Homestead was a minor New York landmark, an old steak house off Fourteenth Street.

She just laughed.

Claire and I were friends and colleagues who liked and respected each other and agreed on almost everything. But food was one of those areas where Claire and I just didn't agree. I still ate red meat, although not more than once a week, but Claire had opted out of the food chain and ate only fruits and vegetables, which included large quantities of green leafy things, lots of seaweed stews, and whole platters of cooked grain.

The restaurant she took me to, Tatiana's, was one of those converted diners so popular among the Unrepentant Yuppies of New York City. It gleamed of chrome and neon and looked like an art deco railway car that might break loose from its moorings at any moment and go careening down First Avenue. It was *upscale* vegetarian—no leftover hippies with ponytails, jeans, and acoustic guitars in this joint.

They knew Claire at the door, but then she never took me anywhere where they didn't know her.

"You'll like the food," Claire said as we opened our menus. "Besides, they have eggs and dairy so you can have a cheese omelet if you like."

Frankly, I find vegetarian restaurants are to a gourmet dining experience what Christian theme parks are to Amsterdam nightlife, but I try to stay open-minded. A waiter came over and reeled off the night's specials, which included tofu fritters served in a pool of sorrel essence and a ground millet mousse in a light orange sauce, which is what Claire ordered. I ordered the cheese omelet.

"Are you worried?" she asked me.

"Naturally. Whoever killed that guy is still out there, and might have some information about me I'd rather people didn't know."

"Think maybe it's just that fan of yours, Elroy?"

"Nah. He's been my fan for five years now. God, come to think of it, that's one of my longest relationships with a man. Anyway, he doesn't want to hurt me, he wants me to hurt him. Now, Christine Muke, she's got a whole harem of disturbed fans."

Christine was one of our prime-time anchors, an aristocratic-looking black woman with a voice so sultry "men in the deep arctic instinctively mop their brows when they hear it" (*TV Guide*).

"Remember that guy in brown polyester pants with rubber

bands around the cuffs?" I asked. "The one who claimed if he
and Christine didn't merge—"

"Fuse. He said they had to fuse together or else the planet
would blow up."

"Yeah. I dunno, maybe Elroy *did* hire Griff. It doesn't make a
lot of sense to me, but then who else would be so interested in
my past? And was it just me this guy Griff was on to?"

While we waited for our food, I played the tape of my
interrogation for her. "You think someone at ANN killed the
guy, don't you?" she asked.

"I don't know. But I think he had the goods on someone else
and that's why he picked the Marfeles Palace that night."

"Well, like you told the cops, he could have been investigating anybody, or everybody. But why?"

"And why me? It's not like I have power or money—or
influence for that matter, not while I'm in Special Reports."

"Well, you're off the hook with the cops, anyway," she said.
"Too bad the news media was there. . . ."

"Enough about my petty problems. They're too depressing,"
I said. "You wanted to talk about that reporter spot?"

"It can wait. The Browner job may not come to pass anyway.
I would like to get away from Jerry, but I like working with you.
We're a good team."

Yes, we were, but I harbored few illusions about it lasting
very long. Claire assisted me, but she was looking far beyond
me and one day would cheerfully and politely leapfrog over
me. Claire was great at finding the story, the right people to
interview, those proverbial pictures worth a thousand words.
She was fantastic in the edit room, putting sound and pictures
together, and she had two important attributes I lacked, confidence and poise.

Our food came. "Mmm, little chicken embryos whipped into a froth and fried," I said. "Speaking of Spurdle, you know what McGravy told me today? Jerry *wants* me in Special Reports."

"McGravy's right. Jerry's not doing you a favor by letting you live out your exile there. He's got personal reasons," she said wickedly. "He *likes* you."

"That's what I don't understand. I give him shit all day long."

"He's in love with you," Claire said, matter-of-factly.

"Give me a fucking break."

Claire smiled. I think she was enjoying my discomfort with this idea.

"He's in love with you, Robin," she said. "He thinks he can bring you around, like in some Tracy-Hepburn flick where the spunky career woman at war with her boss realizes she's really in love with him and falls into his arms and French kisses him in the last scene and . . ."

"Oh! Stop! That's so gross. Don't say French kiss and Jerry in the same sentence when a girl's trying to eat!"

"Sorry."

"Ugh, ugh," I said, trying to spit the very idea out before it attached itself to my subconscious.

"Well, anyway, they live happily ever after and have sex every night and breed little Spurdles," Claire continued.

"Stop!"

"What do you think Jerry's like in bed?" she went on mercilessly.

"Oh jeez. Oh God. Ick. What's he like in bed? Ugh. Like chiggers, maybe."

"Okay," Claire said. "What about this? If you had to either have sex with Jerry Spurdle or else do a really gross thing, what's the worst thing you'd do before you'd have sex with Jerry?"

Claire often came up with peculiar riddles involving a choice between two or three hellish options. Another of her riddles was, would you rather look good and smell bad, or smell good and look bad?

"I'd rather eat live insects by the handful," I said. "Of course, unlike you, I am a meat eater."

Claire shrugged. "I think it's kind of sweet that someone as disgusting and venal as Jerry Spurdle can still entertain a romantic fantasy."

"Oh God. It *really* bugs me to think that I am in Jerry's fantasies. I wonder what I do in them. Ugh. Something truly foul, I'm sure." I put down my fork, my appetite irretrievably spoiled. "If I have a sex dream about Jerry tonight, Claire, I am going to blame you."

She leaned back and laughed.

I have romantic fantasies too—in fact I think a minimum of four are required just to get through the average day—but mine do *not* include Jerry. I have to admit a bit of inverted sexism, in that I often look on men as sex objects. I can't help it. When I meet an interesting man, I automatically wonder what it would be like to have sex with him. Men are not only sex objects, but they are sex objects also.

The thing is, I still sort of believed in love. I was kind of agnostic about love, actually, but I hadn't lost hope completely. I was waiting for the feminist wet dream, Spencer Tracy. And while I was waiting, great looks and a great bod could tide me over nicely. But Spurdle was not Spencer Tracy and I'd be hard-pressed to find any Hollywood counterpart for Jerry that walked on two legs and had opposable thumbs.

Later, as I rode home from Tatiana's in a creaky taxicab with bad shocks, I thought about how I'd married the wrong man, which meant maybe the right man was still out there somewhere.

So was the killer.

When I got home, I turned ANN on to keep me company while I brushed Louise Bryant. The *Greg Browner Show* was on—the Hawaii version, a taped repeat of the evening show that played during prime time in Hawaii. It made for good white noise.

"Topeka, Kansas, on the line. What's your question for Jack Kemp, Topeka?" Greg said in his warm way.

"Greg, my husband and I think you should run for office in ninety-six."

Browner got several calls like this every night. Some of the Perotist carpetbaggers, who had wandered in the wilderness for many months since their man's defeat in '92, had tried to get Browner to pick up the Independence banner. But Browner refused to run, elevating himself above the fray and giving his show-ender commentaries greater credibility.

But for every call of support he got, he got one like his next call.

"Yeah, Greg, this is Barry from Union City, New Jersey. I want to know if Jack Kemp would support a national holiday to honor Howard Stern's penis?"

Live television. You gotta love it.

Chapter Five

THE MAN WHO SOLD newspapers on Avenue B greeted me with a strange look and kept his eyes on me while I scanned the dailies. When I got to the *News-Journal*, I saw him grin.

P.I. DEAD

IN BAD-LUCK HOTEL

FOUND BLUDGEONED—ROOM 13D

Inset was my picture, coming out of the police station, with the caption, "Reporter questioned in murder."

The *Post* was more succinct. "JINX!" it screamed in large black letters. "PRIVATE EYE DEAD IN MARFELES ROOM 13D." Then, in smaller letters along the bottom of the page: "ANN Reporter a Suspect? Page 3."

"Shit," I said. I took a copy of the tabloids, along with the *Times*, and paid the guy. I opened the *News-Journal* and read it as I walked to the subway. It was unbelievable.

Renegade reporter Robin Hudson, who is perhaps best known for belching loudly on live television, was questioned by police for nearly two hours last night in the murder of Lawrence M. Griff, 38, of Ozone Park, Queens.

Griff, a licensed P.I., was found in a pool of blood in his room, Room 13D, at the Marfeles Palace . . .

Blah. Blah Blah.

Detective Joe Tewfik of homicide said, "Ms. Hudson was questioned as a witness in this case and is not a suspect at this point, although we haven't ruled anyone out yet."

What bullshit, I thought. He knew I didn't do it.

But neighbors and colleagues say Ms. Hudson appeared agitated on New Year's Eve, when the murder is thought to have occurred, and threatened an elderly woman with a tire iron. Later, she was seen talking with the victim at ANN's New Year's Eve party at the Marfeles.

There was more, but I won't bore you with the details.

It's amazing how one disaster can distort the truth of one's life so quickly and so completely. I had held up my tire iron—part of my costume—in the street to ward off Mrs. Ramirez's cane, and the News-Journal made it sound like I was some sort of maniac on a wilding spree that started with a tire iron and an old lady and ended with a man dead in a classy midtown hotel room.

Unnamed "colleagues" and "neighbors" supported this tale of my orgy of violence with telling anecdotes of past bad temper. Most people don't like to get involved, especially with any legal authority, but some people are so eager to please reporters they'll gladly corroborate anything you want with a little factoid or two. I'd seen it plenty of times.

This was bad. If the *News-Journal* kept this up and the police didn't arrest me, the villagers would soon come for me in a torchlight procession.

Work was going to be a bitch too. I went straight for Democracy Wall when I got in to assess the damage to my reputation and found a small mob crowded around something on the board. Before I could make my way through, a hand grabbed my sweater and yanked me cleanly from the throng. It was Jerry.

"You're wanted at the morning editorial meeting," he said.

"Rats."

"Robin, Robin, Robin," he said. He was so smug. "How long am I going to have to keep bailing you out of trouble?"

"Oh please," I said. I pushed open the door to the executive conference room and almost every face in that room turned to me, cold and unappreciative. McGravy energetically worked his modeling clay with his smoking arm. George Dunbar gave me a look of sour anger, like he'd just swallowed a pickled mouse. A miserly man, he could pinch a penny till it screamed. You know the expression "Money talks"? At ANN it didn't just talk. It begged for mercy.

Dunbar rose and spoke. The daily papers were on the black enamel table in front of him, next to his cup of tea and two

Sweet'n Low packets, one empty, the second one rolled up, half used, saved for later.

"We have a *system* here, Ms. Hudson. When a member of our staff gets information, that member of our staff calls up the assignment desk and relays that information. When it's a story about ANN personnel, it is doubly important that we are informed as early as possible, so we can manage the crisis."

"I'm sorry," I said. "I figured it wasn't a big deal for ANN. I'm just a witness in the case and my involvement was personal, not professional. I didn't . . . Mr. Dunbar, the stories in the paper are wrong. I'm not a suspect."

"You didn't do it?" he said, as though he couldn't be sure.

"No! Ask the cops. They don't think I'm a suspect, not really."

"The point is, you should have let ANN know what was going on, so we didn't have to learn it by surprise. Either you or Ms. Thibodeaux should have called us," Dunbar said.

"If Claire didn't call, it's because she's my friend," I said. "Don't take it out on her. She respects my feelings and my privacy. She probably didn't feel it was her place."

Apparently, this was a novel concept to some in the room, who looked at me perplexed.

"You don't seem to understand how much trouble you've caused," Dunbar continued. "The police have been here all morning and reporters have been flooding public relations with calls. It's bad enough this involves you. Other ANN personnel might be involved too. We could have used the extra time to formulate a response."

"What other personnel?" I asked.

"The issue is you, for the moment. And how we should deal with your inexcusable negligence."

Immediately, I tried to excuse it. "You know, I had a very weird night. I kind of had other things on my mind. . . ."

But he cut me no slack. I'd used up my slack allotment at ANN a long time ago.

"You're a journalist, aren't you?" he asked. "You couldn't make one phone call?"

"I think we ought to vote on disciplinary action," said Al Prevost, the morning supervising producer. There was muttering among the middle-aged males and sole female executive around the table.

"We'll vote," Dunbar said. He turned to me. "Please wait in the hallway."

I left and stood in the hallway like a bad kid outside the principal's office, a situation I admit I was once quite familiar with. Through the particleboard door I heard someone yell, "No way."

What did they think? They owned my entire life? I had to tell them everything that happened to me that might reflect on the company? I felt like marching in and saying, "I've had it. I can't take this anymore! I quit!" I have these moments every now and then.

But I mobilized those seven major muscle groups and held my tongue. I couldn't quit, you see; I had this ironclad contract. In 1990, long before my on-air disgraces, Dunbar offered all the reporters long-term contracts with guaranteed job security. There was a catch, of course. If you took the contract, it tied you to a modest salary that would go up only with the cost of living each year. I was just insecure enough to take a job guarantee today over possible big salaries somewhere in the future. A bird in the hand, as they say. A bird in the hand will shit on you, I've found.

So if I quit, I would be legally prohibited from working in any media-related field, which meant I couldn't even do infomercials. Of course, they couldn't fire me either, not without paying out the remaining three years of my contract, an idea so daunting to Dunbar that I'd have to fart on national television while *eating* human flesh before he'd sign that big check. Holy Lump Sum Payout, Batman.

The most he could do was suspend me, like he did after the cannibalism fiasco, and at the moment that didn't sound so bad. I'd just use the time to get to the bottom of this private investigator business and Jerry would have to find someone else to play Mrs. Spurdle for the sperm bank series.

I could hear Bob McGravy defending me. My one and only champion in the executive branch. Unfortunately, my champion was kind of lacking authority at the moment, his power greatly diminished after a serious, quality news show he'd championed—*21st Century*—bombed in the ratings and after the rising reporter he championed—me—embarrassed herself on national television.

On account of having worked for Murrow, having a fairly solid reputation at CBS, and having kicked a serious drinking problem, McGravy still had moral authority. But moral authority doesn't go as far as it used to, and I couldn't call it, how Dunbar would go. Vote, my ass. Everybody would argue their point of view, and then Dunbar would vote. One man, one vote.

How would he vote? As Dunbar wasn't a journalist, per se, I wasn't always clear on his ethics and instincts. He came from sales at DIC, where he racked up a miraculous sales record while at the same time having the lowest budget and expense accounts in the company, forever endearing himself to

Georgia Jack Jackson. When Jackson decided to launch ANN, he knew he needed a man with a tight fist at the helm, and Dunbar was that man, the Tightest Fist in the East.

A year before, Dunbar himself made news with a long piece he wrote for the *New York Times* op-ed page in which he put forth a proposal to reduce the federal deficit through promotional considerations. Sponsors, that's what the nation needed. NASA, he wrote, could make millions by having companies sponsor the space shuttle and satellites. Columbia could be known as Anacin-3, Discovery as Lipton Fine Teas. Eventually, the idea could be expanded to include housing projects, aircraft carriers, and national parks.

The piece was hailed as fine satire, and Dunbar kinda smiled weakly and pretended indeed that's what it was. But those of us who knew him knew he'd been quite serious and was hurt the rest of the country misunderstood him, didn't see the brilliance of the plan.

The door opened and McGravy came out. "You're reprieved," he said. "But don't fuck up."

A ringing vote of confidence from my mentor.

Dunbar filed out after him, walking, as he always did, with his head down. I used to wonder why he did that, if he was shy or something, then one day I saw him stoop to pick up a coin, which he examined with relish and put in his pocket.

Jerry stayed behind while I went to the office alone, stopping by Democracy Wall. Someone in Graphics had made up a wanted poster with my publicity photo.

"Wanted, dead or alive," it read. "Renegade Reporter Robin Hudson."

It was pretty funny, really. Under distinguishing characteristics, it listed "Legs to die for," and noted that, "as usual," I was armed and dangerous. While two producers walked by, watching me but pretending not to, I took out a felt marker and drew fangs and made my eyes look a little wilder. I grinned at the two women, and they hesitated before grinning back at me. If all else fails, laugh at yourself.

All morning, reporters called and Claire cheerfully intercepted and directed them to public relations, except for one: Burke Avery.

"He says it's personal," Claire said.

I took the call.

"I'm worried about you," he said.

"Don't. I'm fine. I'm not a suspect. The tabloids have it all wrong."

"Oh, I know you didn't kill the guy. I know your M.O., Robin, and you are way too sinister to commit such a clumsy crime. Maybe if the guy had been killed with a lettuce spinner or a potato peeler. I use sinister in the sense of the traditional Latin word *sini* . . ."

"And . . . ," I prompted.

"And what?"

"And you know that I am basically a good person with a conscience who could not kill another person . . . except in self-defense."

He didn't say anything for a moment. "Right, that too," he said finally. But he was grinning as he said it. I could hear him grinning.

"Are you still covering this story?" I asked.

"Of course. It's my beat."

"I'm a witness in this case. Don't you think it's a conflict of interest to be reporting on a story in which your wife is a witness?" Channel 3, where Burke worked, wasn't known for its strict adherence to ethics.

"You're just one witness so where's the conflict, realistically? Besides, we're separated and we parted amicably."

Parted amicably?

"Anyway," he said, completing his three-part rationalization for staying on this story. "You're not a suspect."

"I wish someone would tell the *New York Post* that."

"Robin," he said. "It'll pass. How is ANN spinning the story?"

"Nobody tells me anything around here," I said. "What have you heard about it?"

"I don't know. What do you know?" he asked defensively. The reporter in him was kicking into full gear and he was protecting his information while trying to get mine.

So was I. "Nothing."

"I don't know anything more than you do," he said before he hung up. "Do you know how ANN is going to cover this?"

I didn't, but I had wondered about that too, if they'd put a reporter on it or just do it as an on-cam reader. I couldn't cover it, even if Jerry would spring me from Special Reports, because I was a witness in the case, although what I did on my own time was my own business and I did have a strong personal interest in getting to the bottom of it all.

I was supposed to be reading up on sperm, but instead I clipped out all the stories about the case, to read over and put into my scrapbook later.

There was also a blurb on Amy Penny in the TV Ticker column of the *Post*. Amy, reiterating her aspiration to become a "serious reporter," was going to do a series of reports on prenatal diagnostics for her show. Great. She had my husband. Now she wanted to become a serious reporter. I couldn't help feeling that this young, beautiful woman was living the life I was supposed to be living.

I hid out that day, leaving Special Reports only to hit the ladies' room and the cafeteria. Claire thought it would blow over and in the afternoon, when the calls from other reporters subsided to a dull murmur, I thought maybe she was right.

I wondered what Griff had on me. Did he know about that night in Paris? Did he know about my father's death when I was ten? He had the story of my mother's arrest in London. Did he know about the Sesquin murders? Where were pages two and three? And why me, oh Lord, why me?

After work I went to Keggers for a drink and watched evening news programs on the bar television. Gil Jerome, who now had Crime & Justice, did a piece on the circumstances of the murder. Griff had been found facedown in a pool of his own blood by the night maid. He'd been struck on the front of the head repeatedly with the murder weapon. Everything had been wiped for prints except the inside knob on the bathroom door, which yielded only Griff's prints.

To make matters worse, the cleaning lady, Mrs. Jessie Good, had vacuumed the bedroom and disposed of the full vacuum cleaner bag down a garbage chute in the hallway before going back in to clean the bathroom, where she found the body. The bag, compacted with trash from other rooms in the bowels of the Palace, was probably crammed with fiber evidence, evidence lost forever.

Griff, Jerome reported, had worked for Boylen Investigations before breaking away to start his own firm. He was divorced and his wife lived in Florida. No children.

There was no mention of me by name, although there was no mistaking who the "red-haired woman seen lurking around" Griff's hotel room was.

After the report ended, the anchorwoman, Madri Michaels, appeared on camera to read, in a dispassionate voice, the ANN statement about me, how I'd been questioned but was not a suspect and how ANN management stood behind me.

Yeah, way behind.

Chapter Six

"RENEGADE REPORTER MAY HAVE led double life, says neighbor," read the headline in the *News-Journal* the next day. Between the stuff on my mother, which they'd managed to dig up, and Mrs. Ramirez's ramblings about my late-night orgies, I was looking more and more like a menace to society.

At the moment, I was doing a pretty good Jackie Onassis impression, my hair hidden under a black wool scarf wrapped around my head like a skullcap. Oversized dark glasses hid my eyes and cheekbones.

It didn't help. When I went to get my papers, I heard a voice behind me whisper, "That's her. She killed a guy." I turned and saw two adolescent girls waiting for the bus to parochial school. They were studying me, not with fear but with interest.

The other news was, they found my tire iron in a dumpster near the service entrance behind the Marfeles. But what did that mean? Either it was simply taken out with the trash, like the bartender suggested, or the killer ditched it there after wiping it clean. There were no fingerprints except for one partial—mine—no bone fragments, blood, or hair stuck to it, just refuse from the Marfeles kitchen, eggshells and whipped cream and cigarette butts and stuff like that.

I was glad I didn't have to go straight to ANN. We had an interview scheduled with a white couple who had an African-American baby after doing business at Empire Semen. Jim and Ellis, the sound tech and cameraman respectively, were to pick me up on the corner of Fourteenth and Avenue B at 8:30 A.M.

They were late, but by 8:50 we were headed out of Manhattan over the Queensborough Bridge and onto the Brooklyn-Queens Expressway. Ellis turned the car radio to a classic rock station, and we listened to a rockumentary on the blues guitar, an appropriate soundtrack as we passed over the rusty, brown industrial clutter of the Brooklyn waterfront. The show broke for a Dentucreme commercial. On a classic rock station. How depressing.

"How is the house?" I asked.

"It's coming along," Ellis said. For the last year, Ellis and his wife had been restoring a rundown Victorian on Staten Island. "It's almost finished. Cami and I are painting it next weekend with some friends."

I leaned my head against the window and looked out at the neighborhoods that straddled the BQE. There were all these single and two-family homes out there, clustered together in neighborhoods. Sometimes I forget that New York City isn't just the boxy apartment buildings, skyscrapers, tourist traps, and garbage of Manhattan. Real people with real families live here too, with backyards and trees, close to grandparents and uncles and in-laws, in little steamy houses that just then looked so inviting.

Ellis was describing the six-foot round window they'd put in on the third floor to exploit the morning sun and I thought, I want to have a husband and restore a Victorian house and have painting parties. Then he started talking about a carved oak fireplace mantel Cami had found at an auction in New Jersey, and I fell into a deep drowse. When I awoke, we were on the off ramp and he was talking in a low voice about Cami.

"I'm monogamous and couldn't be happier with my sex life," he said to Jim. "I'm sexually gratified by my wife and proud to say it."

Oh, I want a sexually gratified man who boasts about it, I thought.

The Zander Tarsus family insisted on being interviewed with coats over their heads, despite our promise to "gauze" their faces and electronically alter their voices. They didn't trust us, so they sat on their sofa—a man, a woman, and a little brown baby—with coats over their heads. Below the shoulder, they looked just like people, with chests and arms and legs. Above the shoulder, they were coatheads. It was like an evil haberdashery experiment run amok.

Zander, who had come to America as a teenager from some dark Carpathian principality just after the second world war, was clearly the king in this modest castle, which smelled of paprika and roses. He was much older than his wife, who spoke with an indeterminate Old Country accent, and he directed her like a child and spoke for her while she sat silently, holding the baby.

Two years before, he told us through his coat, he'd had prostate trouble and, afraid he would be infertile after his operation, he had banked some sperm at Empire Semen. The operation had, in fact, made him "unable to sire children," as he put it, so Marina—Mrs. Zander Tarsus—was impregnated with his stored seed. Or so he thought, until she delivered the African-American child.

"Look, I don't care what color people are," Tarsus said. "They can be white, black, green—hell, they can be striped if they want!" He laughed, like he thought this was original and hilarious.

"I don't care, but people should be with their own. Their own, you see? This is not my son. This is some other man's son. I paid for some other man's son, a Negro man."

Negro?

"I am expected to pay now and in the future, for some other man's son! Where is my son? Where is my own?"

He was very dramatic and impassioned, and there was a note of deep betrayal in his voice. I felt for him, I did. I mean, his family line was finished if his sperm couldn't be found. There would be no son, no heir. The Coathead Dynasty ended.

But it was extremely prickish of him to speak of his huge disappointment, his great dishonor, in front of his speechless wife, whose skin was moist and whose hands were trembling, and especially in front of the child. It wasn't the wife's fault, it wasn't the child's fault, and yet he aimed much of his anger at them.

"At least you have a child," I offered, hoping to elicit a more humane response from the guy.

"I have no child!" he shouted, his arms waving wildly from beneath his coathead. "I, me, Zander, have no child! You understand?"

Next to him, his wife pulled the child closer to her as he

raged. I felt a pain in my chest. The baby clung to her, his head concealed by a tiny blue parka.

I looked at Zander to see if he had noticed his wife's quiet gesture. It was hard to tell, with a coat over his head and all, but he didn't seem to. I had this powerful urge to take the woman's hands and say, "Leave him now and don't look back. Take your baby and be a free woman!"

But the road to hell is paved with good intentions. This was still a strange country to her. Single mothers born and raised in America have a hard enough time of it—what would it be like for her? Zander Tarsus probably wouldn't pay child support for "some other man's son" and she'd probably be doomed to living in poverty. So she was better off economically if she stayed with this old ungrateful control freak. Boy, that made me mad.

I was fuming by the time I got to ANN. "The guy's an asshole, Jerry," I said, as I showed him the relevant parts of the interview.

"Robin, put yourself in his shoes," Jerry said.

"I'm trying, Jerry. He's growing old and he's afraid of that, and now he has lost his last best hope for some kind of immortality, offspring. But the way he treated that baby, the way he spoke to and about his wife . . ."

"Look, the story isn't about Zander Tarsus. It's about Empire Semen. The only thing we need from Zander Tarsus is a bite that illustrates the extent of Empire's alleged wrongdoing."

He rewound the tape to isolate the bite he thought best, in which Zander Tarsus recounted his father telling him, the day he set off for America, that he was going to the U.S. to make a life not just for himself, but for his children and their children. It was like an AT&T commercial. I half expected the scene to cut to Zander holding baby Zog, dialing grandpa Zog in the Old Country to tell him of the birth. Happy, snappy, sappy music up.

Jerry was right about the old guy and he was wrong. He was wrong about the scene to use too. The scene where Zander raged against the child while the mother drew the child closer to her, their heads in coats, best illustrated the tragedy of Empire Semen. If you ask me.

"Don't let your personal feelings color your news judgment," Jerry said.

"What do you mean?" I asked defensively. What did he know about me?

"I mean, you're at that age, Robin, your biological clock is ticking and you ladies get goofy around babies at this age."

"Yeah, right, it's all hormonal," I said. I popped the tape and went into my own office to log it.

Jerry had it partly wrong again. My biological clock wasn't ticking, but my personal feelings probably were mucking around with my objectivity, since I was infertile. I'm not sure I want to be a mother, I'm not sure I'd make a good one, and I'm not sure what kind of world I'd leave to a kid. But I wish to hell I had the choice, that's all.

Claire was scoping out Empire Semen that morning, posing as an interested customer. Casing the joint, as she called it, in preparation for our undercover shoot that week. I had hoped my newfound notoriety might exempt me from going undercover, but Jerry figured a wig and prop glasses borrowed from JNC's weekly sketch comedy show would render me unrecognizable. Going undercover, in disguise, was all the more distasteful to me.

But not everything was grim. I logged into the computer and there was an E-mail message from Eric.

"My place, Saturday," it said. "Fritz the Cat, a bottle of vodka, and thou."

"I'm busy Saturday," I typed back.

It was one thing going for a drink with him at Keggers, surrounded by colleagues, but Saturday night would be a date, and I wasn't ready for a date. I could envision too many things going wrong on a date, like I might open my mouth to say something and belch, or break something valuable.

Or worse. I remembered one dismal date, when I was just out of college, and I decided to try the direct approach on a guy I was lusting after. My plan was to put a little Sinatra on, dance a little slow dance with him around the living room, and then put my hand assertively on his crotch. Just cop a feel.

But as I was reaching for his groin, I slipped and, to keep my balance, I grabbed the nearest object.

Which happened to be his crotch.

I grabbed hard and he screamed. That really killed the mood. He let me make him an ice bag—to go—and he never called me again.

"It'll be fun," Eric messaged back.

"Busy," I typed.

"Quit chasing me, Robin. You're embarrassing yourself," he answered. While I pondered my response, he said, "In the woods? In a midsize car in the woods? In winter?"

Yes yes no, I typed back. Jeez, he said all the right things. That's what scared me most.

I picked up the phone and dialed his extension. "Eric, I have kind of a lot on my plate right now," I said. "Between Burke, ANN, and the *News-Journal*."

"I can't do anything about Burke and ANN, but the *News-*

Journal will have forgotten about you by tomorrow, I'll bet you anything. Joanne will take the front page tomorrow," he said.

"Joanne?"

There was a long silence on his end of the phone.

"Joanne Armoire?" I said.

"Yeah. She's at Manhattan South now, being questioned. There's an ANN lawyer with her. You didn't know?"

I didn't know, but suddenly I understood why Dunbar and the other mandarins were so concerned the day before. They weren't worried about me, or my reputation. They were worried about Joanne, a star.

"What else do you know?"

"Just that it has something to do with Griff. I mean, I could speculate, but that isn't good journalistic practice," he said.

"Yeah, right," I said, and began to speculate.

Joanne must have been the other ANN person he was investigating/blackmailing. Why, and what was the connection to me?

"Want to know what the rumors are?"

"No—and yes."

"A conflict of interest issue. That she had an affair with a man she was reporting on."

"Who?" I asked.

"Don't know, although I've had a helluva lot of fun today running through the list of her interviewees. Boris Yeltsin, Yitzhak Shamir, that Afghan commander Massoud, that Argentine general, to name a few."

I remembered a past conversation between Joanne, Solange, Claire, and me. We started off speculating about how certain newsmakers sounded in orgasm and then went into our dreams, wherein we discovered we all had recurring erotic

WHAT'S A GIRL GOTTA DO?

dreams about newsmakers. I told of my dreams about me and John Sununu and me and Bishop Desmond Tutu, doing the wild thing in the back of a Chevy at a deserted Exxon station under the silvery city moon. Solange told of a dream involving a remote, snowbound cabin, leather restraints, and Supreme Court Justice David Souter.

We all laughed and Joanne described a vivid fantasy about Boris Yeltsin. Now I wondered if . . .

"So, Saturday?" Eric said.

Oh, I knew his type. I had seen it before—the ardent, earnest pursuit, the promises made to ensure the conquest, the conquest, the sudden drop-off in interest, the claustrophobia, that painful, overwrought farewell scene. . . .

But hell, the conquest was the easy part, the part I had control over, right? It was simple. I would not surrender.

Nothing painful could happen, if I didn't let it. If he didn't get his conquest, things would not progress to that painful, overwrought farewell phase of the game. Do not pass Go. Do not collect $200. Nobody wins and nobody loses.

Shit. I *knew* he was just looking for a conquest, but he was so persistent, and it was so flattering. How we come to love our flatterers.

"Saturday," I said.

Joanne didn't come back to work that day. Apparently, half of ANN's executive committee was at her place on Central Park West, devising scandal control strategy. I tried to call her, but her machine picked up.

In the afternoon, a press release went out: Joanne Armoire would be holding a news conference the next afternoon to discuss her involvement in the "Griff Case."

I called Nora and Tewfik to see what they knew about the

91

forensics on Griff, but they wouldn't tell me anything, due to my peripheral involvement in the case. Although Tewfik seemed sure I didn't do it, not everyone in the department was as eager to rule me out. Or so he said.

Jerry had a meeting with network sales that tied him up for the rest of the day so I made a couple more phone calls and then cut out early to do a little investigating of my own.

On my way out, I ran into Amy in the hallway. At first, she looked like she was going to scurry away in the opposite direction, frightened, as she usually did. But Burke had apparently told her my bark is worse than my bite. She pulled herself straight, fixed the appropriate smile on her face, and came towards me.

"I'm so happy you're not in trouble with the police anymore," she said sweetly.

It was a strange greeting. "Glad to hear you're happy," I said dryly.

"No, I mean it. I want you to know, I have a lot of respect for you."

"You should, but you don't," I said, not softening.

I wasn't going to fall for this I'm-OK-You're-OK rap she and Burke were trying to put over on me. It wasn't okay. "Maybe that crap worked for you as Miss Congeniality, but it doesn't work with me, okay? It's crap. You committed adultery with my husband behind my back, and then smiled at me in the hallway. The least courtesy you could do me now is not to feed me a bunch of bullshit about how much you respect me. Okay?"

"No matter what you say, I will always like and respect you," she said adamantly.

Madri Michaels, who had been listening, came up behind Amy and put her hand on Amy's shoulder for support. They were "friends," if it was possible for Madri to have friends. It was maybe more of an "enemy of my enemy" bond between the two women. Madri had dated Burke, until he dumped her for me. In my defense, let me say that I met him independently of her, during a murder trial, and didn't know at that time he was her boyfriend. Not that it would have made any difference.

"She's trying to be adult about all this," Madri said, to explain Amy's stubborn niceness.

Right. "Amy, if it makes you feel any better, I hate Burke far more than I hate you," I said.

I didn't want to get sucked into some stereotypical cat fight over him, playing the scorned woman role, when clearly he was the cause of much pain for all three of the women present. I didn't buy this crap that men are just horny imbeciles who can be led by their dicks by any woman with a good grip. Burke wasn't "stolen," he came and went willingly.

"Look, you're right," I said, jabbing my finger in Amy Penny's face. "We shouldn't be enemies. We have too much in common. We've shared my husband. Someday, after Burke has ditched you for someone new, let's the three of us—you, me, Madri—go have pedicures and lunch. We'll be like a club. But until then, I do not want to see you, and you can't make me be nice to you."

Amy Penny took a deep gasp, exploded into sobs, and then ran away. Madri turned to me.

"Do you have to be so cruel? What good does it do anyone to be a sore loser?" Her face was lit with indignation.

Five years before, when Burke and I started dating, she spread the rumor that Burke picked me because I was willing to do all sorts of filthy things in bed she would never do. Madri's so out of touch, she thought that old sexist epithet "slut" would disable me, not realizing that her rumor only enhanced my reputation and hurt hers. Come to think of it, it was shortly after that rumor took off that Eric began flirting with me.

As for the filthy things I was supposedly willing to do, I'm not sure which filthy things she was speaking of. What I'm willing to do depends a lot on who I'm going to do it with. With Burke, the sex was never very far from the ordinary, although we sometimes let our cat watch.

Chapter Seven

WHEN I GOT TO Griff Investigations, two rooms on the second floor of a dusty old building on Thirty-Fourth Street, right above the Conway's Discount store, Larry Griff's secretary, Crystal O'Connor, a classic petite with a *lot* of frosted brown hair, was packing up her office supplies.

"Like I told the police, I hadn't been with him long," she said. "He just opened the office six months ago, right? And, like, he didn't talk about his cases much. He was real . . . secretive."

"He must have kept files on his clients."

"Whatever information he had on clients he took with him wherever he went because he, like, didn't trust anyone, not even me. And the cops took all his books and stuff after he died," she said.

Into the box went a framed photo of a guy, probably her husband, a stuffed bunny, the aging Polaroids of her and two girlfriends on vacation on a beach with palm trees—all of them with dark tans and white smiles—a black plastic pencil cup, a tape dispenser, a box of labels, two rolls of white correction tape. She hesitated at the cut-glass bowl full of M&M's, then offered me some. "Please, help me eat these. I don't want to pack them and I hate to throw them out."

I took a small handful. "What books did the cops take?" I asked.

"Oh, phone books, *Who's Who,* stuff like that. Oh yeah, and he had a picture of you on his office wall."

"Me?"

"Yeah. Standing with a microphone in front of a courthouse or something. You were wearing a long coat. It was a black-and-white picture."

That would be my publicity photo, which public relations sends to news outlets and fans. Anyone who wanted one just had to write in and, except for those sent to residents of penal institutions, no record was kept. Cheery thought.

"Did he have a photo of Joanne Armoire?" I asked.

"I don't know who she is," Crystal said. "I know he had yours and he had a thing for you. Like, he'd sometimes ask me to call ANN and find out when your special reports were going to air. He never asked me to call for anyone else, right? When you were on, he turned on the TV in his office and locked his office door."

"Do you know anything about his investigations? Anything at all?"

She shrugged, apologetic. "What can I tell you? I know he did most of his work on the phone, but sometimes he had to go out. Sometimes, he'd call someone and say he was Craig Lockmanetz, a reporter doing a story about ANN. I only know this because he always took his callbacks as Lockmanetz on a separate phone line. I had to answer it People's News Service."

"You don't know the names of *any* of the people he was investigating, or who hired him?"

"All he wanted me to do was answer the phones and do minor, routine paperwork. He even picked up the mail himself at the main post office. I wish I knew more. But I don't. Like, this is a hardship for me too. Now I have to find another job, and I know I'll never get another easy job like this one. My husband hurt his back three months ago, so . . ."

"I'm sorry," I said.

"Yeah, well, it's rough all over, right?" She rolled the last M&M around the glass bowl and then offered it to me. I took it and she put the bowl in the box and closed it up. "I wish I knew more, you know, because I asked Mr. Griff to let me help him more, to teach me the business. But he wouldn't."

"Did he tell you why he wouldn't?"

"Top-secret project," she said with a smirk. "Or so he said. For a guy who poked around for other people's secrets, he sure kept his. I didn't even know he was, like, divorced until I read it in the paper."

"Well, if you remember anything, will you call me?" I gave her my card and we said good-bye.

I was halfway down the airless, dimly lit hallway when Crystal O'Connor came running out behind me. "Ms. Hudson? I remember something." She stopped, huffing, and then said, "I think."

"What is it?"

"About a week ago, or maybe more, I'm not sure—anyway, Griff came back from meeting someone on his case and there was a blond hair on his coat and I, you know, pulled it off, automatically. No big deal, right? Well, he grabbed the hair from my hand and looked at it, and he got this peculiar look on his face. It was so . . . funny, I mentioned it to my husband."

"What kind of look?"

"Like he was angry and . . . hungry."

"Hungry?"

"Maybe not hungry. It's . . . it's the look a cat gets in its eyes, right, when it's playing with a bird."

"Do you have any idea who the bird was?"

She smiled. "No."

"Was he dating anyone?"

"I don't know, but he had to be getting it somewhere, right? We all have to get it somewhere."

"Right," I said.

I had over an hour before my meeting with Teddy Boylen, the last survivor of the three Boylen brothers who founded Boylen Investigations in the 1970s, all ex-NYPD. I took a cab downtown and drank coffee at Raps Coffee Shop on Seventh Avenue, wondering how much Griff knew about me, how much was now in someone else's hands, and how much of it he took to the grave.

It's just like Fats Waller said. One never knows, do one?

That's my problem, or one of my problems. I hate *not* knowing. I can't handle too many unanswered questions in my life at one time. Because I can't find answers for those big Q's—Is there a God? Why am I here? What happens when I die?—I get a little obsessed with finding the true answers for those questions that have answers somewhere. That's one of the reasons I got into news. I hate it when answerable questions go unanswered, like when people get away with murder. It really gets under my skin.

That's another reason I got into news, actually. Murder. Six months or so after my father died, someone walked into a farmer's home on the edge of my hometown and shot seven members of a family to death, sparing only a four-year-old girl who hid in a closet and saw nothing.

For several weeks nobody knew who did it, and for the first time we all started locking our doors, not only at night, which was radical enough, but during the day. In bed at night, I had trouble sleeping, shooting bolt upright every time the wind blew through the trees or a dog barked. When I did sleep, the faces of the dead family, the Sesquins, took over my dreams.

One of the scariest things about it was that it seemed so random, so meaningless, and so immense. And it happened to people everyone in town knew, if only vaguely.

The fear subsided when reporters and TV crews from all over North America and as far away as England converged on the town to cover the story, covering it so well that it would have been impossible for another unwitnessed murder to be committed. The atmosphere of terror was quickly replaced by a media circus.

There seemed to be no motive for the cold-blooded slaughter of the quiet, church-going family, and in the effort to get to the bottom of it, everyone in town was interviewed by reporters and questioned by FBI. We got used to being the center of attention very quickly. We felt almost loved, and we felt safe.

After the killer was found, the reporters and the photographers packed up and left town and I felt their absence sorely. I think that was when I first realized the power of the media to transform, and first began thinking it could transform me.

Later, in junior high school, my career decision was reinforced when I discovered that it was okay to go to the prom without a date if you were covering it for the school newspaper, and that, under the guise of "reporter," you could get away with asking the principal a lot of pointed questions considered rude, even cause for detention, if asked by "civilian" students.

A little before seven, Teddy Boylen showed up. He was an older man, in his sixties, I guessed, with a bright red complexion and a white crew cut. He came in huffing, bringing an aura of cold air with him to the table, where it settled and dissipated around us. I shivered.

After exchanging routine pleasantries, we got down to Griff.

"Larry Griff left Boylen six months ago," Boylen told me. "He didn't take any of our clients with him, but I heard he landed a cash cow. I don't know who it was. I also heard he was working solo. That told me the job was hush-hush, and that he was investigating one person or a small group of people."

"What kind of investigations did Griff do for you?"

"A variety. Insurance, corporate, title searches, employee background checks, a lot of marital. Sometimes we did contract work for attorneys. He worked the phone a lot, worked through the mails. I prefer to work in the field, one-on-one, face-to-face."

"Why?"

"It's a philosophical thing. My generation used a lot of psychology in detective work. Griff's generation is too dependent on high-tech stuff."

"Were you friends with this guy?"

"Friends? No. But we worked together okay for a while. He'd been a cop, like me. I was NYPD for twenty years, he was a Philly cop."

"Why'd he leave the force?"

Boylen laughed. "Taking payoffs, although they couldn't make it stick. Griff was always looking for a big payday."

"Did he have gambling debts? Drug problems? Women problems?"

"Women, that's it, right there! He had a problem with women. He couldn't get enough women, and he liked the real glamorous ones, with . . . good heads of hair—blondes, brunettes, but especially redheads, like you. But dames . . . ladies . . ."

"Dames is fine," I said. "It's the word I prefer for my gender, actually."

He smiled at me. He was a cute old guy with clear, unflinching eyes. I had a puckish urge to rub my hand over his snow white crew cut, which I, of course, resisted.

"Dames cost. Dames like that. I mean, you don't go dutch with them. You met him, didn't you?"

"Only briefly," I said.

"Yeah, I read that in the paper. Anyway, he never had enough money or enough women. He was greedy, that was his true problem."

"Why did he leave Boylen?"

"I think he was blackmailing some of the people we were investigating for clients. . . ."

"But . . ."

"No proof. Just a strong hunch. Griff was working for the client and for himself, I figure, double-dealing."

A car door opened in front of Raps and a woman got out. Boylen watched her until she was almost at the end of the block, then he jumped and said, "Gotta run. Call me if you have any more questions. Hope you find what you're looking for."

"You too," I said.

As I left the coffee shop, a bum sang out to me from the sidewalk, "Got a quarter, lady? When I get rich, I'm going to marry a pretty young woman like you. Help me out, will ya?"

Sexist old fart. But I gave him a buck.

So far, I had a whole lot of nothing and not much choice. I was going to have to break the phalanx of ANN spin doctors and get to Joanne somehow. Fortunately, when I called Joanne again, her machine was off and a human being picked up, saving me having to scheme to get past Joanne's doorman.

Solange Stevenson answered the phone. "Robin?" she said. "Joanne is under a great deal of strain at the moment. I don't think she wants to see anyone else tonight."

There was a noise in the background, and I heard Solange cupping her hand over the phone to muffle voices. When the hand was taken away and the fog cleared, Solange said, "Just a moment."

Joanne came on. "You'd better come up here, Robin," she said. "You know where I live, don't you?"

Yeah, I remembered. Joanne and I had been friends for a time, back when we were both writers for ANN's flagship news program. Six months after she became a reporter, I became one, inheriting her weekend spot while she went to the U.N. full-time. I put in my six months covering dog shows and doing quirky stories about New York, the kind of stories the network relied on to flesh out twenty-four hour news on the weekends, which are traditionally slow news days. Joanne was interviewing ambassadors and visiting heads of state, doing a lot of thoughtful, cogent pieces on foreign policy.

Before long, she was jetting off to wars and natural disasters worldwide.

"Nerves of steel, heart of gold," said *Esquire* in an infatuated essay in its "Women We Love" issue. "Gutsy and classy," said Jack Jackson, when Joanne won her first Emmy for her Afghanistan reports.

I envied her, and resented her a little, but what I envied most was not her job or her fame, but her pragmatic, unflagging savoir faire.

Solange greeted me at the door of Joanne's apartment and we sat down in the cavernous living room, which was oddly devoid of furniture. Just a sofa, a chair, a television, and a liquor cabinet stood in the gymnasium-size room. The red-and-white Baluch carpet was marked by bright, clean squares and rectangles where Joanne's beloved art deco antiques had been. Joanne is one of those women who can combine her job with shopping. When she went into Afghanistan the second time to cover the battle of Jalalabad, for example, she came out with great video *and* antique carpets.

The network mandarins had all left, but Solange stayed behind. It wasn't surprising, as she loved misery and was always ready to dispense her venomous psychobabble to "help" a friend.

"Are you getting enough sleep? You look terrible. I'm worried about you," she said to me.

She does this all the time, preemptively disarming you with a quick succession of blows to your self-esteem. I always look "terrible" to Solange.

"I'm fine. I'm having a bad week, but I'm fine, really."

"Are you sure? You really look tired out. It's understandable, though, I mean, you've had a hellish year, between the belch and Burke and Amy . . ."

"So you keep reminding me," I said.

"Look, I'm just speaking out of concern for you."

Was she? She certainly said that like she meant it, but hell, who likes to be told over and over how terrible they look, how bad their luck is, how miserable their life is?

"Your husband's worried about you too," she said.

Oh, below the belt. "You spoke to Burke about me?" I asked.

"Well, it was just a little remark of friendly concern on his part, that's all. Actually, he called to pump me for information on the Griff murder, but I didn't have any, so we talked about other things."

She made it sound so chatty and intimate. Burke must have flattered her ass off, I thought, in his insidious way. The truth was, Burke could never stand Solange. "Here comes six feet of walking saltpeter," he said to me once when he saw her approach at a party.

But, of course, now he was cultivating a source.

Joanne came in wearing a black silk robe that set off her fair hair and skin and sat down across from me. Her eyes were red, but her expression was almost serene, like she'd been refreshed by weeping.

She turned to Solange. "Thanks for coming by, Solange. It means a lot to me that you did."

Solange, who never picked up on my bare-faced hints to butt out of my life, picked up on Joanne's cues all right.

"Any time. I should be running along now, but call me if you need anything. If I'm not home, have my service track me down."

"Thank you," Joanne said, reaching behind her to squeeze Solange's hand.

When Solange had left, Joanne said, "It was Alejandro De Marco."

"Who?"

"The Argentine general. He's the one I had the affair with. When I did that series of reports on Argentina's military adapting to democracy."

"You slept with him and then you did a story about him? Why?" It was clearly a conflict of interest.

"Why? Hmmm." She paused to formulate her answer. "He was sexy and smart and exotic and enigmatic and, frankly, I felt that having sex with him would give me valuable insights into his personality. I guess it sounds egotistical, but I felt sure I could detach myself emotionally and retain my objectivity."

"Did you?"

"More or less."

"And did you gain valuable insights?"

"Yes, more about my own self than his. But I don't think it really compromised my objectivity. It was after I finished the first piece, which was somewhat critical of him and his political ambitions. The second and third pieces were no less critical."

"But weren't you scared you'd 'disappear' into a mass grave somewhere?"

"Not really. The disappearances had virtually stopped by then. Besides, a little danger is an aphrodisiac. You know, it is probably more dangerous to date in New York City. I don't want to go into the whole long story tonight, but I figured you were burning with curiosity about who it was."

"I thought it was Yeltsin."

She laughed. "No, not Yeltsin. I don't make a habit of sleeping with the people I report on. I've never done it before, but Alejandro . . . he was intriguing and . . . it was right after I broke up with Marty and that was so painful. Alejandro seemed like a good way to be bad and get even with Marty in some way. Does that make sense?"

Marty was the cameraman on her foreign stories and her longtime boyfriend, now ex-boyfriend. He was very macho, very glam. They still dated sometimes—and slept together, I'm sure—and before Burke left me he had held this relationship up as a model.

"Completely," I said.

"It was a mistake, though," she said, standing up and going to a liquor cabinet to pour herself a shot of Jim Beam. "Want something?"

"No thanks."

"I've been trying to decide all day if I am going to survive this or not."

"You're a survivor, Joanne," I said. Joanne was too strong and in control to surrender.

"This kind of thing could be distorted by the news media," she said. "I've been thinking about all the things I've done that could be taken the wrong way if seen in a negative light. You understand."

"Yes, I do."

"Tomorrow I have to appear at a news conference and admit everything this investigator might have found out about me. You'd be amazed how many things like that a person can accumulate in thirty-some years of life. There was this lawn boy in Madrid—he was just nineteen—and a married man in Baghdad and on and on and on. You know what I mean."

"No, but I'd really like to," I said. A lawn boy sounded mighty good right about then.

"The media could distort a lot of stuff and ruin me. You know how we are, Robin. Once we get a taste of blood, we embark on a feeding frenzy. The free press, God bless it. Until it's coming after me."

"So who was investigating us? And why?"

"I assume it was just Griff, investigating attractive women like you, like me, to blackmail us. Cash or trade."

"So he was blackmailing you?"

"Yeah." She poured herself another Jim Beam and came to sit, just down the sofa from me. "He called me, about three weeks ago, didn't identify himself, asked me if the words 'Alejandro' and 'armored personnel carrier' meant anything to me."

"Armored personnel carrier?"

She sighed. "One night Alejandro requisitioned an APC and after dinner, we took it for a spin and then . . . we had sex in it. Apparently, there was a hidden camera. A rival general took snaps, and somehow they . . . circulated among the press corps down there and . . . I guess Griff got his hands on them."

"Holy . . ."

"So I was intrigued, to say the least, when he called. I met him at the Royalton bar and he told me he wanted twenty-five thousand dollars for the report he did on me and the pictures, which he showed to me. I told him it was going to take me a while to get my hands on twenty-five thousand, and then he offered me a chance to work it off. He said he had heard I swallowed. God only knows what's in that report."

"You told him . . . ?"

"That I'd get the twenty-five thousand one way or another.

No way I was going to be this guy's whore. I'd pay him the money and get it over with. Just put it behind me.

"A week later, he called up and said the price was going up, up to fifty thousand dollars. Said he was taking a room at the Marfeles the night of the company party, and he'd contact me there. He told me to bring the fifty thousand with me or else he was going to turn my file over to another reporter to expose me.

"Robin, I had cashed my chips, begged and borrowed, even hocked all my jewelry to get twenty-five thousand. I didn't know where to go to get another twenty-five grand. It was a nightmare. Honest to God, Robin, I have never felt more scared in my life. Not crossing mine fields in Afghanistan, not dodging snipers in Sarajevo."

"You didn't get the rest of the money," I guessed.

She smiled ruefully and nodded around the room. "I raised another seventeen thousand by selling my furniture at a tremendous sacrifice. Really. For a fraction of what it is worth."

"Then you saw him at the Marfeles?"

"I was supposed to meet him at ten-thirty in Room 13D, but when I got to his door, I heard voices inside. Griff said, 'It's too late. It's already on its way.' Or something like that. There was someone in there, speaking softly, and I couldn't make out if it was a man or a woman. Then Griff said, 'She won't know what to look for until I tell her. So you still have time.'"

"'She' being . . . ?"

"Me, I thought," Joanne said. "Anyway, I went back to my room. Around eleven, I made another try. That's when I saw you."

"Did you go back to his room later?"

"Shortly after midnight. And there was no answer."

"You think he intended to give the information to me?" I asked.

"Judging from the suggestions he made to me, he probably would have wanted you to give him a blow job first."

"Why us? Or is it every on-air person at ANN? Was Solange being blackmailed?" I asked.

"It's hard to imagine anyone being able to blackmail Solange," Joanne said.

Yeah, what could they get on her, after all? She'd already admitted to being a victim of incest, the child of an alcoholic, a victim of bulimia, anorexia, lookism, sexism, all for the edification and emotional benefit of her television viewers.

"Some people can't be blackmailed. Exhibitionists like Solange and unrepentant rascals like Georgia Jack. And perfectly honest people, of which there are exactly none," she said, and smiled.

"Where are the pictures?" I asked.

Joanne shrugged. "I don't know. All I know is I saw them, I know they exist, but I don't know what happened to them. They're out there somewhere." She looked out her panoramic window at the dark city. "It's scary, some stranger out there, holding my intimate secrets."

I nodded. "I used to think it was scary that some anonymous, lonely fan could be jerking off to my publicity photo. But this is worse."

"Yeah, it violates the self, as Solange put it. It's like psychological rape. The thing is, I've been on the other side of this. I've learned other people's secrets, dug up dirt without them knowing it. I've confronted them with it. It's my job. I'm an investigative reporter. But I feel like I've been stung by my own tail, you know what I mean?"

I did.

"Did you kill him?" I asked her.

"No," she said. "Did you?"

"No."

"In a way," she said, "I'm glad this is out. All this time, I've known those pictures existed, and I've worried about their disclosure. It's a relief in a way not to have to worry about it anymore.

"So—I told you about Alejandro, Robin. Why don't you tell me what Griff had on you?"

So I told her about Red Knobby, an unpleasant memory but a relatively innocuous one.

This is the deal. I was ten, and had suddenly become interested in boys, but did not know how to get their attention. In my reading and my perusal of art books, I got the idea that what boys liked best was the female form, so I invited a half dozen of the neighborhood boys into my garage one day.

There, I reclined, *Odalisque*-like, under a dusty blanket, facing a semicircle of skeptical boys. I hesitated only a moment, and flung back the blanket.

And there I was, completely naked, expecting adoration and admiration for my daring exposure, when one of them, a boy unfortunately nicknamed Stinky Starko, started laughing and said, "Knobby knees! She's got red hair and knobby knees!"

Mortification spread up my alabaster skin like a fire as the boys began jeering "Knobby! Knobby knees," and then ran away from me, like I was poison.

It was a damning commentary on my early sexual presence, and did a real number on my body image. For several years, I was known as Red Knobby, and every time I heard that name I felt exposed, frightened, and pissed off, in that order.

It set my self-esteem back a decade, my Red Knobby Years, although I got even with those boys. When we were little, they wouldn't even talk to me, they'd just make loud jokes at my expense. But by the time I got to high school, I had turned into a swan, on the outside at least, and I wouldn't talk to them.

Even as an adult, whenever I heard the word knobby, I would smell creosote and timber and feel a flash of humiliation. But now that it was out, it seemed like no big deal. Now I look back on that incident and think, those little boys had a chance to gaze upon this body, and they focused on my knees. It's not a bad body and those boys missed a great opportunity, one I hope haunts them in their dotage. I think of them when I'm working out my hostility in the employee gym and am starting to feel the burn.

But as far as dirty little secrets go, Knobby and the Starko Affair couldn't hold a candle to Alejandro and the APC. With pictures.

Chapter Eight

THE *NEWS*-JOURNAL was not convinced of Joanne's innocence, but while she dominated their story in the morning
edition, they weren't letting me off the hook yet either. Using
innuendos, they even put forward a conspiracy theory, involving me, Joanne, and possibly other women, getting together to
rid the planet of a "sleazebag" like Griff, a service-to-our-
gender sort of thing.

"CIRCLE WIDENS—SECOND TV REPORTER IMPLICATED IN GRIFF
MURDER," read the headline on page three. In the main story, a
"retired homicide expert" said, "The guy was a sleazebag. I'm
surprised some lady, or group of ladies, didn't blow him away
long before now."

Inset, they had a photo of me leaving Joanne's the night
before, with the caption, "Hudson leaves after confab with
Armoire." One plus one equals a conspiracy.

The story was flanked by Kerwin Shutz's column, in which
he cited *Thelma and Louise, Basic Instinct,* and Hillary Clinton
for inciting a "wave of violent, vigilante feminism." Kerwin

moonlighted as the ultra-right-wing questioner on ANN's show *Ambush* and his perennial fear was strong women trying to take his gun away. Gee, what would Freud say? It kind of made me wonder what his parents' marriage was like.

I had to laugh, though, imagining Kerwin Shutz huddling in his survivalist basement on Long Island, his constitutionally protected semiautomatic penis-substitute at the ready to fend off a gang of raving feminists.

I was tempted to log into the computer and send Shutz a message, something facetious like "You are next on our Sworn Enemies of Feminism List," but he'd probably take it seriously and it would end up in the *News-Journal* the next day as a "threat."

Claire gave me the day's memos and my phone messages when I got in. I went into my cluttered office and read through them. Two calls from Elroy and three calls from Burke. He was trying to cultivate me as a source, I guess, the shameless cad. In the message space on one of the pink slips was written, in quotation marks, "Hey, Holden, gimme a call, willya?" Holden was his pet name for me, as in Holden Caulfield and William Holden, who starred in Paddy Chayefsky's *Network*.

I crumpled it up rather gleefully, shot it into my wastepaper basket, and turned on the TV to catch Joanne's live presser (I'd been forbidden to attend in person). It was about five minutes before the ten hour—Joanne was coming up in the first block of the next show—so I watched Sawyer Lash, the network's worst anchorman, misread a story on B-films. He kept saying "marital" for the word "martial."

"A new marital-arts action film," he said, as the screen filled with shots of two ninjas kicking the shit out of each other. At the end of it, Sawyer stopped reading and cocked his head slightly, like a hound. I could almost hear the producer screaming at him through the IFB in his ear.

"I'm sorry, that was a *martial*-arts film, not a *marital*-arts film," Sawyer said, and then teased Joanne's live presser at the top of the hour before the show went into terminal break, network ID, and commercial.

I love live television.

At a table in Studio C, Joanne sat before a bouquet of black microphones, flanked by Jack Jackson and George Dunbar, the court eunuchs cringing behind her. The look on her face was perfect—neither chastened nor arrogant, but serene. I knew this serene look of hers and you couldn't argue with it for long. It gave her a kind of mysterious authority.

"Thank you for coming," she said, and went into her prepared statement.

Basically, she said the same things she told me, more or less. She denied any connection to Griff's murder, admitted to Alejandro and the APC, but left out the lawn boy and the married man and all the colorful others, taking care of them with the blanket statement that she was a single red-blooded female in her thirties with a sex drive and a sex life that were nobody's business.

"But," she said, "my brief relationship with Alejandro was a huge mistake in judgment, creating the appearance of a conflict of interest. I take my profession seriously, and I realize I have violated an ethic we hold dear. I deeply regret my mistake, and I have learned from it."

Before taking questions, Georgia Jack came to the mike. "I want y'all to know, Joanne here is a better reporter today for having erred and repented."

Georgia Jack had done a brief turn as a preacher before being defrocked for moral turpitude in 1961.

"Today, she gave me her resignation, but I wouldn't accept it. She's taking two weeks off, without pay, in contrition. I stand behind her one hundred percent. All this sniffing around ladies' petticoats for secrets and love letters is gutter behavior. And I have something else to say. Someone is trying to discredit ANN's integrity and I am going to find out who."

Then he opened up the floor to questions.

In one fell swoop, Jack Jackson had spun the focus away from Joanne and on to some outside force threatening ANN. If you want to debunk one conspiracy theory, give 'em another. From there on, all the questions had to do with which shadowy force was trying to ruin ANN—the religious right, the radical left, rival broadcasters, the Democrats, the Republicans, the print media, sinister foreign powers?

Jackson hinted of vague, suspicious things, and promised that when he knew something, they'd know something.

A reporter then asked Jackson if he had anything he wanted to confess. Jackson said that with all his sins, he'd have to do it in installments, the reporters didn't have that much time, and in any case, most of his sins weren't PG and couldn't go out on the airwaves.

When they broke for commercial, I scanned the day's memos. The first, from Jack Jackson, iterated that he believed in freedom of speech and association, he believed in Joanne Armoire's integrity, and he believed in the integrity of his employees.

The second, from Dunbar, urged anyone who might have some secret that could compromise his or her objectivity to come talk to him about it, so that ANN could share the burden. I'm paraphrasing, but basically it was a call to confession. Voluntary, of course.

And Bob McGravy, now head of ANN's in-house Ethics Committee, had written a memo restating ANN's policies and ethics quite righteously, but also gently reminding us that we are all flawed and should not pass judgment too quickly. Typically, he ended it with a bit of poetry.

> Why should not old men be mad?
> Some have known a likely lad
> That had a sound fly-fisher's wrist
> Turn to a drunken journalist;
> —W. B. Yeats

When the commercials ended, Joanne answered a question about how she knew Griff. I couldn't stay to listen, though; Jerry was standing outside my office rapping on the mottled glass, saying, "Makeup, Robin, makeup. We need time to rehearse, you know?"

Jerry and I were going undercover as Mrs. and Mrs. Eugene Fullmark at Empire Semen that day, and we needed to get ready. I would much rather have watched Joanne talk about Griff, but sometimes one's real life intrudes on, even overtakes, one's problems and crises.

I was going in disguise, with a black wig and thick glasses. It took a long time to get all my hair up under that wig, and the wig was made bigger to compensate, until I looked like Lady Bird Johnson. My eyebrows were darkened too, and in a bit of inspired work, the makeup woman lightly dusted temporary dye across my upper lip, giving me the faint illusion of a moustache. In less than an hour, I was transformed into Ivy (it was Jerry's mother's name) Fullmark, homemaker and help-mate to Eugene Fullmark, tax attorney.

Jerry took one look at me after I got out of makeup and said, "Can't you make her look pretty? I want a pretty wife."

Sometimes he's so outrageously sexist, I can't believe he isn't pulling my leg. Then I remember he has no sense of humor.

"Well, I'm the wife you got," I said, talking tough.

"You aren't going to use that crusty sailor voice today, are you?" he said.

There was something sick about the way Jerry relished this role-playing, us posing as man and wife. There was a powerful element of control in it, in his being able to make me play his wife because he was my boss. Or so I thought, but hey—I'm paranoid.

In any case, the control wasn't overtly sexual. Jerry often made crude, sexist remarks—then again, so did I—but I have to say this for Jerry, he never hit on me, not once. In fact, I always thought he was a little afraid of my body, the way he rarely touched me. It was like there was a one-inch offshore zone radiating from me, a force field he could not bring him-self to breach.

Before we left, we rehearsed our answers and our behavior towards each other in the office while Claire watched. We weren't in sync.

"You should defer to me a little, show me some respect at least," Jerry complained. "We have to convince the people at Empire Semen we *are* married."

"I hate this. This isn't reporting, this is acting."

"You know," Jerry said, his voice rising slightly. "I'm starting to lose patience with you. You're not being a team player, Robin. Just remember this"—he jabbed his finger in my face, careful not to cross the one-inch DMZ—"if you can't stand the heat, get out of the kitchen!"

"It's not the heat I can't stand," I said, grand and self-righteous. "It's the stink!"

Claire came between us, laughing. "Well, you've convinced *me* you're married," she said.

On the way over, we acted even more married, sitting in the back of the surveillance van, fuming, not speaking to each other. Jerry and I didn't see eye to eye on much, that's for damn sure. All the male-female stuff aside, we had different visions about how to present the news. Jerry liked a lot of easily identifiable clichés for our viewers, who apparently don't understand the meaning of tears in an old woman's eyes in closeup as she smiles a little, ruefully, and says, "It's been good and it's been bad." To help the viewer out with this emotional complexity, we cut the bite and instead explain that "Mary has known some sadness in her life, much sadness, sadness and joy." No shit, Sherlock.

Jim and Ellis parked around the corner from Empire Semen and did a quick equipment test. Jerry and I were both wired for sound and we both had small surveillance cameras with built-in mikes. The newsroom had been joking about Jerry's "peniscam," but, actually, his was concealed in a briefcase (his camera, not his penis) and the mechanics of his donation would not be shown, thank God.

My camera was in my purse, or rather, Ivy's purse, a large black vinyl handbag especially made to hold the small camera, with its tiny fish-eye lens and ni-cad battery pack. The network had put big money, for them, into this undercover capability and Jerry was determined to give the network its money's worth. We went undercover a lot. We once went undercover at a church bingo hall for a story on suburban vice.

When everything was checked and working, Jerry and I went into Empire Semen, a large, squat building in the North Bronx. Inside, a receptionist ushered us into an office to wait. Jerry and I still weren't talking.

A densely packed nurse came into the badly paneled room and gave us clipboards. As we filled out the medical questionnaire and a legal form, she sat across from us and watched. Jerry and I seethed at each other and mumbled under our breath. When we handed in our assignments, the nurse spoke at some length about the donation procedure, the storage procedure, and the insemination procedure, which could be performed by a licensed physician affiliated with Empire, by my own personal physician, or by myself in the privacy of my own home. They even delivered. In New York, you can get anything delivered.

When she was through, she handed Jerry a paper cup and a printed sheet of "Ejaculate Handling Instructions."

"Better give me a *bucket!*" he said, winking at me. "Right, honey?" He was really enjoying this.

"Har har har," I said slowly.

When Jerry went to jerk off, the nurse smiled at me. "How long you been married?" she asked. "No, lemme guess. Judging by the way you argue, I'd say ten years."

"It seems like a century," I said, as my camera recorded every word. "I don't believe in divorce, but sometimes . . ."

"Sometimes . . . ," she prompted, expectant of secrets.

"Sometimes, I just want to start over without him. The things he asks me to do . . ."

"What things?"

"You know, in bed. He has disgusting fetishes."

If I had to play this wife role, I was going to play it to the hilt—my own way.

"Disgusting fetishes," I went on. "When he bought that artificial leg, I said enough was enough, you know, because he has two legs already. So we don't have sex anymore. I want to have a baby, but I don't want to have to actually touch him, so this is the next best thing. When I'm ready for a baby, I'll just come make a withdrawal, right?"

"Absolutely!" the nurse said. She couldn't believe I was telling her all this.

I leaned in towards her, confidentially. "Actually," I said. "There's no rule that I have to use his sperm, is there? When the time comes, maybe I could make a switch. You . . . you have any of that Nobel-prize-winner sperm here?"

She shook her head. "A lot of medical students from Columbia University, though."

I asked her to take me on a tour of the storage facility. At first, she resisted, but I convinced her Eugene would be furious if I couldn't at least assure him that his seed would be well cared for.

"Personally, I don't care what you do with it," I said, which was not a lie.

This is where going undercover became valuable, because I was able to see the refrigerated back room, with all its signs of shoddy organization. The sperm was kept in big liquid nitrogen containers, some with faded labels, one of them leaking something. Outside, a lackadaisical attendant watched television.

I asked her all the questions I had to for the piece, and continued trashing Eugene Fullmark and telling embarrassing

120

stories about him, sex stories involving prosthetic limbs and self-abuse. When Jerry and I left, she gave him a strange smile.

"I think that nurse had the hots for me," he said.

"She was fascinated by you," I told him, in all seriousness. It was not a lie.

We gave Claire the tapes to log when we all got back to ANN. Jerry had to run to an affiliate seminar.

"Don't make any dubs of mine," I said to Claire, tipping her off that it was highly dubbable stuff. Tapes that show on-air talent or executives being embarrassed are passed around by the workers to be dubbed for private blooper reels in a kind of samizdat system. I had appeared on several, and had one of my own at home.

"Sure," Claire said, smiling slyly.

What had I accomplished with my performance at Empire? Well, I had assured that my part as Ivy Fullmark would end up largely on the cutting-room floor, so to speak, and only my relevant questions and the video from the back room would make it into the series, thus limiting my exposure to further humiliation.

What else could I do? I have a bad attitude and an ironclad contract.

And, I admit, it was fun.

I started transferring stuff from my pockets back into my real purse (the purse-cam hadn't been designed to hold anything but the camera and battery-pack) and I realized I didn't have my keys. Goddamn it. I started looking around my office, knowing that even if they were there I might not find them. My office, you see, is pretty cluttered, like my apartment, although at work a cleaning lady came in nightly. Newspapers and raw tapes from previous stories were stacked in precarious piles all over the room. Interoffice memos overflowed from the fish bowl into which they were jammed. Papers, yellow Post-It notes, and pens of various colors covered the desk, while along the back wall was a bookshelf holding all the books I thought I might need in writing, all haphazardly shelved. (There was a *Pelican Complete Works of Shakespeare*, the collected works of Mark Twain, a dictionary, the *Columbia History of the World*, collected poems of W. H. Auden and Alfred, Lord Tennyson, Lenny Bruce's *How to Talk Dirty and Influence People*, a few biographies of movie stars, the definitive bio of Edward R. Murrow, and a *Bartlett's Quotations* in a glass case with a tiny steel mallet and a sign that said, "In case of emergency break glass." That was a gift from McGravy.)

I couldn't find my keys. Believe it or not, I misplace them a lot, although never for very long.

I called out to Claire, "Did maintenance empty the trash baskets this afternoon, while we were out?"

"I don't know," she answered back, her voice muted by the wall between our offices. "I was in the library most of the morning, boning up on sperm. So to speak. Go ahead, ask me anything. I'll take seminal fluid for four hundred, Alex."

"I can't find my keys," I said. "Shit."

I closed my eyes and tried to retrace my steps that day, where I last saw my keys and what I then did, like that. Did I drop them somewhere when I was taking stuff out of my purse and putting it into my pockets? But it was no good. I couldn't remember.

As luck would have it, there was only one set of spare keys to my place and Burke had them, which meant I'd *have* to call him and I'd *have* to talk about the Griff case.

I dunno. Maybe a part of me wanted to see him, and the keys were a good excuse. I hadn't asked for my keys back because I still had this romantic idea he would just quietly come back one night, slipping back into my bed as though he had never gone, and my real life could resume. He hadn't given them back to me for reasons I couldn't presume to know.

It was probably time to close the book on that fantasy, I thought. I called Burke and asked him to meet me and bring my keys. I wasn't keen on seeing him, but I had no choice, right?

All the same, before I left I checked my desk one more time, pushing around the loose papers, still hoping to uncover my keys. I didn't, but I found a Xeroxed sheet with a yellow Post-It note attached.

"Squirreled this away from Gil Jerome for you. Eric."

I peeled off the Post-It and read. It was the preliminary medical report on Griff, which Jerome wouldn't give me, me being a witness and all.

Based on the last time he was seen, a partially digested meal in the stomach, liver temperature reading at the crime scene, and lividity (the way the blood settles in a corpse), time of death was guesstimated at sometime between nine-thirty and eleven, New Year's Eve. He had been attacked from the front with the murder weapon, and he was in the bathroom when it happened, judging by blood splatters and fingerprints—his— on the bathroom door. The report speculated that he fell to his knees, holding his bleeding head with one hand. He was hit again, on the top of his head. When he collapsed, facedown on the floor, he was struck sixteen more times.

Chapter Nine

TWO WORDS BUZZED AROUND Keggers that night: conspiracy and confession.

Because it had good prices and because it was in the basement of our building, right across from the subway, Keggers was *the* ANN hangout. Open a bar near a network or newspaper and you can make a fortune. Journalists like to unwind, they like to drink, and they leave big tips.

Keggers catered to us by papering the walls with facsimiles of historic newspaper editions (the ladies' room was done completely in Women Get the Vote! editions of the *New York Telegraph*). Behind the bar were caricatures of ANN personalities and executives (not always mutually exclusive nouns), including my caricature, with my overlarge mouth. If we didn't already feel at home, the bartender always knew our drinks, and the lighting was kept low and flattering.

Keggers was where Burke wanted to meet me, presumably because he could stop by the *Gotham Salon* offices and see Amy on his way to or from meeting me, or maybe so he could cultivate a few sources. However, Burke was not there when I arrived, which was unusual. He was an early person. I, on the other hand, am a late person.

A Willie Dixon blues song was playing on the jukebox when I walked in. The regulars were all there. By the door, a table of senior assignment desk guys were loudly discussing the possible conspiracy against ANN, which preempted their usual war stories: Khe Sanh, Dhahran, Sarajevo. Bullets, booze, broads. Dallas '63, I drank with Ruby. I'd heard these stories a hundred times, and so had they, but they didn't seem to mind the repetition, lubricated as it was by steady glasses of sour mash sippin'.

Louis Levin and a bunch of writers were sitting together in the back, trapped by Turk Hammermill, who was probably the only person not discussing conspiracies and confessions. Louis saw me and waved at me, signaling me to come over. I shook my head—no way—and went to talk to Mark O'Malley.

O'Malley, a financial reporter who once advised me to "think geriatric" in my investments, had a theory that fit his special area of expertise. Jackson had taken the company public in the early eighties to raise cash, but the only way he could get investors to buy into his dreams, which seemed farfetched and quixotic back then, was to give them forty-one percent, with another thirty percent given in royal grants, i.e., stock options, to top employees. So Jackson, chairman of the board, held just twenty-nine percent of the stock, hardly a controlling interest.

Of course, that was never a problem for Jackson. He controlled his stockholders, a disproportionate number of them wealthy feminist widows, with charm. And they were very loyal. Their loyalty increased as JBS took off and the profits rolled in. That loyalty helped fight off takeover attempts.

But everyone has a price and the disloyalty price on the stock was believed to be $50. Fifty bucks, and the devoted suffragettes would hitch up their petticoats and run for the highest bidder. At the moment, it was listed on the NYSE at about 28½. It seemed safe as long as we weren't ruined by scandal and stockholder panic, Mark asserted, before taking his drink and his theory to another group.

Eric Slansky was at the bar. I took a seat between Dillon Flinder and Eric and ordered a lemon Stoly martini from Mickey, the barman.

"Hi," Eric said, flashing his pale blues at me. "I was hoping you'd be here tonight."

I suddenly felt a blush was imminent and I turned away from him, not wanting to reveal myself to him that way, not at this stage of the game.

"Hey, Dillon," I said. "Did I interrupt a heavy conversation here?"

"No," he said. "We were discussing the line of people who stood outside Dunbar's office today, waiting to make confession."

"Hell, his memo worked! Who was there?"

Eric jumped in. "According to my sources, about six people spoke to Dunbar after Joanne's presser, including Mark O'Malley and Solange Stevenson."

"Solange? What could she possibly have left to confess?" Dillon asked, in his class of '55 Hahvahd accent. Dillon Flinder was a second-string medical correspondent who sometimes drank with me at Keggers. "Now me, I could give Dunbar a confession that would be worth his while."

He laughed. Dillon was corrupt, dissolute, and unrepentant. Get a few drinks in him and he'd tell you all kinds of scandalous stuff about people, mainly himself, and would be completely unremorseful for his drunken confessions the next time he saw you. He considered himself a true scientist and had an excessive interest in sexual science and an unhealthy interest in botany.

Once over drinks at Keggers he told me that in pursuit of the perfect sexual experience he had drilled a hole in a watermelon and then made love to it—his words, made love to it. How was it? I asked. I shouldn't have refrigerated it first, he said.

"You know what Mark O'Malley has to confess, don't you?" Dillon asked.

I did, but I wasn't about to say it and confirm Dillon's own speculation. Mark was the best-looking man at ANN, one of the smartest, one of the nicest and—ain't it always the way, girls—he was gay. He hadn't come out because his family didn't approve of that sexual preference and because he felt it would hurt him on his conservative business beat. Man, it wasn't fair, that Mark's private life, which had no bearing on his reporting, could be forced out like this.

I changed the subject to spare Mark's ears from burning, and turned to Eric.

"What do you have to confess, Eric?" I asked.

"Want to give me something to confess?" he asked, and grinned. I felt a sudden, powerful pelvic twinge. I hated that he could affect me this way. I said nothing.

"Well, I don't have to confess anyway," he said. "Obviously, whoever is trying to discredit ANN is gunning for on-air people. They're going after the most visible symbols of the network's credibility, its reporters and anchors. Nobody knows just who, though. Was every on-air person investigated, or just some? By the way, did you get that note I dropped off for you?"

"Yeah, thanks," I said. "How did you get hold of it?"

"I saw Gil Jerome in the Xerox room. He'd thrown that copy out to get one of better quality. After he left, I fished it out of the trash."

"Well, thanks."

I saw Burke's head above the crowd as he squeezed through towards me. When he finally made it, he said, "Sorry I'm late. I had to wait for Amy to bring me your keys. I'd forgotten where I put them. I'd forgotten I even had them."

"But you brought them?" I said. Eric's arm moved across the bar behind me, protectively. Burke looked down at Eric's arm and then back up at me without reacting. Boys, boys.

"Yeah," he said. He pulled them out and dangled them in front of me. When I reached for them, he snatched them away.

"How mature," I said.

"First, I need to talk to you. Privately," he said.

I looked at Eric. He looked at Burke suspiciously.

"You want me to wait for you, Robin?" he said.

"No, thanks," I said.

Eric plunked his money on the bar for Mickey and slid off his stool. "See you tomorrow then," he said, and kissed me full on the lips, quickly, before he left.

Burke said nothing about the kiss as he led me towards the back. We passed Madri Michaels, who saw Burke and me together and cooed, "Way to go, Robin!"

"No, no, it's not what you think," I said.

Madri's assumption that this was a reconciliation pissed me off because I'm not the type of woman who would take a man back that easily. No, if Burke wanted back in my bed now, he'd have to perform feats that would make the twelve labors of Hercules look like child's play.

"Sure, sure," Madri said, unconvinced. The rumor of our reconciliation would be circulating as soon as I left her sight—and she was Amy's good buddy. Fuck it, I thought, as we moved past her, into a booth papered with Dewey Wins headlines. We sat beneath a fake green and orange Tiffany lamp. A waitress came over and gave us menus.

"Have you eaten?" Burke asked me.

"No." I glanced at the menu quickly. I ordered a chili burger and a double lemon Stoly martini and Burke ordered the salad platter and an obscure local beer.

When the waitress left, Burke started rearranging the condiments on the table, aligning the ketchup, sugar, and napkin dispenser, placing the salt and pepper in front of them in perfect symmetry, and putting the small bottle of Tabasco right in front of the salt and pepper. Then he straightened his paper place mat and moved the fork from the right side to the left, lining it up at a perfect ninety-degree angle from the table edge.

Watching him do this, I felt my chest constrict with a familiar tension. "Do you have to do that?" I asked, irritated. "It's so anal."

"Do what?"

"Straighten the table."

"Did I do that?" he asked innocently. Ah yes. When you're married long enough, you can annoy each other without even being conscious of it.

"Forget it. So what do you want to talk about?" I asked.

"How's your mother?"

"I can't believe that is what you want to talk about, but since you asked: She has her good days and her bad days. Her bad days are real bad."

"Does she still believe she's the queen of England?"

"She never believed she was the queen of England, Burke. She believes she ought to be."

One of my mother's delusions of grandeur involved her belief that her mother had mated illicitly with King George VI during a royal visit to the States that coincidentally took place nine months before my mother's birth. My father, bless his heart, loved her despite this cracked view, and convinced her of the need for discretion. But occasionally, when she felt she wasn't getting the respect she deserved, she would announce her alleged parentage to any and all. This often happened during disputes with Safeway checkers and once with a Woolworth fitting-room attendant, who curtly told my mother she didn't care if she was the queen of bloody Sheba, she still couldn't take more than three items into the fitting room.

"She has some good days, though?" Burke prompted.

"When she takes her drugs she's fine, except for a few minor lapses. I mean, she talks about my father like he's still alive. I hate to call her because she'll say, 'Let me get your father. He'll want to say hi,' and she'll leave me hanging there indefinitely while she looks for my dead dad. The long-distance bills are hell. She stills asks about you all the time. Well, she calls you Frank for some reason, but she means you. So—what is it you really want?"

"Robin, word on the street is Griff turned some kind of information over to you the night he was killed. What can you tell me about it?"

Word on the street. Burke liked to talk as though he were Hildy Johnson, as though he were plugged into every waterfront bar and hood hangout in the city.

"They say lots of things on the street. Not all of them are true. Who told you Griff turned info over to me?"

"Someone saw a guy fitting his description handing you something during the party."

"Who?"

"A source," he said. "Then Joanne said he threatened to turn info on her over to another reporter, and I put two and two together . . ."

The waitress brought our food and drinks. I bit into my burger.

"Seriously, can you tell me what he gave you?"

I had a mouth full of food, so no, I couldn't tell him just then. I purposely chewed very slowly, making him wait, and then I said, "If I knew, which I don't, I wouldn't tell you, Burke. We're rivals now." I emptied my martini and waved at the waitress to bring me another.

We'd met on a story, Burke and I, the murder trial of a mobster named Lonnie Katz who was believed to have killed a dozen men with no penalty, but got in hot water when he killed a woman. A woman he was married to at the time. A woman with a suspicious mother. When Lonnie tried to buy his mother-in-law's silence with a bookmaking concession, Ma turned state's evidence and sent Lonnie away.

Burke was at WOR at the time and we started dating. I always thought that was kind of romantic, meeting on a murder.

"If he gave me anything, don't you think I would have turned it over to the cops?" I said. I was thinking about that sheet I hadn't given the cops, the one that was all blacked out. Once I'd kept it from them, I couldn't hand it over without making them suspicious, even if it wasn't relevant. Guilt for this omission was starting to weigh heavily on me.

The page hadn't seemed important to anyone but me. But was it? Did it contain some clue? I wanted to leave, go home, look at the sheet again, but I was midmeal and Burke was on my case.

"We used to tell each other everything once upon a time," he said wistfully.

Jeez. This guy just didn't get it. He cheated on me. He left me for a younger woman. He did all this while I was in the midst of a professional crisis. I was no longer required to like him.

"We used to *trust* each other once," I said. "The rules have changed slightly."

"Let's not fight."

"But we're so good at it," I said. "It seems like from the moment we got married we fought. We're such opposites. Given all this, Burke, what made you marry me? Just out of curiosity. I've been wondering."

"What makes a man throw himself on a grenade to save his buddies?"

"That's funny."

"How about this then." He grinned. "What makes a man who is standing at the edge of an abyss looking down want to jump into it?"

"Oh, that's a much nicer analogy."

"It's the thrill of the fall," he answered for me. "When I was falling in love with you, it was the greatest time of my life. But sooner or later, I had to hit solid ground."

"You're doing a great job of getting into my good graces with all this fawning flattery," I said.

"You know what I mean. When we lived together in that big apartment in your funky neighborhood, I never knew what the next day would bring, and it was exciting in a way." He averted his eyes. "But I can't live with you. You wear me out. I want a peaceful home life, a normal wife, and . . . and children, a house in the burbs, once in a while, maybe, a home-cooked meal. That's not such a radical concept outside New York. You don't really want me back anyway, do you?"

"I want somebody," I said. "But I don't think it's you anymore. Good thing, since you've found your beauty queen."

"Well, Amy and I may be very compatible, but she's no Robin Hudson," he said.

"Meaning what?"

"Amy . . . she doesn't make me laugh like you do. You really made me laugh and I never realized how nice that was until it was gone. Sometimes I really miss you."

"Nice try," I said. "But flattery will not get you any information I might have."

"I wasn't flattering you . . . I was opening up to you." He smiled and flashed that endearing Correspondent's Squint.

It softened me up. By now I had decided to reduce his sentence to eleven heroic labors.

"You're one in three billion, Robin," he said, and signaled the waitress to bring more drinks. "I think we should try to be friends. To be honest, it's too exhausting fighting you, it's debilitating being married to you, and friendship seems the only other option you'll consider."

"Oh, I can think of another. Of course, it would probably mean life without parole . . ."

"You're drunk."

"No, I'm not." I reconsidered. "Well, maybe I am. I've had a helluva week, and not much sleep, and the *News-Journal* thinks I'm a menace to society and . . . Well, anyway, you're here and you want to be my friend. What kind of friend? The kind of friend who brings chicken soup, Puffs tissues, and French *Vogue* when you're sick with a really horrible, contagious disease? Or the kind of friend who sends a belated birthday card every year?"

"The kind of friend who really cares about you but can't stay married to you."

"That's a very narrow category," I said, and waved for another drink. When the waitress brought it, Burke asked for the check.

I took a big sip and after giving it some impaired thought, said, "Okay. You can be my friend. But only on the third Tuesday of every month." I was talking too loud and slurring my words. Even I could hear it. "And I still won't tell you anything about this murder. Even if I knew anything. And I don't."

"I think you've had enough to drink, Robin."

"It's no longer any of your business," I said. "And it's a conflict of interest, because you slept with me, and now you're reporting on a story I'm involved in. Oh wait, things like that don't matter at Channel 3, do they? Ethics and stuff."

"You're drinking too much," he said. "Maybe you'd better get some air. Come on. I'll take you up to get a cab."

He helped me to my feet and supported me as we went up to the street. After hailing a cab for me, he insisted on seeing me home. I was, in fact, pretty drunk. Halfway back to my place I started feeling green.

"Oh, shit," I said.

"What's wrong?"

WHAT'S A GIRL GOTTA DO?

"I'm not feeling well," I said, rolling down my window.

"Are you going to barf?" Burke asked with some alarm. Even in my troubled state I could see how the idea of his estranged wife puking in a cab distressed the ever neat and tidy Burke Avery. I exploited his anxiety by hanging my head over his lap.

"Robin, don't throw up here, please," Burke beseeched.

"Oh," said the Egyptian cabbie. "Oh, and I just started my shift."

"Put your head out the window," Burke said, and without waiting for me, he shoved my head out for me. I felt like a German shepherd going for a ride with Master, but the cold wind was effective. It washed over my face and calmed the nausea.

"Breathe deeply," the cabbie implored me. He ran a red light in his haste to deposit me at my destination.

"I'm okay now," I said, pulling my head back in.

"You're drinking a lot more than you used to," Burke said.

"I don't drink every day and I never drink alone," I said, which wasn't really true.

"I'm just saying you should watch it. Just some advice from a friend."

"Here we are," said the cab driver and his whole body slumped down in the front seat with visible relief. Burke paid him and helped me out of the cab.

"You're not walking very steadily. I'd better take you up," he said.

I protested at first, but then gave in. In the elevator, I continued to lean against Burke, using him as a crutch. The light was out in the hallway—again—making it seem treacherous. For that reason alone I was glad he had seen me to the door.

"Don't come in," I said.

"Let me just get you in and get some water and aspirin down you."

"Is this part of this friend stuff?"

"Yes, sure. Why not?"

"I'd really rather you didn't . . . ," I began, but the lock popped and he opened the door before I could finish.

"I see your housekeeping habits haven't changed much," he said, dragging me inside and plopping me down on the couch. He surveyed the mess, the clothes and papers and greasy pizza boxes and empty soda cans strewn all over the room. "Christ!"

"Don't start with me."

"There are flies in here, Robin. You're the only person I know who has a fly problem in the middle of winter."

"I've-been-a-little-depressed," I said.

If you're a slob, it helps to have a low comfort level. A mess doesn't really bother me, but Burke grew up in a home kept like a national monument and even a little dust makes him rabid. Bottom line: He was a Felix and I was an Oscar and we couldn't seem to keep a maid. We were doomed.

Louise Bryant came out of the bedroom, absolutely delighted to see Burke. She started rubbing against him and meowing and if she had been capable of intelligent thought and speech, I'm sure she would have begged him to take her away from here. Too bad Amy Penny was allergic or didn't like cats or whatever it was.

"Hello, Louise," he said. He leaned over and scratched her head. "Are you hungry?"

"You'd better feed her before she gets combative. Her food's in the refrigerator in a Corning casserole. It's already prepared. You can just zap it in the microwave."

"You first," he said, handing me a tall glass of water and two aspirin coated with Maalox. "I'm going to make tea."

"Thanks," I said.

I was starting to feel more sober. It was strange to have him in the kitchen, our bedroom door open and our marriage bed there in full view.

We drank tea together and talked about the murder until ten, when he tried one more time to get the dope on Griff from me. He was convinced I knew something because someone had convinced him I did, someone belonging to his vast network of cultivated sources.

I wanted him to go so I could look over that page, but he wouldn't take the hint. Finally, I said, "Look, I'm tired. I've got to get some sleep. I have a big date tomorrow."

"Eric," he said, in an oddly wounded tone of voice.

"Yeah."

"He always liked you," Burke said. He gave me a sad look. "I need to ask you another favor, a personal favor."

"How awkward for you. What is it?"

"Be nice to Amy. . . ."

"Oh pulleeze. Why should I be nice to her?"

"Because you'll feel bad about it later if you don't."

"No, I won't."

"I know you. You will. Let's do this again soon," he said, and kissed my cheek.

As soon as the door slammed, I went to the Webster's and opened it to where the word "blackmail" was defined, which is where I had hidden the page Griff had given me.

I looked at it up against the light, in case there was invisible writing or something. Remembering how I wrote notes in invisible ink as a child, with sugar and water that caramelized over a flame, I ran a match under the sheet, but nothing turned up.

I replaced the book on the shelf. There was nothing on the page of any interest to anyone else. But I decided not to tell Burke. I kind of liked the idea that he was on a wild goose chase, and I was the wild goose he was chasing. There was a certain justice in it.

This made me feel something like happy and I went to bed and began easily drifting off to sleep, only to awaken with a start just as I was about to abandon consciousness.

Something was wrong with the apartment, I thought, but was too drowsy to make the synaptic leap as to what it was. I rubbed my eyes and went out to look around.

Something about the place jarred me, but thanks to all the lemon vodka I'd had earlier in the evening, I couldn't think what it was. I felt sure that someone, someone other than me and Burke, that is, had been in my apartment. But I didn't know why I thought that. My apartment is always so messy it was hard for me to tell if anything was out of place. I went back to bed and fell asleep again.

It wasn't until the next morning that I realized what was wrong.

Two days before, Louise Bryant had knocked over a vase of dried flowers on top of a file cabinet and I'd been too harried/indifferent to deal with it, so I'd left it on its side. But somebody had righted it.

I knew someone had been in my apartment because it was tidier than when I left it.

Chapter Ten

"YOU THINK SOMEONE WAS in your apartment because it seemed tidier?" Detective Tewfik said, as he walked around, surveying the mess. "What is tidier, exactly? And how on earth can you tell? What tipped you off? Is some dust missing?"

It was a pigsty, I won't kid you, but there was no need to be sarcastic. Since Burke had left, I'd let it go completely, and even in the best of times I'm not much of a housekeeper.

In fact, I am a slob. I admit it. It's not that I'm a lazy person. I tend to workaholism and when I do clean, I clean compulsively, unable to stop until the place is completely spotless. But housework just seems so insignificant and, as men have always known, there's always something better to do. I haven't read *Moby Dick* yet. I haven't seen Fellini's *Satyricon*. There are dozens of countries in the world about which I know nothing and billions of people I haven't yet met.

I told Tewfik about the vase but saying it out loud made me realize how stupid it sounded and my voice wavered and lost confidence in the telling. The thing is, I *might* have righted the vase myself, automatically, without thinking about it. Maybe I was paranoid.

"Did you make this up to get me over here to answer your questions?" he asked, annoyed.

New York homicide detectives are terribly overworked and Manhattan South had a lot on its plate, including a dead stockbroker found in an alley outside a Wall Street strip bar, an artist and his dancer wife dead in an apparent murder-suicide, and a tourist from Gary, Indiana, killed for his wallet in Times Square. Tewfik was understandably a little testy.

"Make it up? That would be dishonest," I said, in my best Girl Scout voice.

He looked at me, trying to figure out if I was on the level.

"Well," he said. "We haven't found the killer in this case so it wouldn't hurt to be extra security-conscious until we do. Although, you know, there are a lot of burglaries in this neighborhood. There's no necessary connection to the Griff case."

"Okay, okay."

"Wouldn't you like to live in a place that wouldn't frighten your mother?" Tewfik went on. "This neighborhood is scary after dark."

"I know. But I have this theory that a little terror is good for you. Like, fear is the aerobics of the mind," I said. "Besides, I have never been robbed, knock on wood. And look at the size of this apartment, and the rent I pay."

"You're muy macha, I know," he said.

"My keys," I said suddenly, thinking out loud. Tewfik looked at me, his heavy, dark eyebrows raised. "I thought I lost my keys yesterday . . . but maybe someone at work took them."

This made him pause. "You better take my direct number,

just in case," he said, and wrote it down for me. "And be careful. If you don't feel safe, go stay with a friend or in a hotel. And if your apartment gets mysteriously cleaner, let me know."

"Yeah yeah," I said. "Who do you think hit Griff sixteen or so times with a tire iron–like instrument?"

"It wouldn't be professional of me to speculate," he said, smiling now. "Who do *you* think killed him?"

"Who do you think hired him?"

"Who do *you* think hired him?"

"You know, officer, sir, lately I'm having a lot of conversations consisting largely of questions with very few answers."

"It's an occupational hazard for both of us, isn't it?" he said, before putting on his hat and coat. Tewfik wore a hat. McGravy wore a hat too. I liked men in hats, it made me think of my childhood.

When Tewfik left, I picked up the phone and started to call Eric, but after three digits I put the phone back in its cradle. It was Saturday and we were supposed to have a date that night at his place, but he hadn't said at what time. And he hadn't called me to confirm.

I was going to call him, but then I thought, what if he was just flirting, just kidding around? Will I look like an ass if I call, thinking it's for real?

Like I said, I was a little rusty on this dating stuff. For years, my radar had been jammed by monogamy and marriage, and now the single signals confused me.

Maybe if I came up with a pretense to call him, I thought, but caught myself. Resorting to feminine wiles, shame on me.

I picked up the phone and dialed.

"Hi, you've reached 1-900-CONFESS," his answering machine said. "After the beep, please leave your name, number, the date and time you called, and a salacious tale of personal misconduct. I'll get back to you as soon as I can."

"It's Robin, it's Saturday noon," I said, thinking to myself, if he calls me back, I'll cancel the date, I'm not ready. "Today I took the Lord's name in vain, I had impure thoughts about George Stephanopoulos and . . ."

The machine clicked off. Eric came on.

"Robin?" he said. "Sorry, I've been screening my calls this morning. Greg keeps calling from Grand Rapids."

"What's he doing in Grand Rapids?"

"A trade show, meeting sponsors, the usual PR stuff he loves so much. Calling me and annoying me. So. You miss me?"

"No." My voice sounded strange to me, soft, sexy, roughened. No, I said, in a way a woman usually says yes, trailing the vowel to a fade-out. I hadn't been speaking this way consciously and was only then aware that this was a different voice for me, that I only used it with Eric.

"Are we still on for tonight?" he asked. "You're not calling to cancel, are you?"

"No. I was calling to see if I should bring anything."

"Just your sweet self. Eight o'clock all right? I'll meet your cab downstairs."

"Okay."

"Come unarmed," he said, before giving me his address.

It was okay, I told myself. It was just a get-together. As long as I didn't kiss him, I was safe. I had control over this.

Still, when I went to the corner bodega to get milk and newspapers, I hesitated for a moment at the sight of the little condom boxes hanging on hooks behind the counter and considered buying some, just to be safe. I passed on them in the end. Nothing was going to happen. I mean, it was a first date, sort of.

Although a new disaster took the front page ("WATER PIPE EXPLODES AT CAFÉ MARFELES. ELOISE MARFELES BLAMES UNION 'GOONS'"), the tabloids were full of Jackson's theory that someone was trying to destroy ANN through its reporters. Various possible villains, ultra-right-wing "watchdog" groups on jihad against the "liberal media," media competitors, and vague political cabals were suggested. Paul Mangecet's name was mentioned, as he was believed to control some of the stock, but he vigorously denied any sinister intentions.

There was just one problem with all this: Why would anyone trying to destroy ANN bother with me? Go to all that trouble and expense? I mean, I was not a major player at ANN and I had very little credibility left. Why pick on me?

Some of the details of Griff's death were reported too, and there was also a boxed story at the bottom of the page, a sidebar on Griff, which detailed his alleged "history" with attractive women, using quotes from First Avenue bartenders. First Avenue, once the place fashionable singles bed-hopped, was now where the recklessly unhip went searching for meaningless sex. It said something about Griff that he was so well known in anachronistic singles bars.

The bartenders said he flashed a lot of money around and sometimes used pseudonyms and "cover stories" with the women he picked up, telling them variously that he was a cop, a magazine reporter, an art forger, and—get this clunker—Elite modeling agency boss John Casablancas.

He regularly employed "escorts," preferring redheads, according to one "escort agency insider." "But only real redheads, which are hard to come by," the insider added. Well, I thought, at least I've never had to pay for sex. Let me rephrase that. At least I've never had to pay *money* for sex.

If that wasn't bad enough, Griff had made surreptitious films of several attractive young women who lived in his building, using concealed cameras in their bathrooms to film some of their most intimate moments. Man, this guy made Jerry Spurdle look like Germaine Greer.

I put down the papers and, although it was only the early afternoon, I started getting ready for the evening, taking a long, hot shower.

It had been years since I'd dated a man other than Burke. The last time was shortly before we got engaged, when *we* agreed to see other people while *we* evaluated our relationship. Well, really *we* agreed that *he* would see other people. He was the one pushing for it but he didn't expect me to do it too.

It's that old double-standard bullshit. He gets to go off to the Crusades, wenching all the way, while I stay home watching the rust grow on my chastity belt.

I didn't.

I put myself on the arm of every interesting man in New York who'd be seen with me in public, and back then there were a few, believe me. This went on for about a month, and then, suddenly, Burke was at the door with a bouquet of roses, saying he figured we might as well get married. I'd had fun dating around but he gave me that Correspondent's Squint and it took me just fourteen seconds to bargain away my freedom. Okay, I said, let's get married.

What sorry sequence of events had brought me to that disastrous pass, and how could I disrupt the sequence this time around? I wasn't sure I could trust myself around a cute guy in my weakened, vulnerable state.

As I was dressing, I set out two underwear sets. On one side of the bed was the creamiest, slinkiest fuck-me lingerie on the island of Manhattan, lingerie that felt so good on my skin it qualified as foreplay.

On the other side was what I jokingly referred to, when Burke and I were still together, as my anti-adultery underwear, big old ugly granny underpants with goofy flowers on them, underwear no man could see me in without laughing. I knew I wouldn't commit adultery while wearing this underwear be- cause I wouldn't be caught dead in this underwear and, as I was still married in the eyes of the law at least, I hoped it could prevent adultery one more time.

My choices suddenly appeared very concrete. There was the dangerous underwear and the safe underwear. Which would I wear that night?

I chose the granny underpants and wore them around for five minutes before deciding they just didn't feel right, opting for the slinky stuff over which I wore a sweater and jeans. Another spray of L'Heure Bleue on my pulse points and a final sweep through my hair with a natural-bristle brush and I was ready to go.

There is Murphy's Law and there are Robin's Amendments. Number one: The guy with the biggest tub of popcorn and noisiest eating habits will always sit directly behind me in a movie theater (or else a hearing-impaired foreign national with his translator, so that every line of on-screen dialogue is repeated in loud German). Number two: The amount a man adores me is roughly equal to the number of his faults. Number three: When I'm already running late, something will inevitably happen to make me even later.

Something like, say, Mrs. Ramirez. When the elevator doors opened on the first floor, there she stood with Señor.

"You!" she shouted, coming at me. I tried to press the Door Close button but it was too late, she had her cane in the doors, forcing them open again. The old lady, the dog, and the leash effectively blocked my exit.

"You whore!" she said, raising her cane. I put my hand up and grabbed it before it hit me.

"Mrs. Ramirez, you're mistaken in the head again," I sang sweetly.

"You had a transvestite orgy in your apartment last night. Don't deny it! It woke me up and then I couldn't get back to sleep."

"I did not have a transvestite orgy," I said, knowing it was useless to try to reason with Mrs. Ramirez.

"Don't yell at me!" she shouted.

Apparently, she hadn't taken my advice about turning down her hearing aid, because I was talking quietly.

"I saw one of the transvestites," she said. "The man in the blond wig dressed up like a woman."

Mrs. Ramirez thought all my friends were transvestites or hookers. She thought I was a transvestite *and* a hooker. A week before, she'd been raving about "Negro prostitutes" working out of my place. Her eyes weren't so good either.

"That probably *was* a woman, Mrs. Ramirez. Probably coming to visit someone else in the building."

"Don't lie to me!" she shrieked. "I'm eighty years old. You

think I don't know the difference between a man and a woman? What kinda fool you take me for?"

I considered this. "An old fool?" I guessed.

"The police are on to you, missy. And the newspapers too!"

Her cries of "Whore" and "Sodomite" followed me as I pushed past her, and rang in my ears as I left the building.

Some people have luck with cabs; I am not one of them. Claire can hail a cab at any time of day, in any kind of weather, in any neighborhood in New York. The cabs come looking for her. They pick up her scent and zoom in on her from all directions like hounds. But me—I always have to work to get a cab, and tonight was no different. My apartment building is in a "marginal" neighborhood and not too many taxis cruise the area. My best bet was Fourteenth Street, four blocks away.

Thanks to a brutal wind-chill factor the streets were pretty deserted and between me and Fourteenth Street lay a long stretch of dubious real estate. My own street was a nosy and neighborly sort of street for New York. I felt relatively safe there. But the streets around it were less residential and less friendly. There was a whole stretch of buildings that could have been Berlin during the blitz—burned-out shells with blackened windows and doors boarded over with cheap plywood; shops covered with corrugated steel bearing the bright, ugly spray-paint graffiti of the local youth gangs. KILL THE SKINHEADS! screamed a choice bit of blood red graffiti, to which the skinheads responded, DIE NIGGER-SPICS! signing it with a swastika. Over both of them, in yellow paint, someone had written PEACE.

I finally hailed a decrepit cab. It began to rain.

When my taxi pulled up, Eric was waiting outside his building, huddling under an umbrella, his free hand jammed into the front pocket of his jeans. He looked thin and a little tired, which just heightened my desire. A girlfriend and I discussed this once, how a touch of pathos, a hint of haggard, makes a man more attractive to a woman. When courting hesitant females, the males of other species cinch the biological deal by puffing up their brightly colored plumage. All our men have to do is not shave for a day and stint themselves on sleep.

When the cab stopped, Eric came forward and reached into the driver's window to pay him, over my objections. I got out and he held his umbrella over me, wrapping his other arm lightly around my waist. We walked this way, touching under his umbrella, into his building and his apartment.

The apartment was warm and masculine, but not in an overpowering way. It wasn't neat but it wasn't messy either. A floor-to-ceiling entertainment center dominated the wall across from me and the two adjoining walls were lined with books.

He *reads*, I thought, with some surprise.

While Eric poured drinks in the kitchen, I scanned the titles, from *Crowds and Power* by Elias Canetti to a book of critical essays by Northrop Frye to Stephen King. I hate to admit this, but I checked the spines and the pages of some of the books to see if they were largely ornamental or if he had actually cracked them and read them. He had. He'd even underlined passages and made funny notes in the margins.

Eric came in with a glass of seltzer for me and a beer for him, which he put down on the coffee table in front of the sofa. He came up behind me as I looked at a cluster of family photographs.

I could feel him standing there. I could smell him, that great clean man smell. I was holding a small, framed photograph of a little boy in black martial-arts garb of some kind.

"My nephew, Patrick," he said. "He's into ninja. Only seven, but smart. Last time I talked to him, he told me ninja is—these are his words—'the art of escape, essentially defensive, not aggressive.' Invisibility is apparently a big part of it. Smart kid, huh?"

"The art of escape," I repeated.

He went back into the kitchen.

"Are these your parents wearing the fishing hats?" I asked, picking up a picture of an older couple with their arms around each other.

"Yeah. Alf and Irma," he said.

"What are your parents like?" I was nervous and when I'm nervous I tend to turn social situations into interviews, which are easier to control.

He came and stood in the doorway, holding a handful of mushrooms. He was cooking dinner, I realized.

He *cooks.*

"Mom's a rock-of-Gibraltar type—kind of a martyr sometimes. Six kids—I was the second youngest—four boys and two girls. Seven, if you count my dad. Mom always did," he said. "You're not allergic to anything, are you?"

"No."

"Any foods you don't like?"

"Blue cheese and anything that comes from a goat."

"Great," he said.

"What is your dad like?" I persisted.

"My dad," he said. "You really want to know?"

"Yeah." I followed him into the kitchen and watched while he sliced mushrooms.

"There's this one story that . . . well, my dad drove a cab for a while, here in New York, and one day he came home with this enormous box. He'd bought it off a customer, he said, for twenty-five dollars, which was a lot of money in our household. My mother, when she was mad, didn't frown or yell, she just went blank. She looked at him like that, and he said, 'Wait until you see what's in here. Just wait until you see.'"

"What was in it?"

"Well, Dad wouldn't let us see right away. He liked to build up the suspense. It was dinnertime, so we all sat down for dinner, for about an hour, while the box sat in the living room, unopened. After dinner, we all had to watch Cronkite, silently. By this time, we were bursting with curiosity."

"So am I," I said.

"After Cronkite, Dad said, 'Mother, you know that wall-to-wall carpeting you wanted?' Well, my mother's face lit up a little, but only a little, because she had been with my father a long time and she knew better.

"'Ta da!' my father said, and he opened the box." Eric stopped talking but continued chopping, smiling to himself.

"Well? What was inside?"

"Hundreds of broadloom samples, ten-inch squares, in dozens of colors and textures, samples from the season before. Got 'em from a carpet salesman who took his cab. Anyway, my mother's face dropped because she had always dreamed of a soft blue carpet and Dad knew it. Dad always seemed to be raising her hopes, and then he'd deliver on 'em in a way that completely . . . confounded her expectations. She was let down a lot."

"That's too bad. What happened to the carpet squares?"

"Mom and us kids, we spent two weekends sewing the whole mess together, a white shag next to a nappy orange square next to a shaved blue patch. Dad got a cheap carpet and Mom got a conversation piece, an excuse to tell the story about Dad and his carpet of many colors to every person who walked through the door. She scorned that carpet, but when Dad could afford to get her a nice one, she kept the old carpet, put it in the bedroom. She said she was kind of getting used to it."

He put the knife down on the cutting board and looked straight ahead.

"My dad died last year. . . ."

"Oh. I'm so sorry," I said.

"Yeah, and after he died, Mom moved into a retirement community and she had that old carpet rolled up and shipped to her new place. Isn't that romantic?"

I wanted to have his baby.

"It's . . . beautiful," I said.

"Yeah, ain't it though." He scooped up the mushrooms with the knife and the palm of his hand and dropped them into a wooden bowl into which he sprinkled olive oil, wine vinegar, and a bunch of spices. I liked watching him.

"I'm not really much of a cook. I make a few things over and over again, but I make those few well," he said. "In our house, everyone had to help out with everything."

"I don't cook," I said. To me, a meal is something eaten standing up more often than not. For example, breakfast is eating dry frosted mini-wheats straight from the box and washing them down with periodic gulps of skim milk straight from the carton.

"I know," he said, and grinned. "And you're a rotten housekeeper."

"How do you know that?"

"You have a reputation, Robin."

"A bad one?"

"Well, an interesting one," he said. "So tell me about your family."

"My mom lives with my aunt in my hometown. All my mom's sisters are there. My dad died."

"When?"

"When I was ten."

"Wow. How did he die?"

"Well, you know how you can't get a traffic light at a bad intersection until somebody dies?"

"Yeah."

"My dad was the guy who died. My father was a real safety nut, you know? He was *always* warning of the hidden menace in things, and looking for ways to thwart it. Anyway, he was one of the organizers of a petition drive to get a light at this intersection in the middle of town. It was a really bad one, a blind corner with the streets crossing at funny angles and a lot of thick bushes on one side."

"What happened?"

"Well, that day he was taking measurements of the street dimensions for the committee's report, and a truck barreled around the corner and killed him. There's a little plaque there with my dad's name on it, near the traffic light."

"That's terrible. You were pretty young," he said.

He took a cut mushroom from the board and put it up to

my mouth. I ate it. His fingers touched the tip of my tongue.

"Yeah, you know, life's a bitch," I said. "I used to imagine my dad was in those traffic lights. Oh God, does that sound crazy?"

"Not really. . . ."

"I didn't *believe* my father was reincarnated as a traffic light, or anything. It's a metaphor for a kind of . . ."

"Benign authority," he said.

"Exactly!"

"Something telling you stop, go, caution."

"Yeah. So—how did your dad die?"

"Um, massive coronary," he said, almost apologetically. "In the bathtub. He smoked, ate, and drank himself to death. Slowly. He was sixty-nine."

"I'm so sorry."

There was an awkward moment. We had divulged too much. Or I had, at least. Eric, actually, seemed unbothered, but I felt like I had made a tactical error.

The bowl went into the fridge to marinate, and Eric wiped his hands on his apron before taking it off and hanging it on a hook.

I loved the way he dressed, a navy blue corduroy shirt over faded jeans. He had a great physique, like he worked out, but not too much. He didn't have that bowling-balls-in-pantyhose look of muscle men or anything like that.

Did he have a hairy body, I wondered? His arms weren't very hairy, but just above his open collar there was a nice hint of dark hair on his chest. Too hairy didn't turn me on, but some strategically located body hair would be nice. Burke was almost hairless.

"Have a seat and I'll plug in the Fritz tape," he said, but then the phone rang.

He took it in the bedroom. The door was open and I could see him sitting on his bed, a four-poster. I sat down on an overstuffed sectional sofa, which sank comfortably as I nestled in. It was warm in Eric's apartment, a nice contrast to the icy rain outside, and I was feeling very good and very pretty.

When he came out, he said, "Sorry, that was Greg, about some show plans for next week. The guy never stops. Never. He wants me to watch *Greg Browner Weekend*."

"He has a weekend show now?"

"It's highlights from his live shows the previous week. We repackage the stuff and sell it to a new advertiser. Do you mind watching? He thinks he wants to change the lighting. He thinks it's making him look old."

"Age is making him look old," I said.

"I know, but I don't say stuff like that to my boss, Robin, unlike you. I like my gig."

He flicked on the television and sat down on the sofa next to me, just six enticing inches between us.

"I don't know how you work for Browner," I said. "Are you a saint?"

He smiled. "No. I'm just not a news moonie, like some of you. For me, it's a great job. Technically, I work for Greg's production company—I don't actually work for ANN anymore—and I make twice what I made when I worked on *Ambush*. I give him that youthful edge he's missing. I do what Greg tells me to do, and if I have a better idea I tell him and he turns thumbs up or thumbs down. I don't sweat it, and every two weeks I get big bucks, relatively speaking. I have money for my real life."

"What is your real life?"

He thought about it and said, "It's an endless search for true love. How about yours?"

I gritted my teeth and, through sheer force of will, sucked a blush back from my skin. "I don't really believe in love," I said. "I think my life is an endless search for the guilty party."

He didn't laugh. Instead, he looked like he found this . . . interesting.

The show was starting so he turned up the volume. We watched a montage of Greg shots—chatting with guests, laughing at Eddie Murphy, earnestly quizzing Richard Nixon, leaning on Elton John's piano, singing along. Over this was the Browner theme music, friendly but newsy, like a Stephen Foster song played on typewriter keys. The announcer read off the list of guests, three always and always in this order: celebrity, politician (there to tell America something we don't already know about them), and a "regular guy" to whom something irregular had recently happened. At the bottom of the screen, a super told weekend viewers the show was taped and not to call.

Greg, looking handsome for an older man with kind of a blond, Robert Mitchum thing going, conversed with the famous guest and then opened up the phones to his millions of viewers, many of whom had his toll-free number programmed into their phones. They loved Greg and he had good demographics, if not the numbers Larry King had—yet. Ironically, Greg skewed very well with college-educated women. On the air, he was very appealing, I'll give him that, but that was his TV persona. A TV persona is kind of like a whalebone corset. When you take it off, everything goes flying.

"First-time caller, Greg," a male voice drawled. "Want to say I love your show and I wish you'd run for office."

"Thanks a lot, Chicago, but I've already got a job I love. Did you have a question for Cher?"

"Think he'll ever run for office?" I asked.

"Never," Eric said, snorting. "Look, he likes a few of those callers every show asking him to run, because he likes to be flattered, but he *loves* television. He has more influence with his talk show than he would have as president."

"Not quite."

"Pretty close. On his show, he's in control of his image. He gets to be the voice of reason between warring extremes. Nobody can run for office anymore without checking in with him and Larry King, and Greg is the wave of the future because he's younger than Larry and he's better looking. Jackson gives him autonomy. Women viewers write him erudite love letters. People admire him. If he went into politics, all that would be over."

Eric was *smart*. Why did I think he was a bimbo?

"I see your point. But people think Greg might do it—run, I mean. Doesn't he risk a backlash if he doesn't run? Like Ross Perot when he pulled out of the presidential race?"

"Nah," Eric said. "He's more like Will Rogers than Ross Perot, on the air at least. If he refuses to run, it just endears him more to his viewers. If he actually ran, all that would be over."

"Do you think Greg was being blackmailed too?"

"Greg says no."

"Do you believe him?"

"It's not my job to believe him or not, just to implement his managerial edicts," he said tersely and looked back at the television.

He was a little sensitive about working for Greg. I didn't press him.

"Yeah, it's time for the diffusion filter," Eric said, referring to Greg's lighting complaint. "Lighting isn't good enough anymore. We need to blur his edges a bit too."

"You aren't serious? That's so dishonest."

"This isn't news, this is talk, and things are looser in the talk format. Solange uses a diffusion filter too," he said. "It's human nature to want to appear better than we really are. You wear makeup. All you on-air people wear a ton of it on the air just to look 'natural' and not washed out on video. So why sweat it?"

"Oh, it gives me a chance to get self-righteous," I said.

"You're cute when you're self-righteous," he said. It was such a corny thing to say that it caught me off guard. He caught me off guard a lot. That worried me.

We watched the rest of Greg's weekend show and talked some more about our families, a subject Eric kept bringing up. I was an only child. Eric came from this big Long Island family, and he had twelve nieces and nephews. Once a month they all got together at his brother's house in Long Beach to argue, insult each other, and eat grotesque amounts of food.

He made it sound very appealing. I bet other women eat this stuff up, I thought. A bachelor could do very well with this kind of family values rap. I, however, was impervious.

After declining my offer to help, he went back into the kitchen, and we continued our conversation between the two rooms. I knew what was going on. I'd heard the old wives' tale, that a guy who cooks dinner for a woman gets laid that night.

"Here we go," he said, putting place mats, silverware, and wineglasses on the coffee table. He went back to the kitchen and returned with condiments and wine, red, which he poured for both of us, leaving the bottle on the table. On his third trip, he came back with two steaming plates, filet mignon covered in marinated mushrooms, shoestring french fries, and glazed carrots.

Thank God, he's a meat eater, I thought. I have a soft spot for men who are meat eaters. There's just something about a carnivore.

"It looks wonderful," I said.

"Thanks." He sat back down next to me, a little closer this time. "I thought after everything you've been through lately, you could use a home-cooked meal."

Well bless you, I thought, crossing my legs and bouncing my foot slightly.

We watched *Fritz the Cat* and drank some wine and I started to think it might not be such a bad idea if Eric seduced me. God knows he was attractive, and he had a powerful, primal sexuality. So what if he was just casting a role for his memoirs? So what if I would just be the Older Married Woman who follows the Danish Exchange Student? Maybe he could be the Younger Stud in my life story, who comes between the Philandering First Husband and The Kids in the Hall.

Normally, I'm not quite this brazen and desperate, but I hadn't had sex in months, and I hadn't had good sex in about a year. My husband, on the other hand, was presumably having lots of good sex with his younger paramour, and all my friends and foes knew about it.

After Eric cleared away the plates, he made coffee, which he served with a basket of anisette biscotti. His grandmother's recipe.

"The *News-Journal* described you as 'kind of a loner' today," he said, smiling.

"Well, in the last six months I haven't been out much." I

didn't want to go into it. "Thanks again for that police report. Sixteen to twenty whacks with a blunt metal object, huh? What a way to go."

"It must have been bloody," he said.

"Yeah," I said, thinking aloud. "Yeah, it must have been, which means . . . the killer would have been covered with blood afterwards. He, or she, couldn't have gone back to the party without changing clothes. *That* means it was probably someone with a room at the Marfeles that night, someone who could kill Griff and then go change clothes."

"Yeah, or someone who could hide his bloody clothes under a costume," he said, but without my enthusiasm for the topic. "Murder's kind of a hobby of yours, isn't it?"

"Yeah."

"Why are you so interested in it?"

"The usual reason, I guess. We are most fascinated by what we most fear, right? For instance, Claire, who is flawlessly gorgeous, is fascinated by disfiguring diseases, especially if they are mosquito-borne and capable of being transported to this country in tires or produce," I said. "She can go on for hours about biting flies that lay their eggs in your bloodstream, eggs that hatch into these long, slender worms that come out of your eyes. Or that disease that makes men's testicles so large they have to carry them around in a wheelbarrow."

"I get the picture," he said, pained.

By this time, I noticed that we were sitting just an inch apart. Had I unconsciously inched closer to him, him to me, or had we inched closer together, drawn simultaneously by forces of mutual attraction?

At this rate of geographic progress, actual penetration was only hours away. I was in no hurry. I had nowhere else to go and the wine and the stories had lulled me into complacency. I felt at that moment like I could stay where I was forever and whatever happened happened.

I looked up and he was staring at me, into my eyes. I smiled and stared back, just as intensely. At first it was silliness, a staring contest. We had to hold back laughter.

But then it got serious.

Eric has these blue eyes, not just blue, but cold, otherworldly blue eyes. Have you ever been on a glacier? I was once, and when you look down a crevasse, you see this pale, foggy blue ice, deeply buried, prehistoric ice, holding old secrets.

That blue.

It was almost painful to stare into his eyes for too long, and yet I couldn't have looked away if I tried because there was a commensurate pleasure. So I kept staring, watching different emotions flicker below the surface of his eyes. Suddenly, I wanted to run for my life. Instead, I blinked, slowly and deliberately.

He leaned over and kissed me. Or did I lean forward and kiss him? Or both? I don't remember now.

I just remember a kiss and then a jolt of the most tremendous fear I've ever experienced. I bolted upright and sprang to my feet.

"I have a lot of work to do on this sperm series," I said. "And I have this murder on my mind so . . ." I looked around. I don't know why. Looking for an escape hatch, I suppose.

He grabbed my hand, tried to nudge me back to the sofa. "What are you afraid of?" he said.

"Oh God. Nothing personal, but you have a reputation as a terrible playboy, and I've been warned away from terrible playboys by my culture and my womenfolk and, come to think of it, my own experience."

Yeah. I looked around me with some surprise, asking myself, Where am I? How did I get here? In what hormonally induced stupor did I wander into this trap?

"Robin," he said, in a tender voice I'd never heard him use before. It touched me so deeply—a sudden, rapier thrust of tenderness—that my immediate reaction was pleasure, followed by an icy gust of fear.

"I am not a playboy. Do you want references? Call up some of my ex-girlfriends. Investigate me," he said. "Or trust me. What will it be?"

I opened my mouth but said nothing.

"Wait—don't answer now. You're upset. You've had a bad week," he whispered. "Think about it. Sleep on it tonight and call me tomorrow."

Why was I afraid of him?

Later, alone in my bed, windows and doors locked and heavy bits of furniture barricading them, I read over my file of stories on sperm, fertility, and artificial insemination and thought I found the answer in a paragraph Claire had highlighted from the *Encyclopaedia Britannica* entry on reproduction:

Although fertilization in the higher terrestrial forms involves contact during copulation, it has been suggested that all of the higher animals may have a strong aversion to bodily contact. This aversion is no doubt an antipredator mechanism: Close bodily contact signifies being caught.

Chapter Eleven

THAT NIGHT, I HAD this dream again. I was writing a script for the eight o'clock news show and I had writer's block. For some reason, I thought I had plenty of time, but when I looked up at the clock I saw it was three minutes to eight.

A sudden panic gripped me. Sweat sprang like leaks from my pores, rolled down my face, grew legs, and turned into insects. A mob of large, angry show producers and anchorpeople bore down on me. I was ruined.

Now, this deadline dream shouldn't disturb me, because far scarier, far more humiliating things have happened to me in real life. And yet, this dream of inadequacy represents the greatest terror in the world to me.

And then it gets worse.

The anchorpeople and show producers are bearing down on me, my sweat is turning into Mesozoic bugs, and the clock is ticking towards deadline loudly, like a bomb, when suddenly former White House Chief of Staff John Sununu rushes in from behind a blue curtain and whisks me away to safety, where he takes me in his beefy arms and kisses me.

I awake screaming.

Instead of the sound of my own scream, however, I hear the ringing of a phone come out of my mouth. Another ring, and I am almost conscious and reaching for the phone, buried beneath some dirty clothes.

"Robin?" a woman's voice said.

"Yeah. Who's this?"

"Susan. Susan Brave. I hope I didn't wake you."

"Actually, you woke me just in the nick of time," I said.

God, I hate it when I have those Sununu dreams.

"I wondered if you'd meet me for lunch. It's, well, an emergency and I can't talk about it on the phone."

"What kind of an emergency?" I asked, groping for my clock radio. It was almost noon and, I remembered, Sunday.

"It's about Griff," she said. "Will you meet me? I've beeped Joanne too."

"Of course," I said, still fuzzy with sleep. I rummaged for a pen and took down the information on the restaurant I was to meet her at, A Real Dive. Only after she'd hung up did I think to ask: Why would *Susan* want to talk about Griff?

Louise Bryant looked at me with scorn.

A Real Dive was housed in a renovated bar on West Street, overlooking the Hudson. Every table had a view of the big Maxwell House sign across the river in Jersey. A trendy, self-consciously seedy place, it was popular with Boomers because it specialized in the cuisine of their youth, or imagined youth.

The white formica tables were veined with gold and the menus and place mats had faux coffee rings and faux grease stains printed right into the paper.

I guess I'd describe the decor as Mel's Diner meets 1950s Waterfront, complete with such appetizing accoutrements as faux bait buckets. It was very faux. In fact, the only thing that wasn't faux about A Real Dive was its prices—a very real $15.95 for the meat loaf platter with mashed potatoes and green peas. For a dollar less you could get the tuna and potato chip casserole platter or the macaroni and cheese with franks platter.

Susan was already there, sitting in a booth by herself looking uncomfortable, when I arrived. A sweet dame, bless her soul, Susan is a perennially awkward adolescent, the timid girl (despite her valiant last name) who joined every club she could to make friends and didn't fit into any of them. In a way, she was perfect for Solange, her boss, because she was a born martyr who could absorb Solange's psychological abuse and come back for more.

"Takes a licking, keeps on ticking," they said of Susan in the newsroom.

When I approached, she started to rise but the paper place mat stuck to her hand and came with her, sending silverware and condiments spinning all over the floor. Everyone in the restaurant looked up, and then looked away, nonchalant, as busboys came over to wipe up the broken glass and ketchup.

Susan makes me feel graceful.

"Oh, God, I'm so sorry," she said to the kneeling Guate-malan bus guy.

"'Sokay, 'sokay," he said.

She looked at me. "Hi, Robin. I'm so embarrassed."

"Don't worry about it," I said. "I'm the queen of public humiliation. Not that you should be humiliated," I hastened to add.

We sat down and another busboy brought Susan a new stained place mat and fresh silverware.

"I'm just not myself these days," she said. After ordering drinks from an indifferent waitress in a starchy pink uniform and cat's-eye glasses, Susan said, "I was hoping Joanne would get here. . . ."

"What's going on, Susan?"

"Weelll," she said, twisting her fingers nervously. She looked around, everywhere but at me. "Griff?"

"Yeah."

"He was . . . blackmailing me too."

"He investigated you?"

"Yes," she said. Every word she spoke came squeezed through some dense filter of fear or embarrassment, or both.

The waitress brought our drinks. Susan had a double scotch, I was having mineral water. It was way too early in the day to drink, even for me, but Susan downed hers.

"Why was he investigating you? I thought only on-air people . . . it doesn't make sense."

Susan was Solange's producer. As they had no idea who she was, how could her credibility be ruined with the public? What would be the point of investigating midlevel producers, when there were so many riper targets around?

"I don't know why, but he did. I don't want to tell you any more until Joanne gets here," she said.

"Well, okay."

But I couldn't stop asking questions. "Did you stay at the Marfeles that night?"

"No," she said. "But Solange did. She let me use her room to change into my costume."

"So Solange stayed at the Marfeles, and Joanne did. Do you know who else stayed there?"

"No. Why?"

"I dunno. It might matter," I said.

There was a familiar voice behind me and when I turned around I saw the waitress guiding Joanne to our booth.

"Sorry I'm late," she said, looking very early Grace Kelly in dark glasses and scarf.

"Where were you?" Susan asked.

"Don't laugh, but I went to Eileen Lane Antiques in Soho to visit my furniture. You know that vanity I had, the one I bought in Paris with the teardrop-shaped mirror and the mother-of-pearl accents?"

I didn't, but I nodded.

"Sold," she said.

"I'm sorry."

"Yeah. But I'm going to be able to buy most of it back, I think. Oh, there was a photographer on my tail too. He took my picture coming out of Eileen Lane. Wonder what spin they'll put on that in tomorrow's paper? Don't worry, though, I lost him."

"You're sure?" Susan said.

"Positive," said Joanne. "He's somewhere on the New Jersey Turnpike in a New York City taxi looking for me right now. Meter running at double fare."

Joanne had a round-the-clock tabloid photographer following her. I did not. I felt strangely miffed about it.

We ordered lunch and then Susan reprised what she'd told me. Then she paused, reached out and grabbed our hands.

166

"Before we go on, we should agree that nothing we say among ourselves goes beyond this circle."

"But if it . . . ," Joanne began.

"I don't want to go to the police. I'm afraid I'm going to end up on the front page of the *Post* or the *News-Journal,* and my mother—she still goes to church almost every day. She thinks I'm still a virgin."

We had no choice. Joanne and I both promised secrecy. This, my friends, is a conspiracy—of sorts.

Above us, the minute hand on a clock featuring the Cream of Wheat man clicked loudly forward.

Susan went on. "He called me up about three weeks ago, told me some stuff about myself, and said he knew a lot more, stuff I'm not going to tell even you two. I met him the first time in that restaurant in Macy's Cellar and he showed me a sheet of paper with most of the information blacked out."

Joanne and I nodded. The very pink waitress brought us our meat loaf platters.

"He said he had two more sheets, and if I wanted them, I could have them for ten thousand dollars."

"Only ten?" Joanne interrupted.

"Well, I'm not as well-known as you," Susan said. "You're more famous, so you had to pay more. Anyway, I told him I didn't have ten thousand. I have about five in my 401(k) but I can't get at it, and I have a little more in CDs I can't get at and . . ."

"What did he say?" Joanne asked, between bites of the mealy meat loaf.

"He swore and said he hated the nineties, because nobody was liquid."

"Hard times for blackmailers," I said.

"And he said I'd better find the money, or he was going to turn over all the information on me to someone at ANN. I wanted to know who, because I was afraid he'd turn it over to Solange. I . . . I don't want anyone to know my private business, but especially not her."

"She'd probably do a whole show around you and your private problems," Joanne said.

"Yeah," Susan said, picking at her meat loaf, which was growing cold in a congealing pool of amber gravy flecked with green peas.

"What happened next?" I asked.

"He called me up a couple of weeks after that, and insisted on coming to my place."

"Uh-oh," Joanne said.

"I didn't have any choice. So he came over, and when I told him how much I'd been able to raise, selling my grandmother's jewelry, he got upset."

"And—"

Another drink came, and she halved it in one gulp and emptied it in the next.

"So, he offered me an alternative."

"A blow job?" Joanne said. "That's the deal he wanted to make with me."

"Well, I . . ." Susan stopped.

"Don't go on if . . . ," I began.

"I performed . . . um . . . manual masturbation on him. A—a—what would you call that? A hand job?"

Joanne and I nodded.

"Once, only once. And you know, that worm still didn't give me the information."

"I'm sorry, Susan," Joanne said, giving Susan's hand a

squeeze across the table. "Robin's right, don't go on if you feel uncomfortable."

"No, it feels good to talk about it, to tell you the God's honest truth," Susan said. "It's been awful carrying it around these last few weeks."

She stopped for a drink of water.

"So, anyway, on New Year's Eve he called and told me to meet him at the post office with the money."

"Which post office?" I asked.

"The main one on Eighth Avenue, across from Madison Square Garden. He came, I gave him the money I had, and then he told me he didn't have the information with him. He'd already sent it to a certain reporter at ANN, but he said she wouldn't actually be able to *get* it without first talking to him. But if I didn't show up at the party that night with another five thousand, he would hand over his information about me to this reporter."

"Who?" I asked.

"I asked him again who it was and he said it was *someone down on her luck who would be real grateful to get a scoop*."

She and Joanne looked at me.

I said, "Why would *I* be interested in his information? He was taking a chance if he thought I'd rat out my colleagues. How did he know I wouldn't take the information and burn it? Or . . . or turn it over to Standards & Practices for an endless, discreet, internal investigation. Besides, he investigated *me* too."

Joanne snorted. "Maybe he thought he could use it to get a blow job from you. I hear he had a thing for redheads."

"The way he described it, it did sound like he meant you," Susan said.

"And you do have kind of a whistle-blower pathology," Joanne added. "Not to sound like Solange. . . ."

"I've been worried sick the last week," Susan continued. "It hasn't shown up in your mail, has it, Robin?"

"No, of course not!" I said at once. Did they believe me?

Despite our benign relations in the past, we were suspicious of each other now. I was beginning to experience that universal feeling of guilt. Once I stole a package of Life Savers from a five-and-dime and to this day whenever I walk into a Woolworth's I feel a little shabby and a little guilty and I always keep my hands where the clerks can see 'em.

"He said I had to know something in order to get it, right? Well, except for the initial phone call and a brief encounter on the dance floor, I didn't see or talk to the guy, okay? When I went up to meet him, there was no answer. You remember, Joanne? You were coming out of your room when I was knocking. . . ."

"That's right."

"I figure he was already dead at that point. If he was going to tell me something, he took it to the grave."

"Well, I know this sounds terrible, but I'm glad he's dead," Susan whimpered. "I don't think he ever would have given me that information on me."

"Probably not," Joanne said. "Sounds like he was building a harem. Women he could control through information."

Susan, who had rather an unfortunate love life, worse even than mine, launched into her ritual condemnation of the entire male gender. Men were brutish, lying, hypocritical traitorous shits, she said, adding, "And they never call when they say they will," as though this were the worst offense. "I hate men. Don't you?"

"I love men," I said. "In general, I love them. We're just as bad as them and we're just as good as them, I think."

"Some of them can't accept that, though," Joanne said.

"Some of us can't accept it," I said.

When dessert came—layers of lime Jell-O alternating with layers of Cool Whip for $5.95—we got into the trickier aspects of the situation.

"So the question," Joanne said, "is, why us?"

"Yeah. And is it only us?" I asked. "And who hired him? Who else from ANN had a room at the Marfeles that night?"

"A bunch of us," Joanne said. "Most of the execs, some 'talent.'"

Talent is the term we use for on-air people, provoking much mirth among the writers and producers.

"Solange had a room, I had a room . . . let me see . . . Sawyer Lash and his wife stayed there that night, and Greg," she continued. "Who else? Oh yeah, Pat Lattanzi and Elsie Ormsby Ward." Pat and Elsie were married. They anchored the 6 P.M. together and earlier shows separately.

"That's it?"

"Oh no, there were others—execs, some civilians. But I didn't keep track. I didn't know at the time it would be important," Joanne said.

She went on. "Robin, are you *sure* Griff didn't slip you something or tell you something that . . ."

"I'm positive!" I said.

We went over the events of the evening, where we were and when, what we saw and when. Of course, it was a New Year's Eve party and we were all pretty liquored up, so the details were blurry.

They were particularly blurry for Susan. "When Griff was

killed," she said, "I was passed out in a stall in the bathroom. Remember, Robin, after I spilled that drink on Solange, I went to throw up? I . . . I was there until about midnight, when someone found me and put me in a cab."

That sounded reasonable enough. I did remember my last vision of Susan that night, green and weaving, as she headed to the john. No, I didn't think she had done it. But then, how well did I really know her? What were her secrets? Surely more than a fear of an unlikely *Post* headline: FLORENCE BRAVE'S DAUGHTER NOT VIRGIN.

"What about Solange? I heard she 'confessed' to Dunbar. Any idea what that was about?"

"She told me she didn't confess anything," Susan said. "She said she went in to give Dunbar advice."

Then Susan said she had to go. She was cooking dinner for her mother that night at her apartment in Brooklyn. We all agreed to honor the omerta and not speak of our meeting.

As soon as she left, Joanne turned to me. "Think she did it?"

"I don't know. What do you think?"

"I don't think she's capable," Joanne said. "I hope she doesn't get mucked up in this in the papers. It's awful to be tried in the press. Oh, the irony. When you're exposed, you start thinking about all the people you've exposed, and how their stories were warped or distorted by your own bias without your even being aware of it. And yet, it's our job to expose hypocrisy."

"Even though we're all hypocrites too."

"It's the human condition," she said. "Strange to find ourselves on the receiving end."

"Who do you think is investigating us?" I asked her.

She smiled. I couldn't help noticing how immaculately dressed she was. I don't think you could even find a piece of lint on her. How did she manage it? In my haste that day, I'd thrown on a big gray shirt and faded black jeans. My hair was loosely tied back and unkempt.

"Between us, since we're sworn to secrecy, Jackson really thinks it's Paul Mangecet. It makes sense."

"The holier-than-thou man?" I asked.

"Millennial Broadcasting is doing great, it's a money machine for Mangecet. But imagine what a guy like him could do if he had Jackson's global reach," she said. "Only I doubt if Jackson's stockholders would sell to an archconservative theocrat like Mangecet. They're very liberal and he thinks interracial dating is unholy and feminism turns women to witchcraft."

"Yeah, too bad there aren't really witches. Too many tel-evangelists in the world, not enough frogs. One twitch of Samantha's nose could fix that little imbalance."

"Oh, I loved Samantha when I was little," Joanne said, whooshy and girlish all of a sudden. "I used to sit in class and if I didn't like my teachers, I'd pretend I was Samantha, cast spells on them under my breath. Poof! You're a bag of shit!

"But . . . back to Mangecet. He could have hired Griff, and then Griff could have turned on him, played both sides, for money and for sex."

I trusted her just then. Later, in the taxi home, I wondered if I trusted her because she didn't seem to trust me. You know, the best defense is a good offense and all that. On paper, she made a damn good suspect, but in person you couldn't entertain the idea seriously because she seemed too . . . real somehow. None of the revelations about her were that surprising; she'd made no bones about her sexual prowess in the past, but, gentledame that she was, she never named names and left out telling details, like armored personnel carriers.

. . .

When I got home, I pushed all my heavy furniture back in front of the door and the windows, just in case. I had considered staying with a friend—for about ten seconds. Due to my rather careless lifestyle and housekeeping habits, I've often lost friends by staying with them too long. So friends were out, and I couldn't afford a hotel. I compromised by making it impossible for anyone but the Terminator to get into my place while I was there, although I was in big trouble if there was a fire.

Actually, it made me feel very cozy, all locked up like that. I kicked off my shoes, untucked my gray shirt from my jeans, and listened to my answering machine, Louise Bryant in my lap. I was hoping for a message from Eric, but he hadn't called and, despite my fears and doubts, that disappointed me.

There were two hangup calls (I'd had a few the day before too) and several messages from tabloid reporters who had, like any persistent journalist, obtained my unlisted home number. I zoned them out and thought instead of what Joanne had said about Susan not being capable of killing Griff.

In my experience, we're almost all capable of killing under the right circumstances, even if it's only in self-defense—and self-defense in the eyes of some people is a pretty broad category.

I started doodling on a yellow legal pad, making a list of all the reasons a person could be incapable of murder. There weren't many. I wrote down saintliness and then struggled to think up another reason someone couldn't kill under the right circumstances. Coma, I wrote finally.

And what was it Griff was going to tell me? What did I need to know in order to find the information everyone was so anxious about?

My head shot up at the next message on my machine. "Ms. Armoire, this is Mary Coffield at the *News-Journal*. I'd really like to give you a chance to tell your side of the story before I talk to Robin Hudson. Please call me at . . ."

I laughed, because she'd dialed my number and asked for Joanne, and because reporters always say they want to give you a chance to tell "your side of the story." If Joanne did tell "her side of the story" to an outside reporter like Coffield—and there was a better chance of her mud-wrestling with Jeane Kirkpatrick—Coffield would then use that to get at me, or someone else in the story. "I just talked to Joanne and she told me you did such and such. . . ." Then you have to explain, and you get drawn into it, and she takes your information back to Joanne with a slightly different spin and so on, provoking the information she wants for the story she wants to write.

That got me thinking again about that murder in my home-town, where all but one member of the Sesquin family were killed. I had been thinking about this a lot lately, how the police and reporters were sent on a wild goose chase, about how easy it is to follow your own imagination and lose sight of the truth.

This is what happened: One of the Sesquin teenage girls was quite beautiful, and the popular theory was that a rebuffed suitor, a mysterious dark-haired boy, had killed everyone to avenge his broken heart.

It was a wildly popular theory.

The only problem with it was it drew on an outright lie. I know, because I'm the one who made it up, who told a reporter that a week before the killings I'd seen a boy trying to kiss the beautiful Frances Sesquin behind the Strand Theater, and I'd seen the girl push the boy away. A dark-haired boy. It was too dark to see the boy's face, but I'd distinctly heard him say, "You'll be sorry. I'm going to get you."

I didn't tell this lie out of malice. I told it for two reasons, one noble, one ignoble. First and most important, I wanted to steer suspicion away from my mother, who had been a little less sane than usual after my dad died, causing some talk after the murders. Second, I wanted to please the nice reporter who was interviewing me in front of the Central Café.

And he was pleased. This was just what the national news desk in New York wanted. A beautiful girl. A spurned lover. A fatal kiss.

With shock and fascination, I watched the lie grow greater and greater as respectable grownups corroborated and enlarged my story, which made the front page of every major newspaper in the state and led the local newscasts, further legitimizing it.

I imagine this must have been a difficult time for dark-haired boys to get dates, but maybe not. I'd guess the parents in town weren't keen on their daughters meeting dark-haired boys during this period, but that may have enhanced the allure of dark-haired boys. If parents forbid a teenage girl to date someone, she almost always sneaks out and dates him secretly, and with a great deal more enthusiasm than if the parents approved. Add to that the outlaw love factor, the possibility that any given dark-haired boy in town was the love-crazed killer.

But I'm only speculating about how my lie enhanced or changed the social lives of dark-haired boys in my home town. I know it had other, unhappy effects, but I try not to think about that too much. I mean, I didn't do it alone. A lot of townspeople, many of them grownups, fed the lie. I was just a kid. What did I know? Why did they listen to me?

Chapter Twelve

When i got to work on Monday my keys were at the lost and found, turned in Friday night by an anonymous samaritan, so I relaxed a little. I told Claire about my "fastidious burglar" and she laughed, both of us completely unaware that all hell was breaking loose around us.

It was Jerry, that baying hound—no, braying ass—of hell, who bounded in late that morning to tell us about the upheaval all over the network. It seems a lot of people, not knowing who Griff was or whether he had investigated them, were preemptively confessing. At the end of their morning shows, Pat Lattanzi and Elsie Ormsby Ward had each read brief statements in which they admitted taking junkets paid for by travel organizations, ones they had reported on in the past. They then announced their own one-month suspensions, pending further disciplinary action.

"The rumor is they confessed to the junkets to cover up some serious swinging in the late seventies," said Jerry, always ready to promulgate truth. "But they have an airtight alibi for the time of death."

Mark O'Malley, award-winning business reporter, issued a press release stating that he had spent the weekend with his family informing them of his homosexuality and, with their unanimous support behind him, he was now coming out to the viewing public.

"No one should be forced 'out,'" he said. Although he had no knowledge of an investigation into his affairs, he went on, he felt in the interests of honesty he should come out now and not be forced out by scandalmongers later.

Mark also had an alibi for every moment between nine-thirty and eleven. Part of his alibi, Jerry informed me, was Jack Jackson. Another part was Burke Avery. Seems Mark and Jack were chatting when Burke finally got up the nerve to approach the great man.

"And *you'll* want to watch *Gotham Salon* this morning," Jerry said, waving his melon-inspector coffee mug at me. "It's on in, oh, about a minute. But don't get too caught up in it. I want a script for the first part of our sperm series on my desk by six."

"Why do I want to watch *Gotham?*"

Jerry just smirked, but he didn't have to tell me. I knew.

"Excuse me," I said, going to my office.

Claire followed me. "You really want to be alone for this, or just away from Jerry?"

"Just away from Jerry," I said. "Come on in."

I flicked on the monitor and sat back to watch as Amy, visibly distraught, told her viewers she wanted to come clean about some things and called on them for understanding. And then she got my respect, because she came right out and said, "I have committed a sin and broken a commandment I was raised to believe was sacred. I have committed adultery."

Whew! Claire and I looked at each other. Amy really was coming clean, but as admirable as that was, I wasn't keen on watching my dirty laundry exposed to even more complete strangers in TV land.

"I fell in love with a married man and he fell in love with me. We tried to avoid each other, but we couldn't. I want you to know, though, that he and I did not become intimate until he and his wife had already taken steps to dissolve their marriage."

I didn't believe this for a minute. This smacked of rationalization, backdating. But she seemed to be genuinely suffering for her sin and she didn't name names. And while I was deeply embarrassed that my friends and colleagues watching this knew she was talking about me, even I couldn't find fault with her performance.

Only Amy Penny could confess to adultery and come off looking like the piteous victim of Cupid. She quoted Pascal—"The heart has its reasons that reason cannot know," a favorite of Burke's—and, with tears in her shimmering eyes, she asked her viewers once again to understand and to believe in the redemptive power of love.

Then she got carried away, confessing to all this diddly stuff too, like she couldn't stop herself, she just had to unburden to two million or so of her closest friends: a bird she killed with a slingshot at age eight, a girl she teased to tears when she was ten, a scarf she stole from a friend in junior high school, and so on and so on, until she was radiant, approaching rapture, the burden of her guilt lifted. Redeemed.

I came to Carthage, and all around me in my ears were the sizzling and frying of unholy loves.

No, I wasn't quite ready to let bygones be bygones.

"It isn't fair," I told Claire after the whole ridiculous episode was over and Amy had moved to the kitchen set for a segment on cooking for wheat-allergic children. She teased the segment and then tossed to commercial. "She thinks she can just confess and then have it be over. Confess, go to commercial, and then—time for cooking! No, she hasn't suffered enough."

"Life isn't fair," Claire said dreamily. "Let it go."

Claire had fallen in love with a new guy over the weekend, a news producer for MTV, and she was "happier than a bee in a Burmese poppy field," as she put it, which made her a bit unbearable.

She put her hand on my arm. "It's time to heal, Robin. Forget about Burke and Amy. You need to fall in love."

"Yeah, like I need a tax audit," I said, but it was false bravado. The fact is, I still hadn't heard from Eric and I was concerned. It had been so long since I'd been single and dating that I'd forgotten how to handle the guy who forgets to call you after a date. The correct way, of course, is to forget about him completely. He's either gutless or inconsiderate. The wrong way is to make excuses for him. He was probably just busy. Couldn't get to a phone. Was involved in a disabling accident.

"That's my vice—love, I mean," Claire said. "Seriously. My therapist says I'm addicted to love, like in the Robert Palmer song. I just go from man to man constantly seeking the first flush of love."

"So what? You're young, you rarely drink, you don't do drugs, and you don't eat meat. Love is a legit vice because it's worse for you than all those other things."

"Love is better than all those things," she said.

"Not any love I've known. Look at my example, Claire. Or look at Joanne Armoire, for that matter. I don't think she'd give a ringing endorsement of love these days. I mean, look where it led her. To blackmail and disgrace," I said. "Were you being investigated and/or blackmailed, Claire?"

"No," she said.

"How can you be sure?"

"Who'd investigate me? I'm a producer in special reports, an embarrassing network cash cow."

"I'm a reporter here and I was investigated."

"That's different. You're on the air and, besides, the guy had a thing for redheads, didn't he?"

"Yeah. Still, how can you be sure? You've got secrets, right?"

"Not one," she said sunnily.

"Sure you do."

"What are my secrets?" she challenged.

"Um, I bet on weekends you dress in camouflage and liberate lab animals, right? Or you load up a Supersoaker with red paint and mow down fur-bearing widows on Fifth Avenue from a moving vehicle."

"Not even close," she said, very Mona Lisa, impossible, as always, to provoke. She gathered up a pile of medical tapes that showed swimming sperm and went to isolate some good wallpaper—background—shots.

As soon as she left, I logged into the computer, thinking perhaps Eric would contact me this way. A message blinked in the corner of my screen. I retrieved it.

As I read it, icy fear cracked up my back like lightning. It came from the generic log-in "Intern."

"I know what you did," it said.

I know what you did.

That spooked me. Someone knew what I did. Who was it? What did he know about me? Was he the killer?

At lunch, I skulked around the cafeteria, looking at everyone sideways. Was it you? Or you? Whoever you are, will you expose me? Or will I expose you?

I noticed a few other on-air people looking suspiciously around, but it wasn't until the afternoon that I found out *all* the on-air people had received this same message and it was believed to be a prank, something one of those boho writers would pull.

In response, Dunbar ordered two security guards to stand guard at Democracy Wall. This caused an outcry among the writers, who said it was a freedom of speech issue, that the anonymity of the board ensured a free forum without fear of management reprisals. "Now," they said, "such speech will be inhibited by the presence of 'The Man.'"

If Dunbar's purpose was to stifle dissent, it didn't work. The writers, led by their producer/peasant-king Louis Levin, quickly opened a secret file in the computer, hidden in an obscure corner, and locked with passwords that changed every couple of hours. Louis messaged me to look under "Research. Writers" for a file called "Radio Free Babylon," Password: "dirt," where I found a neatly organized, concise catalogue of ANN personalities who had confessed and what they had confessed to, along with little satirical comments contributed by the newsroom.

There was a fair bit of résumé padding among the correspondents, widespread pot smoking in college, minor conflicts of interest, one old drug conviction, the employment of illegal aliens to help around the house, like that. Madri Michaels's "real" age was revealed, as was Dillon Flinder's.

Among the on-air people conspicuous by their absence were Greg Browner and his ex-wife Solange Stevenson. I was surprised Solange hadn't confessed to something new and then made a show of it. It wasn't like her to pass up an opportunity like that. Odd too, that both Greg and Solange had nothing to confess—at least about each other. I concluded that after fifteen years of marriage, they probably had equal amounts of dirt on each other and a no first-strike agreement.

I put my feet up on my desk as I scrolled down through the list. I was supposed to be thinking about sperm, but I couldn't stop thinking about the Griff murder. While I was stuck in the office, others were searching for answers and, I was sure, finding them.

I searched the computer list for Susan Brave, but there was nothing. Everyone else thought it was just "talent" who had been targeted, and until Susan came forward, they would go on believing so. Shit. I shouldn't have promised not to repeat what Susan told me. I wondered if Joanne's conscience was bothering her on this.

What goes around comes around, right? History was repeating itself, with a twist. This time, because of information I was *withholding,* the police might very well be off on a wild goose chase, and a killer might go unpunished. First I kept that worthless sheet of paper and now I was keeping Susan's secret.

Susan. Poor Susan, who spent the first half of the party downing Jonestown Punch and the second half ridding her system of it in the ladies' room, "puking purple," as it was commonly known.

I sent her a message to see how she was doing—and maybe get a little more information from her—but she wasn't logged in.

I was hyperaware, sitting in front of the computer, that just a hundred or so feet of fiber-optic cable was all that stood between me and Eric. I could almost feel it humming beneath my feet. But I wasn't going to message him first.

Maybe he'd thought I would be an easy conquest, vulnerable as I was, and when I proved difficult, he'd given up the fight.

Well, I had bigger fish to fry, I thought, rolling a piece of six-ply script paper into my typewriter.

Jerry poked his head in. "I have an executive committee meeting," he said. "Do you have a script coming? I want to see it when I get back."

"Yeah, yeah," I said.

Before I could write, I needed four cups of coffee, each with three sugars and three creams. After performing all the necessary rituals, I sat down to confront the judgmental paper in my typewriter. My stomach gurgled and cold sweat sprang from my neck and ran down my back. I typed a lead, then tore it out of the typewriter in disgust and put in another piece of copy paper. I typed another lead and this time ripped it out midsentence. Once I get the right first line down on paper the rest of the story pours itself out on the page. But the first line, the hardest line to write, just wouldn't come to me. I reminded myself what Hemingway prescribed for writer's block: Just write one true sentence.

Then I swore.

"God bloody son of a bitch damn it all," I shouted, and the glass walls of my office shook.

Swearing often helps, I've found, but not this time. I felt the frustration build inside me. Clear your head, Robin, I told myself, and just write it. Just get the first word down.

But I couldn't even summon a first word. I got up and kicked over my trash can and that did the trick. As I was cradling my bashed foot, I saw clearly and very suddenly just how to begin and immediately hopped back to my typewriter. After I hammered out the lead the rest of the story wrote itself.

Jerry wasn't in his office when I finished, so I dropped the script on his desk. Then I couldn't resist sitting in his nice, padded chair and spinning around, putting my feet up on his desk and doodling on his blotter/calendar, where I noticed a very interesting thing. All the birth dates of key ANN and JBS executives were dutifully noted, along with a suggested gift. On February 11th, for instance, he'd written "Rupert Regelbrugge, Napoleon brandy." Regelbrugge was vice chairman for all of JBS, Jack Jackson's right-hand man.

I don't know why that surprised me. Among ass kissers, Jerry was always the first to pucker.

Unfortunately for him, Jerry had written these dates down in pencil and it took me less than five minutes to erase the old information and replace it with new. I swapped Regelbrugge's birthday with Dunbar's and made the gifts more imaginative.

"Rupert Regelbrugge," it now read, "large black dildo."

I got as far as the month of May when Jerry came in. As I looked on, seething, Jerry read over my script, moving his lips as he did, an annoying trait many people in television, particularly anchors, have. After fifteen minutes of red penciling, he handed me back a red-crossed mess.

"The stuff of life itself, his precious seed, a small vial that could have launched a hundred generations of Tarsus men, lost, perhaps forever," I read. "You're kidding, right?"

"I want to make it more dramatic."

"You know, Jerry, we're not in the drama business," I said. "We're in the *news* business."

"I know that, Robin. But what you don't realize is that our job is to help our viewers find the natural drama or pathos or whatever in a situation. We locate it for them . . ."

"And then hit them over the head with it?"

"Track it and cut it tomorrow," Jerry said, grabbing his coat. "I've got to go. I'm having dinner with a friend of mine from *60 Minutes*."

Not all the news was bad for ANN that day. As the dirty laundry was being displayed—resulting, incidentally, in higher ratings all over the schedule—PR was flacking positive stories to friendly media columnists, stories on nice anchors with strong families and a commitment to their communities.

For example, Sawyer Lash was happily married to his child-hood sweetheart and had three kids. As a family, they sponsored a pile of overseas orphans, fasted and marched and bike-a-thonned for charity, and built houses with that group Jimmy Carter was associated with.

Public Relations even called me, late in the day—I was obviously way down on their list—to find out if I had any redeeming qualities.

"Did you ever do anything really good for someone?" the PR intern asked me. "Something we can throw to the tabloids?"

I used to read erotic books on tape for blind people, in a very torchy voice, before books on tape became commonplace, but that was a while ago. I made a note to get more involved in my community in the future.

"I hope to one day become an organ donor," I said. "And once a month, I beat myself with a spiked stick."

"Weird," said the intern on the other end of the phone. But he wrote this down and thanked me.

Mark O'Malley was at Keggers with some of the business-news people when I arrived. He told me he didn't know if Griff had been investigating him—Griff had never contacted him. He just decided it was better to come out than to live in fear. I bought him a drink.

"What do you think about the Mangecet threat?" I asked him.

"He's a threat, all right," Mark said. "He already controls a bunch of JBS stock through a Christian no-load mutual fund in the financial-services arm of his empire. The fund holds ten percent of the stock, accumulated over a six-year period."

"But ten percent isn't enough to pose a real threat, is it?" I asked.

"A lot of the stockholders have died in the last few years and their kids have sold already, not caring who they sold to. Maybe Mangecet is planning to ruin ANN to get at Jackson, affect the stock price, and make a play at the next stockholders' meeting."

"But the next stockholder meeting is six months away," I said.

Others at the bar jumped into the discussion. Mangecet had been building liquidity since he bought out Pilgrim Publishing (with its profitable Christian sci-fi line) and that theme park in Arkansas with the world's tallest freestanding Jesus at the entrance. Did he have the liquidity to pay the "disloyalty" price? Or just to be a spoiler, get enough stock to harass Jack Jackson and influence his programming and news-gathering decisions?

The Mangecet theory was picking up steam when Mark, ever the reporter, began to argue against it.

"Jackson, Regelbrugge, and Browner control fifty-nine percent of the stock," he said. "I can't believe Mangecet would make a move on us now, with only ten percent. But he might have wanted to exert influence over our news policy."

"Maybe it wasn't planned the way it went," Mickey, the barman, said. I hadn't been aware he was listening as he shot back and forth with beers. "It coulda backfired on them when Griff turned double agent."

I had an additional problem with the Mangecet theory, which I couldn't divulge. Why would Mangecet have someone like Susan Brave investigated? Or me? Maybe he didn't want me investigated. Maybe Griff just added me because of that redheaded thing?

I saw McGravy over in the restaurant, so I said good-bye to Mark, and went to sit with Bob, who was alone at a table for two eating a bowl of soup with his left hand while squeezing modeling clay with his smoking hand.

"Bad day?" I said.

He gave me a look as he squeezed his clay. Stupid question.

"At least you're not being demonized by the tabloid press," I said.

"Not personally. Have a seat," he said. I did. "I've had reporters from other news organizations up the wazoo today."

"Was anyone else at ANN being blackmailed by Griff?"

"No one else has admitted it." An important distinction. "You know, while this media circus is going on, there's flooding in the South, blizzards in the Rockies, fighting in the Balkans. There's some kind of flu going around so we have sick-outs. Now five of our anchors and reporters are on suspension for ethics violations and three others are at home with the flu. *Goddamn it,* I wish I could smoke a cigarette! Did you see the six?"

"No."

"A disaster, complete disaster. You know that young woman from Gallaudet, the deaf university?"

"Chrissie something."

"Yeah. I brought her on as an intern to run tapes and write a little. The girl—lady—is a fine writer. So what does Kevin Peet do with her?"

"I don't know."

"Puts her into the newsroom assistant rotation right away and forgets about her. Then the prompter girl—*lady*—gets sick, and he grabs the nearest intern, who happens to be Chrissie, and puts her on TelePrompTer for the six. Puts her on *headsets.* Says something to her she can't understand because she can't lip-read that fast, and he takes off. It's six, the show's on, and she's running the script through the prompter, just trying to figure it out as she goes along and make the best of it."

When you're running prompter, controlling how slow or fast the script feeds through, you follow the anchor's reading for pace, which means you have to listen to him carefully on the headsets while following the text.

"And?"

"Sawyer Lash is the anchor," he said.

"Uh oh."

"He's reading, and she can't hear him or see his face. She

189

starts to speed up the prompter a bit, so he reads a little faster, and Chrissie's so engrossed in what she's reading, and she reads so quickly that she speeds up the text even more without being aware of it. Sawyer is reading, faster and faster—straight from his eyes to his mouth without passing through his brain. He's starting to sound like a Looney Tune.

"Finally, the producer gets through to him on the IFB and tells him to read off the hard copy in his hands. So Sawyer stops reading—all of a sudden—still live to the nation and the world, and looks down at the pages in his hands, surprised, like he thought they were props."

Bob squeezed the clay hard and a dollop broke loose and landed in his soup with a dull splash.

"He knows they're not props," I said.

"Yeah, but he *looked* like he didn't know, you know what I mean? So he read the rest of the story, head down, word for word off the page."

"But he's such a nice guy."

"Yeah, and we needed someone to jump into the spot and fill it on short notice, someone with"—he paused and made a face, like he was quoting someone else—"credibility."

"Sawyer? Credibility? The guy who referred to Yeltsin in a phone interview as *Doris* Yeltsin?"

"I know. We're going to become a laughingstock. *Entertainment Tonight* is doing a story on Sawyer's screw-ups and the cult following Sawyer now has among college fraternities. They use his show as part of a drinking game."

Every time Sawyer fucked up, stuttered, or mispronounced the name of a foreign capital, you had to drink. If he mispronounced the name of an American city (he liked to pronounce

La Jolla, California, phonetically, for instance), you had to drink twice. Ratings were up.

"Such a nice guy, and not a speck of dirt on him," McGravy said, digging back into his soup. I guess he'd forgotten about that lump of clay. I was about to remind him, when Burke appeared.

"I have to be running," McGravy said quickly, wiping his mouth with his napkin and then pushing himself back from the table. "Left my flak jacket in the office. I'll talk to you later, Robin. Nice to see you, Burke."

In the last week, I'd seen Burke more than during any other week since the first days of our marriage. I was starting to realize how little I actually enjoyed being in his company. I was starting to feel kind of happy that he'd left me.

"I thought you'd want to know," Burke said. "The police have picked up a suspect in the Griff murder."

"Who?"

"Buster Corbus, a union goon, a troublemaker hired to harass Eloise Marfeles," Burke said.

"Really?"

"Apparently, Marfeles interrogated every member of the staff on duty that night as well as a union informer or two, and got a tip that this goon was hired to sabotage the lights and plumbing in the rooms on the thirteenth floor, while everyone was at the party. Marfeles had your ANN folks up there for publicity, and these renegade union guys were going to take advantage of it."

"Wow," I said. "Eloise, not only a hotel queen, but a crime fighter as well."

"Well, the publicity is bad. She's been putting a lot of pressure on the cops to solve this case, bossing them around, nagging them, berating them. I guess she decided to get the goods on her own. I bet the woman's got a wicked touch with an electric cattle prod," he said, and laughed. "My scoop on this should be airing, oh, about now. I told you it wasn't really a conflict of interest."

"Please! It's still an enormous conflict. Perhaps not at Channel 3 but . . ."

"Can I sit down?"

"Sit at a table that hasn't been bussed yet?" I asked.

"You aren't being fair," he said deliberately and uncomfortably, ignoring the postmeal slop on the table, just to show me. Still, when the busboy came and cleared the mess away, Burke's jaw unclenched and his shoulders relaxed. With his thumb and forefinger, he nonchalantly flicked a cracker crumb off the heavy laminate table.

"You know, it's a good thing we're getting divorced," I said, watching him. "If we'd stayed married, I swear they would have found you one day face–down in your poisoned spaghetti."

"Aw, be nice, Robin," he said in his sweetest voice, the kind of voice you use to reassure wild animals.

"So, tell me, why did this union goon kill Griff?"

"It's speculation but they believe the guy went into the room, maybe through a heat duct, thinking Griff was at the party with everyone else, and surprised him. What do you think?"

"I think you can make a case against anyone if you try hard enough. I have firsthand experience with this now, unfortunately. So the cops get a suspect and Eloise Marfeles gets to screw the unions. Happy ending."

"You prefer the feminist conspiracy theory? Or the religious right?"

The waitress came and we ordered drinks.

"No, I hope they've got the guy, really," I said. "But it still doesn't answer a big question I have on my mind. Who hired Griff?"

"Joanne told Amy she thinks Griff was trying to build a harem of submissive professional women," Burke said, laughing. "Submissive. Imagine including you."

"Yeah, it seems like a lech of his caliber would go after babes—young, dewy models—instead of dames—troublesome women journalists in their thirties. No, it makes more sense to me that Griff was working for someone else, and just using this as a sideline, to make a few bucks and get his pole greased, but who was he working for?"

"Mangecet?"

"I just can't put Mangecet and Griff together in my mind."

"Yeah, Mangecet strikes me as the kind of guy who'd have his own in-house investigators, clean-cut guys with a mission," he said, and stopped. He didn't want to give anything away to me, so he changed the subject.

"Did you see Amy today?" he asked.

"Yeah."

"Well? What did you think?"

"My teeth ached afterwards." But even I was getting tired of this adversarial stance. It was wearing me out. The problem wasn't Amy Penny, I told myself grudgingly. The problem was Burke Avery. And Robin Hudson.

"We were doomed. We always knew it," I said.

I saw Eric come in and walk to the bar. He looked at me but

didn't wave. Burke followed my glance to Eric and back and said, "You and Eric have something going?"

"What do you mean?"

"I saw the way he looked at you," he said. "Did you sleep with him?"

"I'm allowed to now. I think I'm going to like this single stuff."

The last sentence was barely out of my mouth when Burke grabbed me by both shoulders, looked at me with an expression of terror, and kissed me hard. I was so surprised by this move that it took me a moment to recover but when I did, I was decisive. I pushed him back across the table and slapped his face.

The slap was unnecessary, but I didn't know if I'd ever have another justifiable opportunity, so I seized the day.

"You're an engaged man," I said. "You can't kiss me anymore. You waived that privilege."

"I know," he said, contrite. "I know. I'm sorry. I lost my head. I still have feelings for you and, and . . . I guess I got lost in the moment."

"Are you trying to completely confuse me?"

"No! It's hard getting divorced. I mean it when I say I still have feelings for you. I feel kind of mixed up too," he said. "All week I've been debating whether I really wanted to end it. I mean, divorce is so . . . final."

I was at a loss for words momentarily. I looked around while I got my thoughts together. Now Eric had his back to me, but he was looking into the mirror behind the bar and his reflection was staring at me.

"When you were with me," I said very slowly, spelling it out, "all you wanted was other women. Now that you're a hair'sbreadth away from being single again, you think you might want me?"

"I don't know. I mean, yeah, I want you, but I don't want to be married to you. I wish we could date every Friday night or something like that."

I arched my left eyebrow and opened my mouth to comment on this childish, utopian vision of his, a world where all women loved him and were willing to share him freely.

Before I could say anything, Burke said, "I know that's stupid. You don't have to tell me. It's just, everything has happened so fast this year. You know, you and me, then Amy and me. Before you know it, I'll have a family and a big house. I'll never again be the person who lived in the East Village with a buxom redheaded wife. It makes me feel kind of . . . sad."

He smiled at me, certain that I would find this somehow charming.

"You always wanted a family and a house, with lots of trees and streets where your kids could bicycle in safety."

"I did," he said. "I still do. I'm just having a weak moment."

Have it somewhere else, I thought, but I didn't say it aloud, a sign I was getting soft.

"Look, I appreciate your telling me the stuff about Griff."

"I knew you'd want to know."

"That was thoughtful," I said.

"Let me see you home, make sure you get home safely."

"No, thanks, I'm sober and besides, I'm not going straight home."

I slapped a five on the table for my drink and got up. Burke got up too. He leaned over and kissed me again, this time on the cheek.

We said good-bye and, to vex him, I walked over to Eric.

"Did you hear about Griff?" I asked. "They've got a suspect."

"Just heard," Eric said. His tone was clipped.

"So I guess Browner isn't going to confess to anything?"

"Doubt it," he said. He raised a long-necked bottle to his lips and drank. His Adam's apple bobbed. It turned me on.

He looked away.

Well, it's been a long time, but this man-woman stuff was starting to come back to me. If he doesn't call and he gives you the cold shoulder when you run into him, do not chase, because it will make you look really foolish. Looking foolish was something I wanted to avoid at all costs.

"I figured you'd want to know," I said, my chill, clipped tone matching his. "See you."

I turned to go. He turned away too.

Chapter Thirteen

THE SUBWAY PLATFORM WAS JAMMED. On a bench in the center of it slept a reeking homeless man whose clothes had all turned to the color of sludge, while an old woman in a cheap coat and orthopedic shoes stood nearby, probably going home after a long day at work.

That put me into a foul mood. In another time, the old woman could have prodded the vagrant with her cane and shamed him into giving up the bench: On your way, young man. In the nineties, you couldn't be sure the vagrant on the bench wouldn't jump up and blow you away, or shove a screwdriver into your skull. Where oh where is Batman when you really need him?

Kissing Burke made me feel sort of sick inside, a feeling intensified by the presence of several young couples in love on the subway ride home. Antiromantic epithets formed in my head as I watched them, and I had a sudden urge to warn them: Stop! Go back! Abandon yourselves to meaningless sex! But just then the Susan Brave light flashed on in the back of my brain, the light that warns me I am crossing a line from cynical single to bitter spinster. I checked my thoughts.

Susan Brave. Why was Griff investigating her? Susan, Joanne—both people who had paid special attention to me the night of the party. Now I knew why. They thought Griff had given me something on them.

Susan, Joanne, and me—the only people I knew for sure he was investigating. What did we have in common, aside from the fact that we were all women, roughly the same age, single, in television, and had all, at one time or another, worked for Greg Browner?

We had all worked for Greg Browner and it was fair to assume Greg had hit on all of us.

Perhaps Paul Mangecet did hire Griff to investigate us, I thought, as the train lurched and staggered through the semi-dark tunnel. Maybe he wanted control of Greg and Greg's stock and was trying to get the goods on him. Not only would Mangecet get Greg's stock, but he could get Greg's "credibility" and win more of the stockholders to his side. So maybe he wasn't investigating us so much as he was investigating Greg, and we were just part of the web.

Who else was in the web? Madri Michaels sprang instantly to mind. She and Greg were co-anchors for a while. In fact, he had "found" her at an affiliates' convention and brought her to ANN to anchor weekends, before he elevated her to sit on the evening news throne next to his a couple of years later. I took it as a given he had not only put the moves on her, but that he had succeeded.

When Greg hit on me and, in a fairly obvious way, indicated it could help my career, I didn't file a complaint against him and I didn't really talk about it.

I know, I know. I seem like the type to file a complaint, but I didn't, and precisely because I *am* that type. I have a reputation as a . . . bit of a troublemaker and I didn't think anyone would believe me, a lowly writer with a known bad attitude—and a history of insanity in her family—over him, a millionaire and a media force.

I have wondered since if I should have complained, if it was, you know, my duty as a woman. But I'd been lobbying for a reporter slot and after the stuff with Greg happened and I was fired from his show, they plugged me into the weekend reporting slot. I didn't want to make waves.

This was starting to make sense to me. Griff *knew* we wouldn't complain. We were women who had been sexually harassed in some fashion by Greg Browner and, out of our own self-interest, kept quiet.

When I came up from the subway that night, I had this eerie feeling I was being followed.

At first it didn't frighten me, because it was relatively early, about eleven-thirty. I expected to see a lot of people when I turned onto Avenue B. But instead of the usual people hanging out on street corners, congregating around burning trash barrels to keep warm, the streets were deserted. The weather had turned colder and driven most people inside.

I turned around slowly and saw a tall man walking in the shadows by an abandoned building. I couldn't make out his features, although when he walked beneath the streetlight I thought I caught a glimpse of a tweed overcoat. Damn. I'd been in such a hurry that morning I'd forgotten to put my cologne in my bag, and I couldn't find my Epilady.

Up ahead I saw the red-and-yellow awning of a bodega, a little mom-and-pop Hispanic grocery, and I ran up to it and ducked inside. Behind the counter, a fat man in a yellow T-shirt sat leafing through a Spanish magazine. A portable black-and-white TV was turned to a Spanish game show and all the contestants were laughing at something the host had said.

The man looked up at me suspiciously. I acted like a customer, walking down the shelves of Café Bustelo, dried yucca, guava paste, and blue-and-yellow Goya cans towards the steel and glass cooler in the back.

Behind me the front door squeaked open and a little bell rang. I froze midstep and looked up at the round, fish-eye mirror wedged in the corner above the cooler to see who it was. It was a kid, a teenager, maybe five feet tall.

I relaxed and let out a deep breath, then took a can of coffee and went back to the counter. Above me, a heating vent blew a gust of warm, dusty air.

"Is that all?" the man asked. A tinny cheer rose from the TV set.

"Yeah," I said. I glanced out the window but couldn't see the tall man. Maybe I wasn't being followed, I reasoned. But in the event I was, a can of coffee in a plastic bag could be a weapon.

Burke, after surveying my umbrella, my poison ivy, and my spray cologne spiked with cayenne pepper, once asked me if there was anything that couldn't be a weapon if it fell into my hands. The only thing I could think of was Jell-O.

"To you, the world is just full of weapons, isn't it?" he said.

Yep, and the world is full of reasons to use them, I thought now, as I left the store, prepared in my heart to bludgeon a man to death with a coffee can if necessary.

But the man had vanished.

As I approached my apartment building, I heard footsteps and took off running and when I did the footsteps stopped. But as I fumbled with my keys at my front door, I felt a hand on my shoulder and a woman's voice behind me said, "Robin? May I talk to you?"

I wheeled around.

There was Amy Penny, bundled up against the cold in a preppy camel-hair coat, standing behind me blowing warm air into her gloved hands.

"You scared the shit out of me," I said.

"I'm sorry," she said. "May I come in? It's really important."

"Oh, why the hell not," I said. I was really aggravated now, but I wasn't about to leave her alone on my street. With her Upper East Side dress and affected ways, in my neighborhood, she was a property crime just waiting to happen.

"No point freezing your ass off out here." I opened the door for her.

"That perfume you're wearing," she said as we waited for the elevator. "Is that . . . L'Heure Bleue?"

"Yes," I said. The elevator came.

"I thought so," she said, and started crying.

Mr. Grooper from the third floor got off as I shepherded her into the elevator. "Don't cry for Christ's sake. Please? Tell me what's bothering you, and then tell me why I should give a shit."

But Amy Penny was crying so hard she couldn't talk through her convulsive sobs.

"This is my floor. Come on," I said, leading her through the dim hallway. I opened the apartment door and waved her in.

"Don't mind the mess. I never do. And don't talk too loudly. The woman downstairs . . ."

"I didn't know what else to do but come here," she blurted.

"Have a seat," I told her as I threw my coat onto a pile of newspapers. The poor girl looked helplessly at the sofa, which was covered with magazines and clothes.

"Just brush them off onto the floor," I said. "Seltzer?"

"Thanks."

"Tell me why you're here."

"This is really awkward," Amy said. I handed her a glass and she dipped her beak before resuming. It was amazing how she could drink without getting her lips wet.

She continued nervously. "Burke has been spending a lot of time away from home the last week and he's been really moody too, ever since the New Year's party."

"So?"

She didn't hear me. "I just knew he was having a change of heart," she said, tearing up again. "And then I realized he was cheating on me."

"Man, he doesn't even wait for the body to cool off, does he?"

"It isn't funny!" she said sharply. "I *know* what's going on. Madri Michaels called me last Friday when she saw you and Burke at Keggers so I followed him. I saw him come in here and I saw him leave! I beat him home, just barely, but when he walked in he was reeking of liquor and . . . and . . . L'Heure Bleue. I know it was L'Heure Bleue, because I went to Macy's at lunch today and smelled it. And then he kissed you tonight in front of people I know at Keggers. . . ."

It was delicious. She thought her fiancé was cheating on her with his wife.

She started to sob again and only the pathetic sight of her tears kept me from laughing out loud at the ridiculousness of the situation, at the two of us sniffing around each other like dogs over a sorry piece of animal carcass like Burke Avery.

"Robin," she said. "Are you having an affair with Burke?"

"Oh, for Christ's sake," I said.

"You know what I mean. Are you?"

"No. Burke and I were discussing the Griff case. We drank a bit and he helped me get home because I drank too much. He probably soaked up L'Heure Bleue in the taxi."

"But Madri said—"

"Madri is full of shit, okay? Burke and I are *not* reconciling."

"How can I believe you?" she asked, then she turned her dewy, fresh face and looked up at me with her Bambi brown eyes.

"It's not me you have to believe," I said. "Listen, I don't like you. So you understand that if I was a malicious person I'd tell you I *was* having an affair with Burke. I'd give you dates, times, and motel room numbers. But I'm not sleeping with Burke. Believe me when I tell you this, Amy. He really hurt me and embarrassed me. That jerk kicked me when I was down. All's fair in love and war, and people fall out of love and it's nobody's fault and all that, but I'd dance naked at Sing Sing before I'd take him back."

"Would you really?" she asked, apparently cheered by this thought.

"Yes."

I wanted to hate her and I would have been ruder to her, but she was being very nice and in contrast I felt like a bit of a bitch.

"Frankly, Amy, I don't think he's worth all your tears. You'd be better off with a less good-looking, less mixed-up fellow."

"No, I wouldn't."

"Oh yes, you would," I insisted. "Living in a constant state of jealousy isn't a nice way to live."

"I know," she said softly. Our eyes met. "But I can't leave him now. I'm pregnant."

I groaned. "He didn't mention that little detail to me."

"He didn't want to tell you. He thought it might hurt you because you can't . . . you know."

"Have children . . . the conventional way."

"Yes." She burst into tears again. "I'm sorry you can't. I'm sorry, Robin. I'm sorry, so so sorry."

"Well, it's over. Forget about it. Burke must be really happy. He always wanted to be a daddy."

I was behaving very reasonably, I thought, but inside I was burning: I wasn't humiliated enough already, now you tell me my husband has impregnated his fertile young fiancée. What other hell lay in wait for me?

"I'm sorry I bothered you," she said, taking a monogrammed handkerchief out of her purse and delicately wiping her eyes.

"It's all right."

She probably wasn't such a bad sort, I thought. I was probably biased because my heart got broken. The image of Burke and Amy together flashed in my mind, and for the first time it looked right to me. Well, not right, but it didn't make me feel sick anymore.

"Did you follow me from the subway?"

"No. I waited outside for you, inside the doorway of the video store on the corner, until I saw you come up the block."

"Oh."

"I'm really sorry to bother you this way. But I had to know. I'm carrying his baby. . . ."

"I get the point," I said. "Congratulations and all that. Forgive me if I'm not completely overjoyed."

"I'm so sorry. You know, I couldn't help but fall in love with him. . . . I wasn't trying to break anything up."

"Yeah, he's got a way about him, doesn't he?" I said.

I changed the subject as I didn't much feel like saying nice things about Burke to salve Amy's feelings. Besides, I just realized Amy could be very useful to me.

"Listen, Amy, I understand you shared a cab with Madri on New Year's Eve. Who got dropped first, you or her?"

"She lives a little closer, so I dropped her. Why?"

"Did you see her go in?"

"Yes," Amy said.

"Hmm. But she could have gone in and come back out after you'd left, couldn't she?" I mused aloud.

"She had to change to go on to another party, she told me. So when I had to leave early, she was happy to go with me."

"Oh. Amy, I'm sorry if I drove you away from the party," I said, immature enough to try to salvage some small victory from this whole situation.

"You didn't. Not at all," she said. "I said it was flu, I know, but really it was morning sickness. They call it morning sickness, but it hits at all different times."

"You had morning sickness that night, and you got into a New York taxi?"

She smiled. "I'd already thrown up my dinner. Madri brought me a glass of soda and Eric helped us get a cab."

"You threw up in the ladies' room?"

"Well, not in the cab," she said.

"A lot of people throwing up that night. Susan, for example. Did you happen to see her in the next stall?"

"I don't remember seeing her," Amy said.

It didn't matter, because I remembered now; *I'd* gone into the ladies' room, and it was empty. I made a note to call Susan.

"Hardly anyone knows about the pregnancy yet. You won't tell anyone, will you? I have my image to consider and the divorce isn't final. . . ."

"Not if you don't want me to," I said.

"This is difficult for you. But you know, there are silver linings. You can date again. *And* you get rid of your in-laws."

I didn't want to let her off this easily, but she'd managed to find our common ground here. My soon-to-be ex-in-laws, who live in East Percy Township, New Jersey, the preserve of pearls at lunch and the Pat Nixon hairdo.

"Have you met Eileen and H. A. yet?" I asked.

She nodded and smiled a small, wicked smile. "They don't like me so much. When Burke left you, Eileen was . . . um . . ."

"Ecstatic," I suggested.

"Um, well, happy. But then she met me. I don't come from a pedigreed family, you know. I come from people who did fifteen cents' work for every nickel they got paid."

These folksy aphorisms of Amy's were kind of her on-air trademark, that and her repeated assertion that she came from "salt-of-the-earth working people," despite the fact that she looked and behaved like an Upper East Side princess.

"You know, my father was a salesman. He couldn't give me an expensive college education," she continued.

She was very defensive about all this. I gathered these were all the things she wished she had said to Mrs. Stedlbauer—Eileen.

"I had to work my way up. Like you did, Robin."

It's true I didn't grow up rich. My father had a college education, but we never had any money. By day he taught high school math, by night he toiled in the garage, "trying to make the world safe for children like you," as he explained it to me. When he died, he held the patents on two safety valves for natural gas equipment and this generated enough income for us to subsist. I have worked since I was fourteen to help support myself and my mother, and I still send her a check every month.

The Stedlbauers, on the other hand, had money, money that had been in circulation for longer than my people had even been in America, which apparently meant something. Eileen seemed to see me as walking anarchy. She was constantly worried that I was going to say or do the wrong thing and bring shame upon my husband, her precious only son.

For example, when we left after Christmas dinner one year, she handed me a book and said, "I thought you could use this."

The book was *Vogue's Book of Etiquette,* 1948 edition, in which I found this gem:

> The whole relation of men to women, as far as etiquette is concerned, is based on the assumption that woman is a delicate, sensitive creature, easily tired, who must be feted, amused, and protected, to whom the bright and gay side of the picture must always be turned.

The table of contents had several listings flagged with red stars and little comments in Mrs. Stedlbauer's perfect finishing-school handwriting, such as, "Formal dinner settings and dinner etiquette are still relevant today! PLEASE read, for your sake."

Jeez. A couple of wrong silverware choices at the dinner table and a knocked-over glass of ice water and the woman thought I was Fred Flintstone. I was so offended. I told Burke I was tempted to show up for the next Christmas dinner wearing a black leather catsuit, pentagram earrings, and one extra-long Lee press-on nail with which to scoop up cranberry sauce.

"You know, Amy, I have a book you'll want," I said, and went to get it. "Eileen would want you to have this. They have to like you now that you're, you know . . ."

She opened her mouth to say the word and I held up my hand to stop her. I didn't want to hear it again.

"Do you know if it's a boy or a girl?"

"It's a boy," she said.

"Eileen and H. A. will *enthrone* you."

I walked her out and as soon as she was gone I went to the phone and called Susan, leaving a message on her machine. Then I started thinking about Burke and Amy, about how I'd trusted him and how I stopped trusting him.

It had been almost a year since I really seriously started to suspect Burke was cheating on me. You know, the classic signs. He was working late a lot, he was distant and preoccupied when he was with me, there were a lot of random hang-up calls at all hours. When I confronted him, he cut me off indignantly. He was merely "cultivating a source," he said, which in one sense could be the truth, depending on how literally you take the statement and how dirty your mind is.

Amy was already worried about Burke cheating on her, and they hadn't even gotten married yet. The irony—and though I had resisted, she was still probably right. She could have him and welcome. I wanted a man I could trust.

Chapter Fourteen

In the morning, the tabloids were all over Buster Corbus, alleged union goon, who had a long rap sheet for burglary, arson, sabotage, and assault with a deadly weapon. Only two convictions on his record, but with this he would be a three-time loser, a habitual criminal; another conviction, especially a murder, and it was a lifetime as a prison concubine. Corbus was naturally fighting this with all his might and had attracted the interest of famous lost-cause lawyer Spencer Roo.

I knew Roo from when I was on Crime & Justice. The last time I saw him, he was defending this guy accused of killing his wife with thirty-six hammer blows to her head. Incredibly, Roo claimed it was suicide. More incredibly, his client was acquitted, albeit on a technicality.

Complicating matters for Mr. Corbus were two well-documented and unlucky facts. One of his fingerprints had been lifted several weeks before from a Marfeles room where the partially decomposed body of a large rat was found stuffed in a bathtub drain. Six months before, Corbus himself had been found in a ventilation duct with wire cutters and burglar's tools at the ultrahip neopostmodern Metro Grand Hotel, which had a contract with one of the same unions as the Marfeles.

In addition, the paper listed all these tenuous connections Corbus apparently had to the union, which in turn had tenuous connections to the Genovese crime family. It also included the interesting fact that Griff was naked when he was found. The paper speculated that he had been coming out of the bathroom after a shower when Corbus surprised him.

Anyway, while Griff's client remained a mystery, the Marfeles story seemed to be tying itself up in one convenient, tidy knot. There was *no* jinx at the Marfeles, Eloise Marfeles asserted to the newspapers. It was all just union mischief and sabotage, which went terribly awry with the murder of Larry Griff. Hotels don't kill people, people kill people.

On the way to work, I stopped at the main post office, where Susan had met Griff. Crystal O'Connor and Teddy Boylen had both mentioned that Griff worked a lot through the mails. I wondered if he had a post office box, and if there was a key out there somewhere that would open the box and spill out all our sins and secrets.

But if there was a p.o. box, it was under a false name, an alias I didn't know. I'd stumbled down another dead end.

It was all very frustrating. I was bursting with information I couldn't reveal, from people to whom I had sworn an oath of secrecy. Trying to keep track of what I was allowed to talk about and what was classified was hard. Under other circumstances, I could take a bit of information from one person and

bait a hook with it, use it to get more information from someone else, until all the bits and pieces added up to something
resembling a clear picture.

It was going to be tricky.

Trickier still was going to be getting away from Jerry to look
into the murder. As soon as I got to work he ordered me into
edit with Claire to finish the first part of our sperm bank series,
or "Sperm—the Last Frontier," as Claire referred to it.

"Don't come out until you've got a finished tape to hand
me," he said. "You're my girls today."

My girls. I just *love* that macho, proprietary crap. I take to it
like a fish to battery acid. I was about to say something but
Claire grabbed my arm and gave me a slow-lidded blink that
said, let it rest.

So I went to lay down my track—the voice-over narration—
and took it into edit, where Claire was waiting with Hosea, a
dreadlocked virtuoso with a Sony edit bay.

"You shouldn't let Jerry get to you," she said. "He's just trying
to get your goat."

A production assistant poked her head in and the frantic
sounds of a newscast under construction blew in. In another
edit room a reporter was yelling, "Back it in!" A feed room
producer screamed, "We lost the feed!"

"Stevenson promo tape?" the P.A. asked. "Oh, wrong edit
room." She closed the door and shut out the cacophony.

"I just don't want my goat to get got," I said, picking up the
narrative thread precisely where Claire had dropped it. "Especially by Jerry."

Hosea laid my track down and then we inserted the sound
bites, which Jerry had chosen. When we began to cover the
rest with video, Claire said she'd look after it and sprang me to

check out the Griff story, promising to page me by my pseudonym when she was done, or if Jerry came by.

I fled down the hallway to the wing where all the features and talk show offices were, stepping lightly past Sports to avoid Turk Hammermill.

I didn't have much luck. Madri Michaels was home with the flu and Susan was too busy to talk. She was at work on a new segment for Solange's show called *Group,* featuring a therapy group she and Solange had "auditioned" in order to get a good cross-cultural, cross-generational, cross-gender mix of neurotics. Twice a week and on the weekend highlights show, Songe would run these ten-minute minidocumentaries following the group through a year of therapy. It was expected to be a big ratings grabber, as viewers became involved with the participants and their real-life soap operas.

So I went to the Browner offices, but Greg's secretary, Frannie Millard, wouldn't let me past to see Greg.

"He doesn't like you," she explained, as though the reasons were self-evident. "He might fire me if I let you through."

"Tell him it's about Larry Griff."

"Well, I can't do that right now," she said. "He isn't even in his office. He's tied up in a meeting."

Frannie had worked for Greg at least ten years and was very efficient. She was also sixty-three, heavy, and had a hairy chin, so I immediately ruled her out as a suspect. She wasn't Greg's type.

"What about Eric? Is he in?"

"He's on a conference call to Los Angeles and can't be disturbed," she said.

"Well can you . . . ," I began.

The phone rang. "Excuse me," she said, in a please-leave tone of voice.

I was going to track Madri down, but when I left the Browner offices, I saw Jerry steaming down the hall towards me. In the next second I heard, "Paging Josephine Tey. Please call the operator. . . ."

I turned around. At the other end of the hall, Turk Hammermill stood, a big book of baseball stats under his right arm. I opted for Jerry.

"You were supposed to supervise this edit," he said.

"Don't you trust Claire?"

"More than you," he said. "That isn't the point. The point is, I told you not to leave that edit room until this piece was done."

He followed—or rather, herded—me back to Special Reports, where he confined me to my office and made me log a graphic medical tape on sperm to find suitable wallpaper video for part two of the series.

Fortunately, I still had my computer terminal and my telephone. As little white spermatozoa shucked and jived across my TV screen, I logged on to the computer and started a Nexis search for newspaper and periodical articles about Paul Mangecet. Then I called Spencer Roo. He claimed to have airtight alibis for Corbus. He was just having a little trouble locating them.

While I was talking to him he almost had me convinced but as soon as I got off the phone I began to doubt. This was, after all, Spencer Roo, who once used a "nicotine fit" defense for a client who went berserk and killed his wife and all her terriers.

I was starving, but I was "grounded," under office arrest, and Jerry was keeping an eye on my door from his office so I couldn't escape. Finally, he went out to a lunch meeting with some Japanese advertising guys and I was able to flee to the company cafeteria, or Bad News Café, as the writers called it, a large room painted in toxic-waste colors with sludge green-brown walls and surface-scum yellow furniture. Rumor had it Dunbar consulted a cut-rate colorist, who determined that these colors would discourage long lunch breaks by creating an uncomfortable atmosphere. The menu, it was said, was designed to reflect the same principles. And, I might add, the same colors.

Eric was there, about ten people ahead on the line for trays. He was talking to Claire, who was getting a diet soda. At first when we saw each other, he turned away, then turned back to me, puzzled. Claire smiled, got out of the way, and Eric came over.

"Hi," I said, guarded.

He just looked at me.

"What?!" I said.

"You were supposed to call me," he said.

"Uh-huh."

Yeah, the best defense is a good offense, I thought, but then I realized he was right. I remembered. He'd asked me to trust him, to sleep on it, to call him the next day—and the next day Susan called and I got all caught up in that. . . .

"Oops," I said. "I forgot, I was preoccupied. . . ."

"Sure. Well."

"No, really. I was wondering why you hadn't called me. God, I'm sorry, I really am. Eric, it's been a long time since I dated, and when I did, it didn't matter so much somehow."

"It's okay," he said, like it was just academic anyway, of no personal interest. "Saw you with Burke. Things going well with you two?"

"With that sociopath? No. Why would you think that?"

"He kissed you."

"And I slapped him. You saw that too, didn't you?"

"Yeah, but I thought it demonstrated a kind of passion for him."

"It wasn't a passion slap. It was an easy shot, a punitive slap. I saw the opportunity and I took it."

"I heard a rumor you and Burke were hot and heavy again." But he smiled. He believed me.

"Where did you hear that?"

"Madri Michaels."

"She is such a troublemaker, man," I said. We had fabulous eye contact for a moment.

"So—are you going to trust me?"

"Sure," I said. Having mistakenly doubted him, what else could I say?

"Say it."

"I trust you."

"Want to do something tonight?" he asked.

"Okay."

"I'd invite you to join me for lunch, but Greg and I are working with a new lighting designer this afternoon, so I have to get my lunch to go."

"Speaking of Greg, I need to talk to him."

He bristled. "Uh-huh, that's why you're being so nice," he said. "You want to talk to Greg."

"No." This came out of nowhere. How do you respond to something like this? God, he was suspicious of me. "No, I was being nice because I like you *and* I need to talk to Greg."

"Well, he doesn't like you much."

"I know."

"For me, that's another mark in your favor," he said.

We had fabulous eye contact for another while as we waited on the tray line. God, he was cute.

"This is like high school, but with all these complications," he said.

I wasn't sure what he was talking about. Did he mean our little romance was like high school, because if he did, I knew exactly what he meant. I hadn't been so afraid of liking someone since this guy in high school, William Sperry.

Or did he mean standing on line in the cafeteria was like high school? I waited for him to elaborate as I reached for my plastic cafeteria tray.

"Do you know what I mean?" he asked.

I barely heard him. "Oh my God!" I said, flipping over my tray. "I got the death tray!" There, in big black letters, someone had written DEATH TRAY.

Eric laughed. "I wouldn't worry about it. Greg got it last week. He's still around."

A stupid prank, a death tray, something one of the younger writers no doubt dreamed up. And yet, I've always had this fearful respect for omens.

"What do you think of Eric?" I asked Claire later, after we screened the finished sperm piece—part one—and put the tape on Jerry's desk.

"He's okay."

"He's okay? That's like saying Michelangelo's *David* is a nice chunk of marble. This guy has . . . he's so, so . . ." There was no appropriate adjective, so I grunted softly instead. "He looks me in the eye and I have a pelvic contraction. You know, the kind that makes you want to cross your legs."

"And bounce your foot," Claire said.

"Exactly."

"Obviously, there is chemistry going on with you two. Enjoy it. Don't analyze it. Have fun, be animals, but use condoms."

"Hey, I'm going to take this slowly. I'm going to learn from my experience with Burke."

"Good," she said. "But don't take it too slowly. I mean, don't just stand there."

"But, Claire, maybe he's a playboy."

"I don't think he's that much of a playboy," Claire said. "He's single, he's cute . . ."

"Gorgeous."

"It's in the eye of the beholder, but he is cute and single and so he dates a lot but he isn't macho about it, except in a joking way."

"How do you know?"

"He dated Amanda in Graphics for three months when Amanda and I were roommates. He seemed like a nice guy, as guys go."

Even though Claire's love life was not exemplary—she was kind of a heartbreaker—her opinion of Eric carried a lot of weight with me, and helped assuage my fears.

In the afternoon, he justified my faith even further when he messaged me: If you come now, I'll get you in to see Greg.

On my way, I typed back. I told Jerry I was going to the ladies' room—then ran, not walked, to the Browner offices. Frannie had been sent on an errand, and Eric was waiting for me.

He kissed me on the lips.

"Greg's in there now. I can't let you in. You'll have to sneak in behind my back," he said. "Understand?"

"Sure."

"I'm turning my back," he said. "In fact, I'm going to the vending machines to get a soda. I'll give you ten minutes. Don't forget, nine-thirty tonight, the Haddock Bar on Ludlow."

"I'll be there," I said.

I gave Eric a thirty-second head start before barging into Greg's office. His back, or rather the back of his chair, was to me.

"Who is it?" he said, without turning around.

"Bachelorette number three," I said.

Slowly, the chair turned.

"Who let you—what do you want?" he asked.

"I want to know about Larry Griff."

Greg was one of those aging men, once handsome, who thinks he is entitled by way of his years, experience, and position to a steady supply of nubile young women. Controllable, nubile young women. As a young man he had had matinee-idol looks, but he had become cynical looking in middle age. His lined face had a taut meanness and his lascivious eyes, once twinkly, had grown cold and glinting. A few more years and they'd be rheumy. Of course, on television he was "avuncular."

His healthy, virile head of hair, carefully tinted to leave just enough silver for authority, was probably a weave, I thought. Had he had surgery? It was hard to tell if he'd had a lift or a tuck, as he was already in full on-air makeup, although his show was several hours away. Today he had an excuse as he had been sitting for a lighting designer, but Greg wore his on-air makeup all day every day, having it touched up several times before air. He claimed this was in case a catastrophic story broke, like a presidential assassination or a nuclear attack, and he was needed to go back to the anchor desk to inform and reassure an anxious nation.

That may be, but I think he just liked the way he looked in makeup.

Browner was taking a long time to respond.

"What did he have on you, Greg?"

Not a muscle in his face moved.

"Who hired him to investigate you?" I asked.

Greg smiled a little and gave me a look, a victorious and condescending look. This guy was good.

"You are a ranting madwoman, Robin," he said. "And I am not going to get caught up in one of your wild intrigues. Now, I have work to do. If you don't leave, I'll call security and ask them to remove you."

"I'm going," I said. "But I think I'm right. He was blackmailing you and the women who worked for you. Do you have an alibi for the time he was murdered?"

Greg reached down to his phone and speed-dialed security. "This is Greg Browner. There is a crazy woman screaming accusations at me. . . ."

"I'm leaving," I said.

I was in enough hot water; I didn't need the added indignity of being escorted out of my own workplace by security.

Before returning to Special Reports, I stopped back by Susan's office and barged in.

"Robin, I'm really busy now . . . ," she said, looking up from her desk.

"Did Greg ever sexually harass you?"

"My employment relationship with Greg is nobody's business," she said.

219

"Aw c'mon," I said. "He fired you from his show. Was that after he sexually harassed you?"

"I'm not going to answer that."

"Where were you when Griff was killed, roughly speaking?"

"I told you," she said, whining. "I was throwing up in the bathroom. . . ."

"That's strange. Because when I went to the ladies' room a little while later it was empty. That was shortly before Griff died. There's something you're not telling me," I said. "What is it?"

She sighed deeply, like she was deflating, took her glasses off and wiped the lenses. I noticed she had the words for the *Mary Tyler Moore* theme song framed and on her wall. Both verses.

"Well, I was pretty drunk that night—," she began. "This is really embarrassing."

"Go on."

"I went through the wrong door and passed out in a stall," she said, her voice cracking slightly. "In the men's room."

"Oh. Anybody see you there?"

"Yeah. Dillon Flinder found me a little later, around eleven or twelve, I guess."

"You're sure?"

"I told you," she said, displaying some backbone. "I was puking in a stall in the men's bathroom, and then I passed out there. Look, ask Dillon Flinder. My glasses had fallen in the toilet. I had vomit in my hair. I couldn't fake that. I was a mess when he found me."

Actually, she could have faked being that much of a mess, under the right circumstances and with the right incentive. But I went to ask.

Dillon didn't see or hear me come up behind him at his desk, where he was hunched over, trying to cut a cantaloupe with a letter opener. Thinking of his watermelon, I smiled.

"Bringing that to room temperature?" I asked.

"Ah, Robin," he said, removing his bifocals and self-consciously running his fingers through his gray hair. "This is my dinner, dear heart. It is far too small for self-gratification. Only a watermelon can accommodate me. And what can I do for you?"

Dillon had such a classy vulgarity, you couldn't help but be charmed.

"Did you find Susan in a stall in the men's room on New Year's Eve?"

"Oh yes! Poor kid," he said, tsk-tsking. "She was so drunk she went into the wrong bathroom."

"You know, I don't understand how she could make that mistake," I said. "I've been in a few men's rooms—well, boys' rooms actually, and it was years ago—but there's usually a long line of urinals. You can't miss them."

"If you're holding back a gallon of Jonestown Punch while diving for a toilet, everything else tends to be a blur. I've been there, haven't you?"

"But are you sure she was drunk?"

"She was passed out when I found her. I'm positive that woman was seriously inebriated, but I'd rather not go into detail. It would be unchivalrous." Even the satyr of medical news had his good side.

So Susan had an alibi. And apparently so did Madri, or at least Amy Penny believed it. But something else she'd said was eating at me: *Eric* had helped her and Madri get a cab. How come?

Unfortunately, I couldn't ask him about it because I'd promised to trust him.

Jerry came back later and ordered a complete recut of "Sperm, Part One," and wanted it and a script for part two (or "Son of Sperm," as Claire called it) on his desk first thing in the morning. After several hours of feverish work, Claire and I turned in our projects and got ready to go home. I put on my coat and stuffed my briefcase with articles on Mangecet.

I couldn't get a cab downtown to the Haddock Bar so I took the bus to East Houston and walked the rest of the way. East Houston was a long stretch of shuttered shops punctuated by the grainy yellow light of the occasional bodega. The sidewalks beneath me were black and buckled and there were little groups of junkies on every corner.

There must be a lot of good, cheap smack around, I thought, because the junkies were friendlier than usual.

"Hey beautiful lady," a stringy and gaunt Hispanic guy said to me. "Jus' seein' you makes my night." He had that lightly glazed, low-lidded look junkies have when high.

I smiled a benign I'm-OK-you're-OK smile, knowing as I do that when junkies are high they're too happy and dopey to pose a serious threat. "How ya doin'?" I asked.

"Better now that you walked by with that smile. That smile knows somethin'," he said to his friends. "What is it you know, pretty lady?"

I was down the block, ten paces past them now. I turned around and shrugged, smiling, and then kept walking away from them. Ludlow was just ahead.

Ludlow had a powerful sub-rosa feel. Thanks to some shifting earth pattern, the street was tilted just slightly. There was a man's suit in the recess of a slumlike, sooty building, as though the man who was inside it had vanished in his tracks—puff—

beamed up to the mothership from where he stood, leaving the suit behind in a crumpled pile on the dark sidewalk.

The purple, blue, and orange neon lights of hip "skank" spots like the Haddock Bar radiated into the dark street while the glowing yellow sign of the EAT HERE café flashed on and off, slowly. The whole shadowy scene had the texture of a dream, peaceful in a sinister way, like the quiet places in nightmares. I walked into the Haddock, wondering why Eric wanted me to meet him here. Something suddenly seemed very fishy.

The Haddock was perfect, though, for my mood of impending darkness and despair. It was an anarchist artist bar. I'd chitchatted with junkies and now I was hanging out at an anarchist bar with plastic skulls on the walls. I was too cool. On an impulse, I bought a pack of Marlboros for more nihilist kitsch. I hadn't smoked in two years.

At the bar, a black bartender wearing Dexter glasses asked me what I wanted.

A morphine drip, I thought, but said, "Absolut Citron martini."

To my left, two men, one American and the other French, were discussing women.

"She said wait for me, don't change, be patient," the French guy said.

From this one sentence I constructed a scenario, unable to hear what the other guy said because the music cranked up at that point. But easy to infer: His lady left him, it wasn't a clean break, she'd gone off on an adventure and now he was sitting in the Haddock on Manic Depressive Night telling his girlfriend troubles to another single guy. Boy, did that get me down.

A pretty woman with unruly brown hair slid up on the other side of me and bummed a cigarette. "Did you pay your taxes yet?" she asked out of one side of her mouth as she lit the cigarette and inhaled.

"For this year or last?" I asked. It was only January.

"For last year. I paid mine today. I had to *fucking* borrow money to pay my *fucking* taxes—to support a government and a system I *fucking* despise!" She spat out the word *despise*.

I didn't know what to say except a deadpan, "Bummer."

"Yeah," she said.

She was about twenty-four or twenty-five, with a powerful middle-class aroma to her. Her hair, while messy, was washed, violating a main fashion tenet of skankness. Her clothes, frayed and self-consciously grubby, were subversively chic and carefully put together. Skank is anarchy, but it's bourgeois anarchy. The fact that she made enough to have to pay taxes said something about how she fit into the class struggle. Also, the drinks weren't cheap at the Haddock. No starving artists sharing a cheap bottle of vinegary wine in this joint. I was drinking Absolut, the guy next to me was nursing Chivas, the anarchette was drinking Dos Equis.

Eric came up behind her.

"Hey, Lisl," he said, kissing the anarchette's cheek before sliding onto the stool next to me. He ordered Wild Turkey. He looked great, very casual and masculine (but not in a contrived, *GQ* way) in a khaki flight jacket and jeans, a look I love for the way it sets off the line of a man's butt and legs. A man has to have the body to carry off a look like that, though, and Eric did, with strong shoulders, a well-toned butt, not too small and not too big, and nice long legs.

She told him about her taxes and said by paying his volun-
tarily he was condoning all the wrongs of the U.S. government.

"When the revolution comes, and they drag me off as an
establishment toady, I hope you'll come to my defense," he
said.

"When the revolution comes, nobody will drag anybody off.
Everyone will be free," she said, and she said good-bye and
went to rejoin a table of her skank friends.

"She's young and Utopian," he said. "I'm sorry I'm late. Greg
had to leave right after the show, had a hot date, and so I had to
look after the show postmortem with the crew."

"It's okay," I said. "Who is Greg dating these days?"

"I make it my business *not* to know what Greg does and who
he does it to," Eric said.

I nodded. "Eric, do you think Griff might have been investigating women who worked for Greg Browner?"

"Do you?"

"I think he was hired to get the goods on Greg through us,
women who worked for him," I said.

"Robin, I don't want to talk about blackmail and murder
tonight. You make me think you're kissing up to me to get
information."

"Sorry," I said. "I'm not kissing up to you for information. Do
you think you're after me because I'm . . . a challenge of some
kind? That conquest thing?"

"Are you just using me to get even with Burke?"

We stared at each other and he said, "You know, there have
been these small, random events that . . . I can't explain this.
On December thirty-first, I looked out my window and saw a
robin on my fire escape, at least a month early. At the Marfeles,
I heard the song 'Rockin' Robin' on the elevator Muzak. Then I

ran into you at the party, a Robin I've always been extremely curious about. It seems like a . . . meaningful series of coincidences, if you know what I mean."

This was the perfect thing for him to say to me as I have always had a fearful respect for coincidences and omens. Was he sincere, or was I just being played by a Master Playboy, who seemed to know me too well?

"And when I looked in your eyes as we were dancing, I thought, 'Yeah, of course. Robin.'"

Oh, this is the final straw, the next most perfect thing to say to me at this point. I hated that he could do that.

"You wanna go back to my place?" he asked.

"Yes," I said, before he'd even finished the question.

We walked to East Houston to get a cab, stopping every few yards to soul kiss. How do I describe what it did to me, kissing this guy on a dark street in a dangerous neighborhood? We got a cab, and as soon as it squealed away from the curb we started making out in the back seat. I felt like I was seventeen and about to lose my virginity. When his hand came up under my blouse, I thought I was going to die.

Chapter Fifteen

WHEN WE GOT INSIDE HIS apartment, he lifted me up and carried me into his bedroom, almost gracefully, stopping only once to hitch my weight up to a more comfortable holding position. I got the feeling he'd done this before.

It's a corny thing, a cliché, but it sure is romantic, and it sure takes care of that awkward transition between rooms when you're about to fornicate with someone for the first time.

There were condoms by the side of the bed, thoughtfully placed, noticeable but unobtrusive, so I didn't have to ask him any awkward questions. That issue settled, we tore each other's clothes off and were pagan and wicked, several times. Okay, there were a couple of awkward moments, a couple of miscues, but for the most part, the sex was great. After months of celibacy, when my intimate encounters generally involved double-A batteries and Henry Miller, it was refreshing to have good sex with a real man.

After the second round, we ordered in cheeseburgers, fries, and chocolate shakes. Between sweaty gropes, we ate and talked. Eric told me his theory of dysfunctional families, which he claimed improved the species by ensuring migration so that different tribes met, mingled, and mixed genetic material. Dysfunctional families were nature's way to prevent inbreeding, he said, because if everyone liked their family, they'd never leave their valleys or islands and they'd just inbreed to extinction—or idiocy.

It made a certain sense.

I lay there, naked, freshly loved, fed, feeling like maybe, just this once, Fortune had smiled on me, that maybe there was such a thing as Mr. Right and one didn't have to settle for Mr. Close Enough.

I could let myself fall in love with you, I thought, as he told me his theory about the future of television, which was that we'd be washed up in a few years because virtual reality was the next thing, the wave. People would live their own sitcoms, instead of just watching them. It'd be like putting yourself in the box instead of sitting outside it because you'd be able to interact with other characters in a 3-D holographic environment with sensory stimuli so you could touch, taste, and feel the imaginary world. Television would become quaint and we'd end up like McGravy, telling stories of the good old days when television was king, when kids had to use their imagination to enjoy a show in two dimensions.

I smiled and rolled onto my stomach to read the titles of the books on the shelf built into his bookcase, a couple of sports bios and several yearbooks. Over his protests, I made him show me his yearbook pictures. Even back in high school he was good-looking, although awfully clean-cut. In senior year Eric Slansky, student council president, lettered in golf and was a Junior Achiever.

"Prediction: Ambitious Eric goes all the way to the White House, if wine, women, and rock and roll don't get him first," read the editorial note below his picture.

"Golf?" I said. "If I looked at this picture without knowing you, I would have guessed you'd grow up to be the CEO of Omnipotent Industries or something. What were your favorite subjects?"

"Math and history. I was a nerd back then."

"What happened? Wine? Women? Rock and roll?"

"Life," he said with mock gusto. "What were *you* like in high school?"

"Well, I was on the school paper, the *Super Snooper,* and I was a cheerleader for a year and a half," I admitted. "Not a very peppy one. I was kind of the squad black sheep. I quit in junior year."

"Why?"

"I read *The Female Eunuch,*" I said.

It was a lie. Actually, my cheerleading career was brought to a sliding halt before a stadium full of my high school peers by a mud slick and an overly ambitious kick. I'd set myself up as the best and then humiliated myself. I was beginning to sense a motif.

"High kicks, huh?" he said. "Splits?"

"Yep."

"Do a cheer for me," he said.

"Make me," I challenged and we had sex again in a completely different position.

Afterwards, he insisted on going out to get my favorite flavor of ice cream. This is too good to be true, I thought, as I luxuriated, naked, between his blue cotton sheets. A guy who fucks like that and then goes out on a winter night to get you

SPARKLE HAYTER

ice cream afterwards. Yep, if the devil wanted my soul, this is the guy he'd send to fetch it.

Eric was gone a long time. I got bored and turned on the news. A woman reporter was live on the scene of a Queens grave robbing, which led the show, and she tossed to another live story, this one with ace reporter Burke Avery outside Spencer Roo's office building.

"Thanks, Carmela. Buster Corbus has not one, but three alibis for the Marfeles murder," he said.

Three alibis, and every one of them a winner—a woman "in the adult entertainment field," dressed in black lingerie and blue jeans, a timid deli clerk, and a parish priest. Buster Corbus and Spencer Roo were taking no chances. The woman and the deli clerk might not have been credible witnesses, but it was going to be hard to shake the testimony of a man of the cloth, even in this day and age, when we know ministers are flawed men like other flawed men.

Normally, three such witnesses in a Spencer Roo case wouldn't be enough to convince me, but the minister really did look saintlike, and the response from the D.A.'s office was somewhat subdued, like they weren't completely sure of their case.

I was hyperaware suddenly that the killer was probably still at large. To quiet the hum of fear inside me, I made myself a drink and then wandered naked around Eric's apartment, looking for clues to his real self. He had very old-fashioned masculine decor, a lot of deep blues and blue tartans, wooden decoy ducks and Remington prints. In a corner, a bicycle wheel was propped up next to a tennis racket missing a string. There were balled-up socks scattered about and enough general disorder to make me feel comfortable.

230

On the coffee table by the sofa, a P. G. Wodehouse book (*The Inimitable Jeeves*) was open, text down. I just love a man who reads, especially a man who reads P. G. The sofa still held the impression of his body, and I sat down there and imagined him stretched out, reading Wodehouse. It was a very pleasant image.

When I went back to bed, I picked up his college yearbook, from his junior year, trying to find the missing link between the upright nerd of high school and the loose, confident supervising producer. Between high school and college, his physical image changed dramatically. The yearbook called him "Tri Kap's Prez and Partymeister." He was kind of shaggy looking, and he appeared to be stoned. He was smiling widely.

I turned to the section on frats, hoping to see more pictures of him. There was only one, and at first I didn't recognize him. He and three of his "brothers" were in drag for a campy, all-male production of Clare Boothe Luce's *The Women* done for charity. Eric made, well, not a pretty woman, but a handsome one certainly.

It was that blond wig that bothered me.

A blond wig. Like a blond transvestite, I thought. Sure, Mrs. Ramirez was always imagining transvestites and call girls coming to my apartment, but maybe she wasn't far off the mark that last time.

Holy shit! Holy Mr. Wrong! I thought as I quickly dressed and got the hell out of there. What a sucker! It all made sense now. Griff would have investigated Eric too, because he worked for Browner and presumably had a lot of dirt on his boss. Well, this answered another question I had: why Eric was so ardently pursuing me. It was plain: He was dating me to find out what I knew, to mislead me. God, maybe to kill me. Of course, I had no proof beyond an old photo in a college yearbook but I had something else—a strong hunch.

All that talk of Eric's about family. "What a crock," I said aloud. After Burke, he probably thought that was the right button to push with me, the solid family-man button.

Thank God I wanted Ben & Jerry's Light Reverse Chocolate Chunk, I thought, my favorite flavor, but not an easy one to find. It gave me time to escape. I ran out to the street and got a cab and I didn't relax until I was back in my apartment, my heavy furniture pushed in front of all the doors and windows.

That night, I slept very badly at first. Every time a car drove down my dark street, the shadows on my wall changed and grew more sinister, until I had to turn my bedside lamp on. The pipes clanked, the iron fire escape outside my bedroom window creaked, and I was sure I heard a woman screaming in the dark distance.

I rolled over and tried to reassure myself, but then, from the living room, I heard a small but very alarming noise: Louise Bryant hissing softly at something.

Slowly and quietly, I picked up my special umbrella and my bottle of cayenne cologne. My umbrella was the telescopic kind that shoots out and opens up with the touch of a button. Strategically aimed, it could disable an attacker quite nicely, at the same time providing a kind of shield. I kept it by the side of my bed.

Holding my umbrella carefully, I crept towards the bedroom doorway, expecting a psychopathic killer to jump in front of me at any moment. Then, my heart pounding and every nerve in my body on red alert, I inched to the very edge of the wall and heard Louise Bryant hiss again.

At that, I stopped. In my wide-eyed rigor mortis I could not move my feet. But something inside me took over—my bad temper, I guess. With a quick motion I reached around the corner and flicked on the overhead light, hurling myself into the living room.

"Ha!" I shouted, brandishing my weapons, umbrella in one hand, perfume in the other. Go ahead. Make my day.

But there was nobody there. Just my cat holding a cockroach firmly under a front paw and looking up at me, contempt mixed with embarrassment in her cold amber eyes. I felt foolish but nevertheless made myself useful, spearing the cockroach with my umbrella and depositing it in the toilet.

By now I was wide awake and pumped up on adrenaline, so I took a sleeping pill, watered my poison ivy, and took down my scrapbooks and started pasting Griff stories into them with Elmer's glue while I waited for the pill to take effect.

I guess it sounds pretty weird, but ever since I was a kid, I've kept scrapbooks of murders. I opened one to an old story about Nannie Doss, the Giggling Grandma, who killed four of her five husbands. Why? She told police she was looking for the perfect husband, presumably by process of elimination. Four down, a billion to go.

In all, I had twenty-four scrapbooks, each with headings like "Mass Murders," "Random Murders," "Family Murders." Some of these had several volumes, and some, like the one I called "Straw that Broke the Camel's Back," consisted of just one scrapbook. The most famous example of the last would be the Papin sisters, lesbian lovers and housemaids who in the 1930s killed their employer and her daughter in a bloody rage of mutilation after a short-circuiting iron blew a fuse one too many times. Jean Genet immortalized them in *The Maids*.

Another slim but spicy volume was "Least Likely Killers."

For example, that upright Midwest preacher who had an affair with a parishioner and then killed her husband so he could be with her, all the while preaching Christian goodness to his unwitting and devoted flock. The upstanding citizen, pillar of the community turned killer, proving that the primal thump of our ancestral jungle beats in the heart of all of us. Thousands of years of religion, hundreds of years of universal public education and good hygiene, and we still cannot contain that native wildness, that killer instinct we share with other members of the animal kingdom.

You can dress us up, but you can't take us anywhere.

A whole scrapbook was devoted just to the Sesquin murders in my hometown and the big-headed blond boy who killed them. I even had a clipping of the story that first broke my tale about the dark-haired boy and the fatal kiss. That made me feel bad, because it reminded me of all the stuff I knew I hadn't told the police in the Griff case. I was probably the reason they hadn't caught the killer.

In the Sesquin case, it took the police three weeks to catch the killer, the big-headed blond boy, after hunting unsuccessfully for the dark-haired boy. And they only caught the guy when they did because his own mother turned him in. His own mother, imagine that. On the morning after the murder, she told police, she found blood on his work boots and trousers. Despite the utter evil and horror of the murders, she waited three weeks to turn him in and before she did, she whipped him with a tree branch until he was black and blue. He told police he was driving down the road after shooting squirrels when the voice of God told him to go into the house and kill all those people.

This is the thing. If I hadn't told that lie about the dark-haired boy, the police and the media might have thought to look at the strange, big-headed blond boy down the road. They might have been able to nab the boy on their own and spare that old widow woman three weeks of soul-wrenching agony before having to betray her own son. Things might have been different.

But once the lie was out, there was no stopping it. Others, older others I'd been taught to respect, took up the lie as though they'd seen it with their own eyes. Other, similar incidents of passion gone awry for Frances Sesquin were cited to support the lie. The mythical dark-haired boy was sighted all over town.

I had only told a couple of people the truth about that murder. When I told Burke, his response was: "She lived with this kid for seventeen years in the woods, and she didn't know he was crazy *before* he killed all those people? It sounds like she contributed."

He had a point, but I still felt rotten about it all. I mean, what if, while the police were on their wild goose chase, the voice of "God" had told him to go into some other house and shoot up some other family?

I closed the Sesquin scrapbook and picked up "Straw." Reading my scrapbooks calms me down. I don't know why. Maybe because it makes murder so one-dimensional and abstract, all written up in black-and-white text that way it doesn't seem so scary. Maybe because almost all of the murders in my books were solved.

Halfway into the Straw scrapbook I started to feel sleepy and a few minutes later I was test-pattern. Lulled, I slept deeply in my frayed blue armchair I've been dragging around since college. I dreamt Eric and I were making love in a series of blue

rooms—it was kind of like a dream, kind of like a nightmare—
and I awoke, cold and shivering, early in the morning to my
clock radio, cranked up full to vex Mrs. Ramirez, and the news
that Greg Browner was dead at fifty-five.

Sometime between the time Greg left ANN the night before
and the time his cook arrived in the morning to poach his egg,
someone put two bullets into his head. Into his face, to be
precise, which I thought, given Greg's vanity, was particularly
vindictive.

Then the news report continued, saying that there were
signs of genital mutilation, and I redefined vindictive.

This was a desperate killer.

I was late getting to work—couldn't find my keys, either set,
or my Epilady. Eventually I found both sets of keys, but I never
did find the Epilady.

When I got to ANN, the cops were in my office, chatting up
Claire. She was on my desk, her legs crossed, talking to four
cops—Bigger, Tewfik, and two uniforms I didn't know. It
looked like a Marilyn Monroe production number. I expected
her to slide off the desk into their arms, singing.

"Robin!" she said. "Some people to see you. Isn't it terrible
about Greg? I'll talk to you later." And she left, taking the two
uniformed guys with her.

"Where were you last night?" Bigger asked me.

"I had a date, then I went home. Look, I didn't kill Greg, but
I . . . know something about it, okay?"

I'd figured they would want to talk to me so before I left my
apartment I had taken that sheet of paper from the dictionary
and put it in my purse. I had planned to courier it over to them.

Now I handed it to Tewfik and spilled my guts. I told him
everything I could remember, what Susan had told me and

Joanne, what I had learned about Browner, my hunches, and, after some hesitation, all my suspicions about Eric—the blond wig, the Browner connection, Eric getting a cab for Madri that night (who, I hinted darkly, was a co-conspirator), and his long absence the night before.

"Eric saw me with my tire iron," I said. "He commented on it. He even convinced me to put it down and dance with him."

"You should have told us all this before," Tewfik said.

"Oh what a tangled web we weave," I lamented. "I got a bad vibe off this guy Eric from the very beginning, but I ignored it."

Bigger was still skeptical. When he looked at me, it was a look that said, I know who you *really* are.

"You got an Epilady, Robin?" he asked.

My heart stopped.

"I had one," I said.

Where was it? I thought about it. Where had I seen it last? By the side of my bed a few nights before.

"Someone must have stolen my Epilady," I said. "Why?"

"An Epilady was used . . . it was jammed into Mr. Browner's genitals and held there with the belt from his bathrobe," Tewfik said. We all cringed.

"Battery-operated?" I asked.

Tewfik nodded. "It was still running when the first police arrived."

Lord forgive me, but the first thing I thought of when he said that was the Energizer rabbit.

"Some angry woman with a bone to pick," Tewfik said. Ooh. Bad choice of words. "Or someone trying to make it look like you did it."

"The Epilady does have my touch. But me, I'd maybe attack a guy with it if he was coming after me, but I wouldn't do it just

237

to be mean," I said. "And I hate guns. I don't have a gun. You know, you're much more likely to be killed with your own gun than someone else's. Also, there's too much temptation on a bad day to deep-throat a .45, you know?"

"We think it was Griff's gun," Tewfik said. "We believe it was taken from his room at the Marfeles by whoever killed him. We found a carry permit for him, but we never found the gun in his stuff."

"I never heard about a gun," I said, in my best Girl Scout, officer-sir voice.

"It was one of the details we kept from the news media to prevent copycats and to weed out the nuts who confess to everything, ya know, to atone for some unresolved guilt from the past."

"Look, detectives, sirs, someone got into my apartment and stole my Epilady," I said. "I lost my keys one day and Eric was in my office that same day, dropping off something. Remember how I thought someone had been in my apartment because it was neater?"

"I remember," Tewfik said. "Anyway, your downstairs neighbor says she heard you in your apartment around the time Mr. Browner is believed to have been killed. Of course, she also says your pimp was there too."

"She hears my cat and she thinks it's my pimp. Like my pimp would be caught dead in that dump," I said.

"Your pimp?" Bigger said, as though he'd caught me in a slip, because I should have said *a* pimp instead of *my* pimp, and the solution to the crime could hinge on this. You had to be very careful talking to him, as he had no sense of humor.

"It's a joke. I don't really have a pimp."

I resisted the urge to say I work solo. I almost said it, but I caught myself.

"A man is dead," Bigger said. "You think that is funny?"

"No, but other things are," I said. I wasn't going to play Ophelia for Greg Browner. I felt bad, in a broad, philosophical, murder-is-always-bad way, but I never liked him and couldn't honestly say I'd miss him.

They asked me some more questions, about my relationship with Greg and the now infamous incident when I wrote for Browner and I told him in the middle of the newsroom to go fuck himself. They told me to "remain available," as they'd have more questions for me later.

After they left, McGravy came in, squeezing a squeezie doll.

"Tell me everything you told the police," McGravy said, sitting on the corner of my desk Lou Grant–style and looking down at me.

But you know, I just couldn't. I already felt bad for ratting out my friends and colleagues to the cops. I mean, I had to do it, legally and morally, but I didn't want to rat them out to the boss-man too, even a boss-man I admired.

So I told him only that I didn't kill Griff or Browner, and that the Epilady the police found might have been mine, in which case it had been stolen from my apartment.

"You don't think I did it, do you?" I asked.

"No, Robin, I don't think you did it. But you yourself told me once that everyone is capable of committing murder under the right circumstances."

"But I didn't," I protested.

"I know," he said. "It's just such a goddamned mess, Robin.

Greg's dead. I was just talking to the guy yesterday, and now he's dead."

"He was an asshole," I said, and reminded him of that bad-smell story he told me about the asshole who died and nobody missed him.

"Being an asshole isn't a capital crime," he shot back. "Although Greg *was* an asshole, a real asshole. Robin, if I tell you something, don't blab it around."

I nodded.

"The cops wanted me to comment on some disturbing things they found in Greg's apartment. There was an anonymous letter that Greg appears to have written, detailing every sexist thing Jack Jackson ever did or said, and every all-white club he ever teed up at. You know, Jack is an outspoken supporter of women's and minority rights on one hand, and on the other, he's a golfaholic and he's been kind of a rascal with the ladies. He's got a past. He's made no secret of it. But, written up that way, all out of proportion, it made him look really bad."

"Greg wrote an anonymous letter about Jack Jackson? Why?"

"Well, they also found a mailing list—JBS stockholders, who, as you know, are notorious for their . . . egalitarian point of view," he said. "That's not all. It looks like Greg hired Griff."

"How do they know that?"

"They found your name and Eric's in a Reporter's Notebook in his desk. It said 'Check out Robin Hudson and Eric Slansky.' They asked me if this could have been a work-related message. I don't see how it could have been.

"It looks like Greg was going to try to undermine Jackson and set himself up as the stockholders' savior when Mangecet attacked."

WHAT'S A GIRL GOTTA DO?

"A palace coup," I said. "But he would have had to shut up the women who had dirt on him, just in case one or all of us pulled an Anita Hill after all these years."

"Yes. Ironically, Greg has strengthened Mangecet's hand. Now we look like a den of thieves, liars, and murderers," he said. "Mangecet will look like Sir Galahad at the next stockholders' meeting."

"Bob, what if they don't catch this killer? Almost half of New York murders go unsolved, and that includes some famous ones. I could be next. I'm not being paranoid this time, Bob, I swear."

"Maybe you should stay with a friend."

"And expose my friend to danger?"

"Then go to a hotel," he said. He crushed the squeezie doll's head between his thumb and forefinger and then flung the head into my wastepaper basket.

"Griff was killed in a hotel. Browner lived in a fancy doorman building. But maybe I'll be lucky, maybe I'll be arrested."

"I'll see what I can get the cops to do," he said. "To protect you tonight, not arrest you.

"I gotta run, though, Robin. On top of everything else, we have to figure out what we're going to do during Greg's hour tonight. The cops were beginning to grill the supervising producer just before I came to see you."

"Eric? Oh," I said, trying not to give anything away, feeling awful.

"So who's hosting Greg's tribute?" I asked quickly.

"Lash. I'll speak to the cops for you, Robin."

I guess I was expecting a little more concern, but Bob saw me as only one of many problems at the moment, not the least of which were a dead, traitorous talk-show host, a suspected killer on staff, *and* a big flood in Mississippi.

I knocked on the wall, but Claire wasn't back. I was all alone.

What was I going to do? If Eric was the killer, if he'd taken my keys from the office that day and had spares cut, then I couldn't go back to my apartment without changing the locks. The cops might be finished questioning him at any moment. He could be there waiting for me when I got home. I wouldn't feel safe in a hotel or at a friend's house. Where would I feel safe?

I could stay here, I thought. Twenty-four-hour news. Always someone here. I could sleep at a pod in the newsroom and wear the same clothes the next day and . . .

But for how long? I mean, who knew how long it would take the cops to sift through Greg's apartment for the one hair or fiber that was going to ultimately lead to a killer, maybe. Sooner or later I had to go home to bathe and change clothes. Someone had to feed Louise Bryant.

So these were my options—sit around and wait for the killer to get me or hope I was arrested. But with my luck, if I was arrested, ANN would bail me out. So that left sitting around, waiting for the killer to get me—maybe a killer I'd just slept with, who knew how to turn me on.

No, that option just was not satisfactory. Somehow, I had to force the killer's hand, because I couldn't stand the fear or the uncertainty. If my suspicion of Eric was wrong, I needed to have it proven wrong. That was the bottom line. I just plain had to know. It was like, you know, a moment of truth.

Where was this information Griff had presumably sent me? Every day, I'd checked the mailroom, but there was nothing. Every day I'd gone through my mail, opening everything just in case it was disguised as a sweepstakes entry or a Con Ed bill.

Nothing. What was it I had to know to find it, and why didn't the police find a copy in his stuff? Surely he'd have kept a copy for himself.

It was so quiet I couldn't think. I turned on my monitor and watched the news. ANN covered the murder with a dispassionate thirty-second reader that lead into Browner's obit, which showed his good side, as obits often do. I hate to admit this, because the guy was dead and all, but it made me laugh a little. Not because Browner's death was funny, but because it got me thinking about my obit.

There was a special section in the obit drawer for ANN and JBS personalities. But if anything happened to me, I wanted to be sure I went out in style, so on a lark one slow Saturday I'd secretly redone mine. With the help of Louis Levin and a genius in Graphics who was able to superimpose me into a number of different historical scenes Zelig-style, I managed to build myself quite an impressive biography.

Twice a year, the obits were updated, and just before updating I'd replaced my fake obit with my real obit. When the updating was over, I switched them back again.

See, I knew that when I kicked, chances were that obit would be run straight to air without being screened by anyone first, in typically sloppy ANN fashion. It happened all the time. So what ANN's viewers would see if anything happened to me was a video that showed me in a minidress and obey-me heels leading an infantry assault in the Battle of the Bulge, dating the Aga Khan in the fifties, advising Kennedy during the Cuban missile crisis, and climbing Mount Everest with a Japanese team in the seventies.

It makes me feel better, knowing I'll get the last laugh, I guess.

Chapter Sixteen

LATE THAT MORNING Claire came back carrying a soggy bag.

"Special delivery," she said. "Eric asked me to give you this. He's really furious with you. The police questioned him for two hours."

"Really?" I said, taking the bag from her. Even though I knew what was inside, I opened it and looked. Melted Ben & Jerry's Light Reverse Chocolate Chunk. A very clever touch. "And they *released* him?"

"Yeah. They've released everybody."

So far, she told me, the cops had talked to me, Eric, Solange, Susan, Dillon, Jack Jackson, and Frannie Millard. According to an informal poll conducted by Louis Levin, fifty-two percent of newsroom respondents believed *I* did it.

"Do you think Eric killed them?" she asked me.

"The thought has crossed my mind," I said, and I told her some of what I knew.

"But Griff was naked, wasn't he?" Claire said.

"So?"

"I've been thinking about this. You know how you thought it had to be someone who had a room on the floor so they could change out of their clothes after the murder?"

"Or someone who could hide their clothes under their costume."

"Griff was naked. Why? Perhaps he was about to have sex with another naked person. He went to the bathroom, and when he opened the door to come out, the other naked person beaned him with a blunt instrument."

"I'm with you so far."

"After killing Griff, the killer washed his blood off her naked body, got dressed, wiped the room for prints. Didn't need a change of clothes."

"Escaped?"

"Service elevator? Out through the underground parking garage? Back to the party? I don't know. There were a couple hundred people in costumes that night, right? Everyone was drunk. Much confusion. My point is, it was probably a woman."

"Well, she may have had a partner in crime," I said.

"Maybe. But not Eric."

"Claire, if you had something really awful in your past, would you kill to keep it secret?"

"But I don't."

"No, neither do I, not really. But what do we actually know about each other, pre-ANN? The killer obviously has a big secret, something Griff knew about, and Greg may have known about, or the killer was afraid he'd find out. It could very well be Eric."

"Maybe Sawyer Lash did it. A career move." She smiled. When I didn't smile back, she said, "I shouldn't make light of it. I know you're really frightened."

245

"No, please make light of it—*because* I'm frightened."

"Stay at my place tonight."

"I can't put you in jeopardy."

"Oh for God's sake," she said. "I have a great doorman. Great locks. I'm not afraid. Really. Trust me."

"Do you have an umbrella at home?"

Before she answered, Jerry poked his head in. There was this split second between the time I realized it was him and the time I started pretending I was busy.

"What are you doing?" he asked, annoyed.

"Um, looking for my part two script rewrite?"

"Robin, you've got other things to worry about," he said, which was so totally out of character that I could only stare at him. Then he went on.

"McGravy says you think this killer is after you, so . . . I brought you this."

He pulled the undercover purse camera from behind his back. "I want you to take this with you everywhere you go from now on, until this is over."

"So if I'm killed you'll have video?" I said.

"Just to be on the safe side," Jerry said. "I would hate for you to die before you've tracked part two of the sperm series. You know I'm not interested in your safety and welfare. I'm only interested in video."

"I'll take the purse-cam."

"Take it with you *everywhere,* even to the ladies' room. Where are you staying tonight?"

"Claire's."

Claire nodded.

"Take a car service."

"Yeah. Okay."

"I'm not kidding," Jerry said. "Two people are dead. You might be next. I'm going to have two of the security guards escort you girls home tonight. You wait here. I'll arrange it."

He went into his office to "make a few calls," despite my protests that I really didn't want to put any ANN security guards in the line of fire. About the hairiest situation they'd had to handle was the occasional fan or schizophrenic soothsayer who wanted to personally deliver the news that the end was near. Their area of expertise was subduing crabby Federal Express guys.

"It's all set," Jerry said. "Security is going to escort you home *and* the cops told McGravy they'll check on you tonight. I'm going to call too."

I had this sickening revelation just then. For all his flamboyant sexism and crass news judgment, Jerry was one of the few people at ANN I trusted.

"Okay. Thanks," I said reluctantly. "That was nice of you."

"It's all who you know," Jerry said.

After he left, I said, "Man, he's getting kind of paternal, isn't he?"

"He doesn't want you to die because if you do, you'll never fall in love with him," said Claire. "Or else it's a way for him to demonstrate his power, that *he* can make you safe and secure."

I wasn't listening. I was thinking about Solange, whom Claire listed among the people the cops had questioned, and how, as Greg's ex-wife, she probably had been investigated by Griff too. How she went up to change when Susan spilled her drink on her and came down just before eleven, when I was going up. That gave her plenty of time to kill Griff, slip into her room, and change clothes. Did that mean Susan's spilled drink was planned? Did that mean a *real* conspiracy?

Then I thought about what Tewfik said, about those nuts who confess to something they didn't do in order to cover up something they did do, or to atone for it. Were all Solange's televised confessions just a smokescreen for some greater, more dastardly deeds?

Add to this the fact that Solange was a tall woman, nearly six feet, with broad, Joan Crawford shoulders and honey-colored hair. It would be easy for Mrs. Ramirez, with her dim eyesight, to mistake her for a transvestite. Then again, she thinks I'm a transvestite and, as you know, I have the body of Rita Hayworth.

It was lunchtime, and Claire wanted to go eat. The special in the cafeteria was broiled tofu salad, one of the few things they did well. Broiled tofu-salad day was a big day in Claire's life every week. But I didn't want to go, fearing my appearance among my peers, after ratting several of them out, would spark a food fight or worse. Oh, for the days of food tasters.

"Please," Claire said. "I'll protect you. We'll get it to go, and bring it back here to eat. You'll be there ten minutes at most."

"You go, I'll wait here," I said.

"Okay. But lock your office door after me," she said, the picture of friendly concern.

God, how long was this going to go on? I wondered. Being babysat, escorted, watched, all for my own protection. When would I get my privacy back?

The Ben & Jerry's was melting through the paper bag with a sickly brown stain. I picked it up and dropped it into the trash can. "Special Delivery," I said.

And it hit me.

Actually, it did a twist and a flop before it hit me. What is the opposite of Special Delivery? General Delivery. Anyone can receive their mail there. Anyone can send mail there. But you

WHAT'S A GIRL GOTTA DO?

wouldn't think to check there, would you, if you had a legitimate mailing address?

Of course. I called the post office and got an automated
recording. General Delivery was open at the James A. Farley
Post Office from 9 A.M. until 1 P.M. It was twenty-five to one.
I had twenty-five minutes to go crosstown and downtown—in
midday New York City traffic.

Well, I didn't have time to wait for Claire or even to have her
paged. I shoved some money into my pockets, grabbed the
purse-cam, and scribbled a quick note telling Claire where I was
going and when I'd get back. I taped it to her door on the fly.

Murphy's Law, right? I'm yards away from the security door
when I run smack dab into Turk Hammermill.

"Robin!" he said sympathetically. "How are you? Where are
you going?"

"I can't talk right now, Turk. I have to be someplace," I said,
staccato.

"What's your hurry? Need a hand? Where are you going?"

"Post office. It's a personal errand. . . ."

"Oh, I need some stamps," he said, digging in his pocket for
change. "Could you . . ."

"Listen, Amy Penny was trying to defend the designated
hitter rule yesterday. You need to have a word with her."

Escape facilitated by a little revenge, two birds, one stone.
Sometimes life just works out that way.

Without waiting for him to answer, I turned and ran out the
door and up the stairs to the street. I stole another man's cab,
just as it was pulling up, by flashing my press pass and shouting, "News emergency!"

"Eighth Avenue and Thirty-third Street, please," I said to
the driver. "I'm in a rush."

"Everybody's in *such* a big hurry," the Sikh cabbie said, and chuckled. "You should take time to look around, enjoy the moment."

Jeez, and I thought Sikhs were martial and aggressive. What a rotten time for a stereotype to fail.

"This is a life-and-death thing," I said.

"Oh sure, I know," the driver said, inching through traffic, not seizing those miraculous traffic opportunities most cabbies do—the left-handed turn from the far right lane, making a lane where there isn't one, skirting around traffic by driving in the oncoming lane. Fifteen thousand cabbies in New York, and I have to get the one who drives defensively.

"It was life or death for me too, last spring," he continued. "Triple bypass. You know, before that operation, I didn't know how old my grandchildren were. Now I know the meaning of life."

Fifteen thousand cabbies in New York, and I have to get the one who speaks English. I took down his medallion number. I don't know why. What was I going to do? Complain? Yes, Mr. Singh insisted on driving safely and being charming and wise! See that it doesn't happen again.

As we crept towards my destination, Mr. Singh went on and on about trees, flowers, birds, children, all that wonderful stuff until I was nauseous with anxiety. He did a long riff about the Empire State Building as we were stalled in traffic beside it.

"Took my grandchildren up to the top a few weeks ago. Most New Yorkers don't think to do things like that."

I had half a mind to jump the seat and yank the wheel away from him.

"You must have passion in your life, and a passion for life!" he said, with gusto.

"Yeah yeah yeah, can we cut over on Thirty-third, please."

He let me out right in front of the Farley Post Office, a Greco-Roman monument to the postal gods, with twenty-five steps up its broad face and twenty stone columns standing guard. Zip code 10001.

I had seven minutes. I ran through the long, tunnel-like hall looking for the General Delivery counter. But there wasn't one.

"Excuse me," I said to a security guard. "General Delivery?"

"That's 390 Ninth Avenue, other side of the building," he said. "You have to go back out to get to it."

I ran out of the building and down Thirty-third Street. There was nothing much on this street—parking lots and the Glad Tidings Tabernacle on one side, the long granite expanse of the post office on the other. The "other side of the building" was a full block away.

As any New Yorker can tell you, the blocks between streets are short; between avenues, long. Very long. I kicked off my shoes and ran in my stocking feet to make better time. I got to 390 Ninth just as the guard was about to lock it.

Inside, panting, I rested against the door and put my shoes back on. There were still a few people on line. When I got to the front, I said, "I'd like to know if you have anything for Robin Hudson."

The guy went away to check and returned with a thick brown envelope.

"ID," he said, releasing the envelope only after I showed him my press pass.

I was about to leave when an idea occurred to me and I turned back to the counter. "Can you tell me if there's an envelope here for Larry Griff or Craig Lockmanetz?"

251

"I can't give another person's mail to you," he said.

"No, I know," I said. "I don't want it. I just work with them and thought I'd let them know if there was mail for them. We all just transferred here from Kansas City."

God, I'm such a liar. But it worked. The guy went to check and there was an envelope for Lockmanetz, Griff's alias. Maybe this was where he hid his copies too.

I went back into the street. It was a bright winter day and I had to cup my hand over my eyes to read the postmark. It was December 31st, the day Susan had met Griff at the post office. Beautiful. He'd probably mailed it just before meeting her. If his pigeons didn't pay up, he planned to tell me about the letter and where to pick it up. Maybe he planned to tell me even if they did pay up, as long as I paid up, one way or another.

I tore open the envelope as I walked down Ninth Avenue towards Thirty-third. Ninth was pretty deserted. I figured I had a better chance getting a cab on Eighth.

I pulled the sheaf of papers out halfway and began flipping through them at the top, reading the names, which were not alphabetized. I hesitated at my own report for a second, then, prioritizing, flipped past until I got to Eric Slansky, in the middle of the pile. That one I pulled out to read.

I had hoped it wouldn't be there.

After scanning the boring parts, I learned that he had smoked a considerable amount of pot in college (big deal) and had a drunk and disorderly for which he was fined while on spring break in Florida (big deal).

On Eighth Avenue, I stuck my arm up for a cab while I read Eric's credit report, which wasn't bad. Bad guy, good credit? His academic record was pretty good too, and for the last twelve years he'd demonstrated a "strong community service ethic" by his work with homeless children, which he had never mentioned to me.

Gimme a break. It meant *nothing*. Hitler was a vegetarian who was able to tame baby deer at his Berchtesgaden retreat.

Sure enough, as I read further, I found what I was looking for, and what I hoped I wouldn't find, Eric's big secret. Not a what but a who. Wynn Codwell-Slansky to be specific, his ex-wife, from whom he was divorced shortly before coming to ANN, and whom he failed to mention to me. According to Griff's report, Wynn Codwell-Slansky was now a realtor in Chicago and refused to discuss her ex-husband.

"Ms. Codwell-Slansky wouldn't take my calls, and routinely hung up on me," Griff wrote. "I was able to get a full credit report on her, but unable to obtain any detailed personal information about her or her marriage."

Maybe Griff couldn't get the information, I thought. But maybe Wynn would talk to me, another woman.

This all made me feel kind of sick. Man, I had *sex* with that guy, I thought. Worse, I had *great* sex with him. It was sick, sick, sick. Like Pascal and Amy Penny said, the heart has its reasons that reason cannot know, which was reason enough not to follow your heart if you asked me.

A cab pulled up. It was a bright, sunny afternoon and there were people all around me. As I reached for the door handle, someone grabbed my arm and I felt a jab in my back.

"Don't scream. This gun has a silencer and I can shoot you and get away before anyone notices you. We're going to get into the cab and go to your place."

It's like McGravy always says, sometimes you find the truth and sometimes the truth finds you. Who knew the truth would look like Fawn Hall?

Chapter Seventeen

WHAT CAN SHE DO TO me here, with all these people, I wondered. But then I remembered, this is New York.

People here don't necessarily like to get involved with cops unless they know you personally or there's something in it for them. She could fill me full of holes and still make a clean getaway. I mean, I heard this story about a guy who was squeezed between automatic bus doors for four blocks on a busy avenue, screaming every minute. It was in all the papers, but when he tried to sue later he couldn't find a single witness.

So I got into the cab and she slid in next to me.

"Please . . . ," I started to say to her.

"Ssssh," she said nervously but sweetly, jabbing the gun harder into that tender area between my breast and my armpit and taking the envelope from me with her other hand.

Weird thoughts went through my head. I was in a pre-apocalyptic daze. I wondered how this cabbie, who spoke little English, was going to feel later, when he found out he had driven me to my death. Or worse, how the sensitive Sikh would feel when he found out my quest really had been a life-and-death matter.

Weird thoughts: My cat could outlive me.

I felt paralyzed and I found it hard to breathe, like a very strong man was squeezing my lungs. My face felt numb.

The city, which I suddenly loved, whizzed by me on all sides, like in a dream. If she killed me, I'd never eat in that restaurant or shop in that store or walk in that park or see that vista again. I'd never sleep with another cute guy. I'd never hug my mom again. The Sikh was right; you have to take time out to enjoy the world. It could be gone tomorrow.

"My keys are at the office," I whispered to her. I couldn't see her eyes, hidden behind oversized sunglasses.

"I have keys," she said.

Yes, that made sense too. Burke had a set of spare keys. Amy must have had them copied before he brought them to me that day I misplaced mine.

"Claire is waiting. . . ."

"Ssssh," she said, with the hiss of a kind librarian. This was the horror of it, that the face of death was such an appealing, gentle face and it spoke in such dulcet tones.

I couldn't stand it but my options were limited. Amy had a gun. I didn't have my cologne, my umbrella, my Epilady, my staple gun, my spray glue, not even a can of coffee in a plastic bag. I was completely unarmed.

Even the purse-cam was useless, in its current position, wedged under my right arm, Amy and her gun jammed against my left. It was impossible to reach over and turn it on, and even if I could it wouldn't do much. Nobody was talking and the lens was pointed at a Taxi Commission decal on the back of the driver's seat.

255

When the cab pulled up, Amy paid the driver and she and I left the cab as one unit, like Siamese twins. She was shaking, not a good thing. Nervous, she might accidentally pull the trigger.

She gave me the keys, made me open the door, and made me hand them back to her. I suppose Burke had told her a thing or two about me and my array of weaponry—which explained the Epilady attack on Greg Browner's genitals—and she didn't trust me to hold the keys.

We took the stairs to avoid neighbors. Now I wondered if she had planned to kill me that night we talked in my apartment, but called it off after we ran into one of my neighbors in the building. But no, she'd been wigless that night. She must have wanted to see how much I knew, feel me out, find out if Burke still had feelings for me.

How could I get that gun, I asked myself as we climbed the dark stairs up to my floor. And, even if I did, could I shoot her?

Knowing how it would look in the tabloids made me cautious. I was already a scumbag in their opinion, while Amy Penny was a popular television personality, Miss Congeniality, the wholesome face that graced that upscale, low-dust baby powder until her ANN contract was inked.

On top of everything else, if I killed her, they'd find out she was pregnant, that I'd killed a pregnant woman, carrying my husband's child. Yeah, that'd make me look real good.

The wig and dark glasses? The tabs would probably say that Amy Penny, in her quest to be taken seriously as a journalist, had gone undercover to solve the Griff murder.

But there was something in the envelope worth killing three people for, and that would be my defense, I realized. Because nothing Griff had found out about *me*, no matter how humiliating, was worth killing for.

It was dark in the stairway—the way my landlord uses light bulbs you'd think they were made of gold—and Amy had on dark glasses.

Her vision can't be too good, I thought. Could I wheel around and grab the gun from her? No, she was holding the gun right to my head.

I was trapped.

And still I couldn't stop thinking what the papers would say, how bad they would make me look after I was gone. Christ. The cops would find my murder scrapbooks and make a link. Amy intended to take not only my life but my reputation, what little there was left of it.

This would push my mother off the deep end, I thought. She'd end up wandering the streets in full coronation regalia— or a reasonable facsimile, using her high school prom dress and various things found around the house—like she did after Dad died.

This is what they call having nothing to lose.

It was dark in the stairwell and quiet. I could hear the whirring of some kind of generator deep in the lower depths of the building.

I didn't lose my temper. I bided my time. When we were coming up to the fifth-floor landing, I suddenly ducked, dodged, and got behind her, wrapping my arms around her in a kind of Heimlich maneuver, purse-cam flopping at my side.

Unfortunately, I failed to secure her gun arm, and she simply pointed the gun at me over her shoulder.

"You can carry me up if you want. I shouldn't be on my feet

in my condition anyway. But we are going to go into your apartment," she said, in a voice I'd never heard her use before, a cold, mean voice that made me think of nuclear winter.

I put her down and let go.

We came to my floor.

At my door, she again gave me my keys and pushed her body against mine so I was crushed against the door as I unlocked it, limiting my movement.

"Push the door open and go in," she said. "Turn on the light." She shut the door with her leg and nudged me into the living room. She put the envelope on a counter.

"Put your purse down," she said. "Slowly."

I followed orders. I set it down on top of the television, and as I did I nonchalantly flicked the record button on top.

Louise Bryant rubbed against my legs, trying to get me to feed her.

"They're expecting me back at work," I said. "They'll be worried. . . ."

"I want you to call in and tell them you're depressed and sick and you've come home to recuperate," she said. "If they ask you anything else, just yes and no answers and then off, you understand?"

"Sure, fine," I said. This was my chance. I'd call Claire and somehow let her know I was in jeopardy and she'd send the cavalry.

I dialed and waited for someone to pick up, but nobody answered in Special Reports. Finally, the switchboard picked up.

"I have a message for anyone in Special Reports, from Robin Hudson," I said. It was hard to breathe. What could I say that would tip someone off and yet slip by Amy? "I'm at home, I'm

WHAT'S A GIRL GOTTA DO?

sick and . . . depressed. I can't meet Claire at Old Homestead later, so . . ."

Before I could say anything else, Amy's gloved finger depressed the phone button and broke the connection.

"Why did you say that about meeting Claire?" she asked.

"So she wouldn't go there and worry," I said.

"What's the Old Homestead?"

"You know, the office, the old homestead, it's a figure of speech."

And, situated conveniently in New York's meat district, it happens to be one of the city's oldest steak houses. You'd see the pope in a whorehouse before you'd see Claire in Old Homestead. But would Claire get the message in time?

"Do you have paper and a pen in your purse?" she asked, heading for it.

"No!" I said.

She stopped.

"In my writing desk, middle drawer."

"Good," she said.

I kept waiting for my life to flash before my eyes, but it didn't, perhaps mercifully. My past completely vanished. It was like this moment was frozen outside time, like I was watching it instead of living it.

I found some of my nerve. "Amy, why did you do it?" I asked in a tiny, frightened voice. "Why did you kill Griff and Browner? Why are you going to kill me?"

She said, "I have no choice."

"Did Browner harass you? Were you up for a job on his show? Did he get you on at ANN? What did Griff have on you?" I was speaking very fast.

"Sit down at the desk and write what I tell you," she said, ignoring my questions. "Dear . . . everyone."

I wrote it.

"I can no longer go on with my . . ." She thought hard. "Guilt. Write that—I can no longer go on with my guilt, which I brought on myself by killing Larry Griff and Greg Browner. I did it to conceal my . . . sordid affair with Greg Browner, which went on while I was married to another man."

Amy wasn't known for her imagination, so I guessed this was her confession, being made through me. It was small consolation to know my friends would realize I'd never write a suicide note like this, that I would never go out spouting clichés, never without a good quote, and never with a gun. I was more a swan-dive-from-the-Statue-of-Liberty kind of dame.

Also, the purse-cam was rolling.

As I was writing, Louise Bryant, sensing that the balance of power had shifted in the room, began to rub against Amy's legs, trying to get Amy to feed her.

"I think you should tell me why I am going to die, at least," I said, adopting my best Nathan Hale expression, honor in the face of death. "You owe me that."

"I don't owe you a thing," Amy said. "Cat, *stop it!*"

Amy tried to kick Louise lightly away, and then she pushed a little harder. Louise Bryant responded in character, faking a retreat, then turning around and jumping on Amy's legs, vertically, digging her claws into Amy's hose and calves.

"Ouch! Goddamn it!" Amy said, stopping to yank the cat off and letting her gun hand relax, fatally, for a moment. Long enough for me, emboldened by the presence of the purse-cam, to twist her wrist and grab the gun.

Thank God for Murphy's Law.

"Okay," I said, standing up from my desk. I took a deep, deep breath. "Now we're in business."

You know how people behave differently when there's a camera on them, especially a video camera? For a minority of people, this brings out their worst selves, but most of the time, people behave like the people they think they really are, their funnier, nicer, more reasonable selves. Like this Afghan commander who, in the heat of battle, told Joanne Armoire to "shoot my good side." It's a most interesting phenomenon.

I was aware that purse-cam was recording me and I wanted the world to see me in a good light, behaving heroically. I would take the moral high ground here and treat my prisoner with honor. I would not pistol-whip a pretty, pregnant lady.

Then I thought: This woman has her own show, she has my husband, and she intended to take my life and my beleaguered reputation too.

"You can't kill me, I'm pregnant!" Amy said. She was starting to weep and shiver.

"Oh well," I said, dispassionately. "The first thing I want you to do is take all your clothes off. Do it!"

There. Now there was something in it for the tabloid TV shows, something they could show with the help of three black strips.

"Good, now walk over to that planter. Pick it up. Rub your face in the ivy. Good. Now, under your arms. Across your breasts. Put it down and rub your butt on it. Good. Now turn around and look at the hidden camera, there, on top of the TV. And now, I want you to tell me everything."

"This confession will never stand up in court. You have a gun on me. It's coercion."

Everything she said while *she* had the gun on *me*, however, was on videotape and that would stand up in court. Now, my purpose was to satisfy my curiosity.

"I'm not trying to get a confession," I said. "I'm just a reporter cultivating a source. Now, what about Eric?"

"Eric who? Eric Slansky, you mean? What about him?" She was puzzled. "Eric has nothing to do with me."

"How did you get back to the Marfeles? Did you get out of one cab, take another back?"

I hoped to get her whole story on the purse-cam recording, but just then I saw the flash of red and blue police lights through my curtains. I figured Claire had gotten my message and called the cops.

So instead of getting Amy's story, I did a very shabby thing. I stuffed the brown envelope I'd picked up at General Delivery under a stack of newspapers so the police wouldn't see it. If I gave it to them it would become evidence. I might never see it again and there were certain things I needed to find out first. I was curious.

You understand.

Louise Bryant, sensing the balance of power in the room had once again shifted, started weaving between my legs.

"Not now, Louise," I said gently.

The cops pounded on the door and I let them in. Bigger, jumping once again to the wrong conclusion, saw me with the gun and grabbed my arm. Amy was crying hysterically. A uniform handed her clothes to her while I tried to explain to Tewfik what was going on. I told him about the purse-cam tape and the envelope still at the post office. Bigger released my arm.

Tewfik went over to the purse. "There's a camera in here, huh?"

"Yeah. It's still recording."

"And what's this?" Bigger asked, checking out the ivy planter by the fire escape, turning the leaves over, stooping to smell it. Probably making sure it wasn't some form of mutant marijuana.

"Don't touch the plants," I warned, but he ignored me. Now that he had made contact, it didn't seem the propitious moment to let him know it was poison ivy.

"You can turn it off now," Tewfik said. "Can you play that in your VCR?"

"Not without A/V cables," I said.

Tewfik turned to Bigger. "Richard, poke your head out the window there and see if that Channel 2 crew caught up with us."

Bigger opened the window, leaning right into the poison ivy. He hollered down to a cameraman and within ten minutes we were all hooked up and watching the purse-cam tape. It was bad quality, it was grainy, and the tiny fish-eye lens distorted it somewhat, but the essential truth was there, in Amy's own words and actions before Louise Bryant and I wrestled the gun from her hand.

Tewfik looked at me with new respect after that scene. But when he watched me make Amy strip and rub her body with ivy, his expression changed. And Bigger started to squirm.

Amy was read her rights, and Tewfik let the Channel 2 guys get some shots from the hallway.

I fed Louise Bryant. A uniformed cop led Amy away, in handcuffs, still crying, insisting that it wasn't her fault.

"Good thing Claire called you guys," I told Tewfik, cheerleading to compensate for not disclosing the envelope in the stack of newspapers next to my armchair.

263

"It was your boss who called," Tewfik said.

"McGravy?"

"Mr. Spurdle."

A bunch of my elderly neighbors were clustered around my door as Tewfik accompanied me downtown for questioning. Mrs. Ramirez was not among them. It was not until I was outside on the stoop that she threw open her window to yell to the police, "Well you finally got her. It's about time. Good riddance to bad rubbish!"

There were quite a few reporters outside waiting for me, taking in every word.

"Her place is full of call girls and transvestites!" Mrs. Ramirez continued as the cameras rolled. I made a note to send her flowers.

Tewfik hustled me past the reporters as they shouted questions, their eyes frantic and demanding. Soon all the shouting just turned to white noise, kind of a low, hollow screech. It was surreal; the sun moved between the buildings across the street and suddenly the whole scene was blindingly white. I felt somehow removed from it all and said nothing, until I saw Claire with a crew and a live truck. I told her everything I could before Tewfik yanked me away.

Chapter Eighteen

JERRY WAS FURIOUS WITH ME because I let the cops have the purse-camera tape without running a dub for us.

"You had the tape and you handed it to a cop?"

"So he'd see I wasn't the killer. It's evidence, Jerry," I said, although I couldn't be too sanctimonious, since I'd returned to my apartment for the brown envelope before reporting back to work. "They'll release a dub soon."

I'd just come very close to losing my life, but, hey, the news must go on.

Claire, because she knew of my involvement more intimately than anyone, reported the story and provided the information that Amy was apparently after the same job Claire had had her eye on, doing on-air reports introducing Greg's celebrity guests. I was assigned to prepare a "reporter's notebook" piece for the eight.

I locked my office, told the switchboard to hold all my calls, pulled out the envelope and, from the wad of individually stapled reports, picked out the one on Amy.

The first sheet, the "stats" sheet, showed that Miss Amy Penny was born Michelle Amy Soxhaug, and remained Michelle Soxhaug until she was sixteen. Her mother was married three times and left her between marriages with a reluctant aunt and uncle in Garibaldi, Alabama.

Not the kind of thing that would go over well with the near-miss in-laws, but certainly nothing to kill for.

The third time around, Amy's mother married George W. Penny, an automotive parts salesman, and Amy moved to Tennessee, where she took her stepfather's name, had a little nose work done, and went on to become Miss Mason-Dixon Line.

Griff's report indicated she'd met Browner at a personal appearance she made as TV spokesmodel for that upscale low-dust baby powder at a gathering of ANN advertisers and he'd invited her to interview at ANN. She came in through the "Greg" door, like Madri, and he had discreetly "mentored" her with an eye to bringing her on to his show in a custom-made job. Claire had never had a chance.

Still, I couldn't see a motive for two murders and an attempted murder—mine.

I read on.

Amy's association with Greg didn't end once she got to ANN. Griff had a photo of Amy and Browner in a torrid embrace. Griff also had some medical records, including a full amniocentesis report on a twenty-five week old fetus, for which Amy had reverted to her old name, Michelle Soxhaug. I didn't understand all the notations, but Griff had summarized the contents:

The fetal blood type is incompatible with the blood type of Miss Penny's fiancé, Burke Avery, a.k.a. Heinrich Stedlbauer. It is, however, compatible with that of Mr. Browner.

Holy shit. Image conscious Amy Penny was not going to have the daddy she needed—and fast—for her baby if Burke learned this. No wonder Griff picked me to dish the dirt to.

Okay, I only *had* to read the report on Amy Penny, and the report on Browner, and the report on me, but I read them all. I know I should have taken every irrelevant report and shredded it at once out of respect for my colleagues. But I didn't. I couldn't resist temptation.

Larry Griff had covered the waterfront. There were credit reports, summaries of conversations with old friends, ex-friends, neighbors, teachers, employers. The stuff about Joanne and the APC was there, with pictures, which, I regret to say, I lingered over. Susan's *many* lovers were listed—including, sadly, Greg Browner, which explained why she didn't want her boss Solange, Greg's ex-wife, to know. Madri's entire sexual history was there, showing that she did, in fact, share a hotel room with "Heinrich Stedlbauer" on several occasions during my marriage.

There was nothing on Solange.

After I read it all, I felt kind of sleazy for invading their privacy. Sleazy, but with curiosity sated. Then I shredded everything but the report on Amy. That I kept.

Claire knocked on the door. "Do you have a script? Jerry wants you to track soon, and I have to re-edit my six o'clock for the eight so I can't help you."

"I'm working on it," I said.

I wrote up my story, leaving out the sordid details about the "innocent" people investigated. Jerry changed the script, I changed it back and tracked it, and the piece made the eight o'clock with two minutes to spare.

Later, Claire and I went to Tatiana's for omelets and grain to celebrate my continued living and her breakout reporting.

"Jerry's making himself out to be your savior," Claire said. "He told me when he saw your message he knew you would never meet me at a steak house. So he called the cops."

"I had Amy at my mercy *before* the cops got there," I said.

"You know Jerry. He'll milk it forever," she said. "So—you were wrong about Eric."

"Claire, I just can't trust my instincts," I said. "I'm not fit for dating. I need to take a refresher course first."

"No, you *can* trust your instincts, but you don't. You listen to all these other voices. What was your first instinct about Eric, the very first, honestly?"

"That I really wanted to have sex with him."

"What was your first instinct about Amy Penny?"

"That I really wanted to punch her lights out."

"And what was your first instinct about Burke?"

"That he was full of himself, almost sociopathic, but he was really cute."

"Right on all counts," Claire said.

"Well, Eric still has some stuff to explain . . . ," I said.

"So do you, my dear."

"Yeah." That's what happens when you're too close to a story—right smack in the middle of it, in fact, instead of on the outside looking on objectively. You lose sight of things and you make mistakes.

"Have you talked to Burke?"

"No. I figure I'm one of the last people he wants to hear from right now. You know, when we first split up, I wished horrible things would befall him, but this exceeds my wildest revenge fantasies. It's really overkill, it's justice of Greek proportions."

Poor Burke. He took a medical leave and went to rest at his parent's country house in the Hamptons. He always loved the ocean. I was going to call him or send a card but I really didn't know what to say. This wasn't covered in *Vogue's Book of Etiquette*. I felt bad for him, though. Poor guy. He used to have such good taste in women.

The purse-cam tape ran all over the news, ours and others, in the next week. Most of the story is out now.

I say most because one never knows when the story is really over. Just recently, I was reading that archaeologists now believe the Philistines weren't the loutish, barbaric beer-guzzlers their enemies painted them to be. They were actually cultured and refined wine-drinkers with highly evolved arts and technology for their time.

This just in: The Philistines were slandered. Forget what you've read. Even back then, there was media bias.

The stock price is up too, slightly. Paul Mangecet is rumored to be gunning for a big Hollywood studio, but his Christian no-load mutual fund still holds ten percent of JBS, and the next shareholder meeting promises to be a media circus.

McGravy made a play to get me back into general news, but Jack Jackson himself vetoed it. "She and Jerry are a bang-up team," he said. "And I'm going to keep them together. If it ain't broke, don't fix it."

Claire, however, is up for a weekend reporting spot.

Kinda like Ruby Keeler—she went in a producer, came out a star.

Even Louise Bryant has had offers. Get this. Some agent saw my cat on the news, and wants to sign her to an endorsement contract. My cat gets an agent before I do. My cat could make more this year than me. It's a strange world.

ABOUT THE AUTHOR

SPARKLE VERA LYNNETTE HAYTER was born in 1958 in Pouce Coupe, British Columbia, at the southernmost point of the Alaska Highway. She grew up in Edmonton where her father was first a newsman and later a prominent politician. Her mother taught English.

Her work has primarily been in television news: for WABC in New York, CNN in Atlanta, Global Television in Toronto, and as a freelance reporter in Washington, D.C. and Peshawar, Pakistan, covering the Afghan War for *The Toronto Star*, CTV, and *The Edmonton Journal*. She also writes and performs stand-up comedy. Ms. Hayter is married to William Dorman, a business correspondent.